I'M NOT
SHERLOCK HOLMES

PART ONE

based on the great works, novels and stories of
Sir Arthur Conan Doyle

M. J. EDEN

I'M NOT

SHERLOCK HOLMES

PART ONE

© 2024 M.J. Eden
Verlag: BoD • Books on Demand GmbH, In de Tarpen 42,
22848 Norderstedt
Druck: Libri Plureos GmbH, Friedensallee 273,
22763 Hamburg
ISBN: 978-3-7597-9979-1

CONTENTS

I.

THE MISSING BOY

There was a sudden ring at the door.

Silence.

Alexandra Green jerked upright. Long before her eyes could focus, the stiffness in her neck made it painfully clear that she had fallen asleep on the couch. A quick glance at her wrist revealed the time - 7:00 a.m. - rubbing the remnants of sleep from her tired eyes, she wondered.

Who on earth would disturb me at this hour?

And on a Sunday, no less?

She yawned, stretching slowly before rising to her feet. The doorbell rang again, more insistent this time.

Irritated, she stepped into the hallway, her beige dressing gown - a cheap imitation of silk - loosely draped over her, revealing the white nightshirt beneath that reached just to her knees. With an air of growing annoyance, she unlocked the door and opened it.

Standing on the threshold was an elderly lady with silver hair pinned up in a neat bun. She wore a pair of round spectacles with thick black rims, and a hand-knit grey cardigan that appeared to be of her own making. The woman clutched a small dark brown handbag against her chest, as if it were a shield, her thin fingers wrapped tightly around the straps.

"Hello," the woman stammered, her voice uncertain. "Are you Alexandra Green? The detective?"

Alex suppressed an awkward smile, tightening the sash of her robe around her waist. With a polite gesture, she invited the elderly lady inside. Guiding her into the living room, she prepared a hot cup of tea to calm the visitor's nerves. Without a word, she pressed

7

the warm cup into the woman's trembling hands. Then, with a measured grace, Alex lowered herself into a broad reading chair, positioned at an angle opposite the couch. The guest unknowingly seated herself where Alex had earlier been napping, blissfully unaware of the fact.

Nonsense, Alex thought to herself.

She must have realized.

Surely, she knows that if I had been in the bedroom, it would have taken me far longer to reach the door.

It's obvious I've just woken up, isn't it?

No, no, she chided herself, rolling her eyes inwardly.

She's too preoccupied, burdened with the grief of losing someone dear.

She wouldn't have noticed such trivial details.

Or perhaps it's simply that most people - normal people - don't follow these kinds of thought patterns.

Alex took a deep breath, her voice calm yet attentive. "How may I be of assistance?"

"It's about my daughter, Maria Drebber. She is… no, she *was…*" The older woman's voice broke, and tears welled up in her eyes. Trembling, she placed the teacup on the slender mahogany coffee table between them, her hands shaking too much to risk holding it any longer.

Alex handed her a handkerchief from the tissue box, which rested neatly in the center of the narrow table. "It's all right," she said, her voice steady - calm, yet neither cold nor unkind. "You don't need to say more, Mrs. Drebber. I read about what happened in the papers. My deepest condolences."

"Thank you," the older woman sobbed, her head bowed. "They told me there are no leads - nothing to trace the culprit - and that for now, all I can do is wait." She raised her tearful eyes to meet Alex's gaze directly. "Detective Inspector Doyle was kind enough to give me your address. He said you might be able to help." Desperation hung thick in her voice as she pleaded, "Please, you're my last hope."

Why, Alex thought to herself with a faint flicker of annoyance.

It seems as though Doyle is practically daring me to join him on another case.

That lazy bastard.

I have more than enough on my plate as it is.

Whenever the going gets tough, he ropes me in.

At times, he's even worse than Lestrade.

Alex scrutinized her visitor with a keen, almost imperceptible intensity. "Can you tell me what happened two days ago?"

"Maria called me, as usual, just after dinner. She said they'd be out a little longer since they had only just left and that I shouldn't wait up for them. But beyond that… I don't know what happened."

Alex leaned forward, her sharp eyes narrowing as though she could see right through the woman. "Did you hear anything in the background? Children, especially when they sense a parent isn't paying full attention - such as during a phone call - tend to make themselves known. Was your grandson with her? Even if it wasn't words, perhaps loud calls or noises?"

Mrs. Drebber hesitated for a moment, clearly grappling with her memories, before shaking her head slowly. "I… I can't be sure. There might have been something, but it's all so hazy now."

Alex studied her guest for another moment, her mind already working through the pieces of the puzzle.

"No," Mrs. Drebber shook her head vehemently. But then, as if frozen mid-motion, she suddenly stopped. Her eyes widened as a memory flashed before her. "Yes," she murmured, her hands trembling involuntarily. "They must have crossed the street during our conversation. Philip shouted 'Red' - as if my daughter was about to step into traffic without a thought. I then heard the screeching of tires and the blaring of a car horn, loud enough to make Philip cry out. Maria scolded him for it, though I suspect they kept walking after that. But beyond that, I heard nothing more."

As Mrs. Drebber spoke, Alex's mind was already racing, constructing the scene in rapid succession - playing out several possible scenarios with lightning speed, each one dismissed or refined until only the simplest, most logical conclusion remained. Without warning, she leapt from her chair.

"Would you be able to show me the location?" she asked, her voice sharp with purpose. "Of course, you needn't accompany me if it's too much for you. I completely understand. Just the address would suffice."

"17th York," Mrs. Drebber replied, visibly taken aback by the sudden intensity in Alex's reaction. "That's where they found Maria, at least."

Alex's mental map of London unfurled in her mind - a vast network of streets, shortcuts, bus stops, and Underground stations. She frowned, puzzling over the details. "That's not on the most direct route to your home." Her gaze flicked back to Mrs. Drebber, scrutinizing her with careful precision. "Does your daughter often take the York Street? The Gloucester would have been much quicker - and shorter."

She began pacing thoughtfully across the room, piecing together the facts as though assembling a jigsaw puzzle. Yet, even as she did so, the conclusion she reached seemed oddly implausible, and it unsettled her.

"What? Wait..." Mrs. Drebber's voice quivered with confusion. "How could you know that? You don't even know where my daughter started, or where I live."

Alex chuckled, her amusement barely concealed. "Of course, I know that." Her tone was almost too light for the gravity of the situation. "As I mentioned earlier, I read quite a bit in the papers."

"But no addresses were mentioned. Never."

"Naturally not," Alex replied smoothly. "But certain other locations were. And by connecting each known place, it's possible to deduce both the starting point and the intended destination."

Mrs. Drebber took a long sip of her tea, her brows furrowing as she glanced up at Alex. "Then I don't understand why you asked where my daughter and grandson were found."

Alex smiled knowingly. "To err is human." She stepped closer, her gaze meeting that of her guest with unwavering certainty. "I simply wanted to ensure I hadn't overlooked anything." She drew a deep breath, her mind already circling the situation like a hawk over prey. "A mother, especially one raising a child alone, rarely wanders the streets late at night with a toddler. They're tired - worn from the demands of the day. And children, even more so." She cast her eyes around the room, though her mind's eye remained fixed on the intricate mental map of London's streets. "Venturing out late would bring nothing but unnecessary complications and stress. Particularly during the week, when both mother and child must rise early the next day. They'd avoid any detours and almost certainly take the shortest route possible." Alex paused briefly, allowing Mrs. Drebber time to digest her reasoning. "So, either they were taken to York Street by force, or they had an urgent errand to attend to before returning home." She turned her sharp gaze back to her client. "Did your daughter have any friends or acquaintances living near York Street? Or perhaps your grandson?"

Mrs. Drebber shook her head, the weight of her grief evident in the way she lowered it. "I don't know," she whispered. "I'm so sorry."

"Please, don't apologize," Alex said, her voice unexpectedly soft, as a strange feeling of sympathy washed over her. "Trust me, Mrs. Drebber - I will find your grandson and return him to you, unharmed."

What am I saying?
I must never make promises. Not ever.

11

Damn.

This isn't like me at all.

Something about this case unsettled her. The boy... there was something peculiar.

Strange.

He reminds me of something...

Upon arriving at the designated address on York Street, Alexandra Green was immediately confronted with a problem: gaining access to the crime scene. The area had been cordoned off, and she first had to come to an agreement with Officer Tobias Gregson of the Metropolitan Police Service - commonly referred to across the country as New Scotland Yard, or simply Scotland Yard.

"What do you think this is?" Gregson asked irritably, his deep brown eyes flashing beneath his furrowed brows. "A circus attraction, perhaps?" His frustration was evident. "There's been a murder here recently, as you're well aware. Otherwise, you wouldn't be here. This is a secured, sealed-off crime scene, full of crucial evidence. Unauthorized individuals like yourself have no business here. So, be on your way!"

"Where is Inspector Doyle?" Alex replied, her calm demeanor in stark contrast to Gregson's irritation. She seemed entirely unaffected by his harsh tone. "Inform him that I'm here at the request of Maria Drebber's mother."

Gregson rolled his eyes, exasperation clear in his expression. "And what exactly do you plan to do now? She's already dead."

"But the boy isn't. Not yet," Alex replied, her gaze piercing. "The longer you leave me standing here, when I could very well help you, the slimmer our chances of finding him alive become."

Her voice was steady, but the urgency in her words was unmistakable.

"Our chances?" He widened his eyes in disbelief, then narrowed them sharply, his voice thick with disdain. "There is no *our*, no *us*, Missy, understand?" His face twisted in unmistakable bitterness. "You don't work for the police, nor the government. You're just some run-of-the-mill secretary for a greedy lawyer, nothing more."

Alexandra wasn't the type to let such condescending words slide without response. In the span of a mere second, she studied Gregson with the meticulous precision of a hawk. His body language betrayed him more than his harsh words ever could. Officer Gregson had a habit of gesticulating wildly with his arms when he spoke, yet he rarely made direct eye contact. When listening or thinking, he would plant his hands firmly on his hips and stand wide-legged, like a stiff toy soldier. His feet, however, pointed away from her, a subconscious sign of his desire to be elsewhere.

His dark grey shirt, faintly worn and visible beneath the heavy black coat, bore the tiniest of dark red specks just below the collar - almost imperceptible to the untrained eye. The fabric on one side was creased, as though he had spent considerable time lying down or pressing against a hard surface, perhaps a bed or something similar. His coat, still slightly damp at the shoulders and sleeves, suggested recent exposure to the elements, though most of it had dried. Beneath the shirt, a barely visible white undershirt peeked out from just above his collar.

Interesting.

The details before her told a far more intriguing story than the man's blusterous words ever could.

"How long?" Alexandra asked, her tone casual yet razor-sharp, after having gathered more than enough details for what was about to unfold.

Gregson stared at her, understandably confused. "What…?"

"How long has it been since you left the Royal Navy? Two years, or perhaps longer?"

His eyes widened in disbelief. "How the hell do you know that?" He was completely taken aback, though suspicion still flickered in his gaze. "Doyle must have told you, right?"

She smiled, a look of triumph playing on her lips. In that instant, Alex knew she had him firmly in her grasp. "Detective Inspector William Doyle? He's an insufferably meticulous man, as stiff as an iron rod, and he would never, under any circumstances, utter a single word about his colleagues. If I were relying on him for information, I'd sooner have learned more from Maria Drebber herself - or perhaps your companion from last night."

Gregson's confusion deepened. "What? How in the hell...?" The fire in his dark eyes flickered and morphed into uncertainty. "Have you been following me?"

Alex chuckled, clearly amused by his naivety. "Yes, of course! I've been trailing you just so I could throw this in your face and pretend to know everything, as if I'd known since yesterday that you'd be standing here today. After all, as a 'run-of-the-mill secretary,' I have nothing better to do, do I?" she quipped with exaggerated sarcasm.

Her wit struck him like a whip, leaving Gregson floundering, while Alex savored the moment, her keen intellect now fully on display.

"But how do you know, then? Did you speak with my girlfriend?" Gregson demanded, bewilderment clouding his voice.

"No," Alex replied with a serene smile. "I've only spoken with *you*, Officer Gregson - just now."

The man shook his head in disbelief, a deep frown creasing his brow. "That's impossible. How could you know? I've never told you anything about that. We barely know each other!"

"Quite right," she said, her lips curling into a knowing grin. "I didn't even know you had a girlfriend."

14

At that moment, Inspector William Doyle appeared from around the corner, his lanky frame casting a long shadow. He was a somewhat gaunt man, with a long, well-formed face and a nose that was both prominent and dignified, though it had a slight curve to it. His head, crowned with dark blond curls, was buried in his hands in a gesture of weary exasperation. But when he heard the unmistakable sound of Alexandra Green and Tobias Gregson engaged in a heated exchange, his sea-blue eyes widened in disbelief, and he reflexively rolled them in annoyance. Sighing deeply, he hurried over.

"What in heaven's name are you two doing here?" Doyle barked, irritation etched in every word.

"Did you know that Officer Gregson used to be in the Royal Navy?" Alex was fully immersed in her game of nonverbal communication, and for a moment, she seemed as arrogant and insufferably smug as Sherlock Holmes himself might have been.

"What?" Doyle blinked, utterly lost. "No," he admitted, shaking his head and looking at Gregson with newfound surprise.

"How do you *do* that?" Gregson was nearly bursting with a blend of awe and frustration. His curiosity was palpable, and far from being angry, he seemed genuinely fascinated.

For a fleeting second, Alex froze, caught off guard by his reaction. She had expected rage - like all the others before him - yet here stood Tobias Gregson, almost thrilled by her abilities. It unnerved her slightly, though it also flattered her in a peculiar way.

Inspector Doyle, ever the pragmatist, rolled his eyes once more before glancing back toward the crime scene. It was clear that he found Alex's habit of drawing out people's secrets uncomfortable, perhaps even impolite. To him, her uncanny talent for reaching conclusions seemed to strip people bare, leaving them vulnerable and exposed. Yet, as much as it irked him, he couldn't help but be intrigued by how she reached conclusions that were invisible even

15

to him. "Stop stringing the poor man along," he urged firmly. "Just tell him how you do it, or he'll never find peace again."

The young secretary smiled, clearly pleased with herself. While she had no desire to appear arrogant or conceited - after all, she was nothing like Sherlock Holmes, nor did she wish to be - she couldn't help but enjoy the fact that she was, at this moment, far cleverer than the two men standing before her. "Only on one condition: I get to examine the crime scene."

"No!" Doyle snapped, his voice sharp and unyielding.

"Okay," Gregson interjected, his eyes wide with curiosity, almost pleading. "Fine, tell me! Go on!"

Alex sighed, a hint of reluctance settling over her features. "All right, but I warn you - the explanation isn't as spectacular as you might hope." She took a deep breath, carefully selecting her words so that even someone unfamiliar with her often-peculiar deductions could follow. It was clear from her expression that this was no longer as enjoyable to her as watching Gregson squirm under the weight of his own bewilderment.

No magician willingly reveals the secrets of their tricks.

But this time, she had no other choice.

I promised to find the boy.

And I will do whatever it takes to keep that promise.

There are far worse things than this.

She exhaled deeply before beginning. "The wide stance you take, with your hands on your hips, is a clear indicator to me that you've spent time either in the military or a similar institution. That posture is almost instinctive among soldiers. The white shirt you wear beneath your uniform further reinforces this, and it tells me with certainty that you served in the Royal Navy. I happen to know several U.S. Navy personnel, and they all share the same habit of wearing white undershirts beneath their clothing. But judging by your accent, it's clear you've never been to America, so the Royal Navy was the logical conclusion." She paused, enjoying Gregson's

16

stunned expression for just a moment. "The faint red wine stains on your slightly creased shirt are another clue. They suggest you were with a woman last night - had it been a typical evening with men, you'd have likely been drinking beer or something stronger. And you didn't return home afterward to change your clothes. However, you did manage to shower and brush your teeth, which tells me you stayed somewhere you frequent often - likely a place where you keep some of your essentials." Her eyes narrowed slightly as she continued. "Your coat is still damp, which reveals even more. You must have been in a bar where smoking and drinking were prevalent, and afterward, you hung your coat outside to rid it of the smell. However, it rained last night - around 3:20 a.m. - and now your coat remains wet from the downpour."

As Alex concluded her explanation, Gregson swallowed hard, clearly astonished. He took a moment to gather himself. "That's... unbelievable," he finally muttered, his voice tinged with awe.

"May I see the crime scene now?" Alex was utterly unfazed by his reaction. While his words and the look of admiration in his eyes were flattering, she remained focused, her promise to Mrs. Drebber hammering away in the back of her mind like an incessant drum.

I must find Philip - and alive.

Without another word, Gregson lifted the police tape, allowing her to pass through.

Inspector Doyle, visibly uneasy about allowing an unauthorized civilian into a restricted area, led her around the corner of the house and into the secluded backyard of the desolate building. "This is a one-time thing," he said sternly, his voice low. "No one must know you were here."

Alex smirked. "Technically, it's your own fault. You're the one who gave Mrs. Drebber my address."

"What was I supposed to do? She was distraught, and I couldn't help her."

"Then don't complain about me being here. In fact, you invited me yourself. I made a promise to Mrs. Drebber to find her grandson and bring him back alive. So, if you don't mind, let's make an exception - just this once."

The backyard was dim and eerily quiet. The forensics team had already done their work. The body was gone, leaving only a white outline marking where it had been, along with a large, dried pool of blood on the ground. Objects once strewn about - Maria Drebber's handbag, the murder weapon - were now only represented by small white circles painted on the ground, each marked with numbered flags.

"It's pointless," Doyle muttered, his voice resigned. "You won't find anything here. Every piece of evidence has already been catalogued and taken away. There's nothing left."

Alex surveyed the scene, her sharp eyes taking in every detail, no matter how insignificant it seemed. She wasn't ready to concede just yet.

The courtyard was enclosed on three sides by sturdy brick walls, with stacks of crates piled up against them, some reaching nearly to the top. The clutter made the space feel even smaller, and at first glance, there seemed to be little of interest. But Alex's sharp eyes caught something that most would overlook - a small, almost invisible niche tucked into one corner, just large enough for a child to crawl into. The opening was so discreet that under ordinary circumstances, it would have gone completely unnoticed. Only someone with Alex's keen sense for the unusual and subtle could have spotted it so quickly.

"What do you do when you're afraid?" she asked, glancing briefly at the man beside her. "When you know your opponent is bigger, stronger, and armed?"

Doyle, slightly bewildered by the unexpected question, answered, "I'd run."

"And if you were trapped, with no chance of escape?"

"Then I'd hide."

"Exactly." Alex grinned, a mischievous glint in her eyes as she approached the small recess in the corner. She knelt down on the rough asphalt, leaning forward. From her coat pocket, she pulled out a fresh handkerchief, wrapping it around her fingers before carefully reaching into the darkness of the niche. To her surprise, she felt something solid. She withdrew her hand and revealed a small toy - an action figure of a superhero, with a plush red-and-gold helmet and matching armor.

Victor.

The name flashed through her mind with a sudden intensity, though she had no idea where it had come from. It felt as though she had known it her entire life. Along with the name came a wave of deep, long-buried pain, rising unexpectedly to the surface.

"What is it? Have you found something?" Doyle's curious voice cut through her thoughts as he peered over her shoulder.

Alex didn't answer immediately, her gaze fixed on the small toy in her hand, lost in the sudden swirl of emotion and memory. With great effort, she tore herself away from the old, painful feeling that had surfaced and stood up. She handed the small toy silently to Doyle, who, with a latex-gloved hand, carefully accepted it to avoid contaminating any potential evidence. Without a word, she brushed past him and continued walking.

"Alex?" Doyle called after her, clearly confused. "What's going on?"

She didn't turn back as she marched briskly toward the exit. "There are skin flakes and short dark hairs on the doll," she said, her voice clipped. "Hopefully, they belong to the suspect, not the victim. Find him, and you'll find the boy. My work here is done." Her pace quickened, her steps growing more urgent as she neared the exit.

Who the hell is Victor?

19

As she approached Officer Gregson, who was standing near the police tape, Inspector Doyle hurried behind her, catching up just in time to grab her arm and pull her back, his face etched with concern. "What's wrong with you?"

Alex tried to pull away from his grip, but the simple motion triggered an unwanted memory - something buried deep for years, long forgotten or perhaps deliberately suppressed. But now, it surged to the surface, vivid and inescapable, as if the past had materialized right before her eyes.

The memory played out before her, as real and immediate as if it were happening in that very moment.

A young boy with a mop of curly red hair and freckles scattered across his round cheeks sprinted through a knee-high grassy field, chasing after a little girl. She had two beautifully braided dark brown pigtails that trailed behind her as she ran ahead, giggling.

"Stop!" the boy shouted, grabbing the girl roughly by the arm.

"I won!" she cried triumphantly, her braids whipping in the air as she tried to wriggle free from his grip. "You're just a sore loser. You're too slow!"

"You cheated," he retorted, sulking. "Girls can't be faster than boys. That's impossible."

"Oh, yes, they can! I won, and you lost!" she shot back, her voice full of defiance.

The boy, his face scrunched in frustration, yanked her arm harder, pulling her back with a sharp tug.

"Ouch!" the girl yelped. "Victor, you're hurting me."

"Cheater!" he shouted.

"Spoilsport!" she countered.

"Liar!" he barked, his voice filled with the indignation of a child who couldn't accept defeat.

20

"Alex!" Doyle's voice, now laced with fear, broke through the fog, and he shook her forearm gently. "Can you hear me? What's wrong with you?"

Victor.

That name was branded into her thoughts, reverberating through her mind in an endless echo.

"What did you do to her in there, Doyle?" Gregson asked sharply, his gaze filled with concern as he studied the ashen-faced woman before them.

We were friends.

But that was a lifetime ago.

Victor... is dead.

Suddenly, Alex tore herself from Doyle's grasp. "I won," she murmured, still lost in the vivid memory that gripped her mind. Only when she saw the bewildered expressions on the men's faces did she realize she had spoken the words aloud. "I'm sorry," she muttered, pressing a hand to her forehead as confusion clouded her thoughts. "I... I have to go."

Without another word, she bolted, darting away like a hunted animal, leaving both men - and the crime scene - behind.

Victor.

What happened back then?

And why did I forget you?

After a restless and sleepless night, Alex dragged herself wearily out of bed. The past hours had been spent staring at the dark ceiling of her bedroom, her mind spiraling through the labyrinth of forgotten memories, trying to make sense of the sudden resurfacing of her past. But no answers came - only more questions.

21

Still half-asleep, she shuffled into the living room toward the small kitchenette, flicking on the kettle. She tossed on her dressing gown and slipped into her fluffy purple slippers before stepping out of her apartment. Descending the stairs, she collected her daily newspaper and a few letters from her mailbox near the entrance. Back inside, she made herself a cup of tea and sat at the dining table with the stack of mail and her mug.

The headline on the front page caught her eye immediately: it reported the murder of Maria Drebber and the disappearance of her son, Philip. In the corner of the page, there was a small photograph of the boy, smiling so innocently and sweetly that it could have softened even the hardest of hearts.

The poor boy.

I hope they've found him.

A pang of guilt gnawed at her as she opened the paper and began reading the article.

At the top of the page was a picture of the small doll Alex had discovered, placed next to a black-and-white photo of the suspect. It was none other than Philip's math teacher, Richard Hoffmann.

His teacher?

How dreadful.

And yet... somehow predictable.

Alex skimmed the last few lines of the article, a wave of relief washing over her. It reported that the boy had been found unharmed and had already been returned to his grandmother later that same evening.

As Alex flipped the page of her newspaper, her phone rang. She answered the call, laying the paper open on the table before her. "Green?"

"Hello, it's Inspector Doyle. I just wanted to check in and see if you're all right." There was a brief pause on the other end. "You gave me quite the scare yesterday."

"I'm fine," she replied quickly.

22

Victor.

The thought of the previous day's events made her uncomfortable. "I just suddenly remembered something urgent I needed to take care of."

Doyle exhaled audibly, a sigh of relief. "Have you had a chance to read the paper yet?"

Good.

He believes me.

Relaxing slightly, she leaned back in her chair. "I'm in the middle of it now. It looks like you've cracked another case. Inspector Lestrade will need to watch his back if he doesn't want to be left behind."

"I wouldn't count on that," Doyle sighed. "Turn to pages six and seven."

Alex did as he asked, flipping through the paper. She read aloud from the article: "A Study in Scarlet. Detective Inspector Lestrade solves an impossible case with the assistance of consulting detective Sherlock Holmes." She rolled her eyes in annoyance. "Without that bastard, Lestrade would be lost."

"Just as I would be without you," Doyle quickly retorted, his voice taking on a more serious tone. It was clear he was leading up to something. "Now, take a look at the article on page nine, bottom right."

Alex turned the page, her eyes scanning the text. "Vivienne Sawyer," she read aloud. "The only daughter of former Congressman Mortimer Sawyer was brutally murdered and nearly unrecognizably disfigured last Saturday. The perpetrator remains at large. Congressman Sawyer has pleaded for the swift resolution of the case."

"I took the liberty of placing copies of the crime scene photos and all the police reports in an envelope in your mailbox," Doyle added, his voice steady but with a clear undertone of urgency.

23

"I have to work today," Alex replied, glancing at her watch. She was already running later than usual. "Besides, I'm just a simple secretary."

"Please," Doyle's voice took on a desperate edge. "Vivienne's father keeps calling me, and I have no idea what to tell him anymore. And you're far more than just a secretary, as we both know."

Alex sifted through the pile of letters on her table, her hand landing on a thick envelope with her name scribbled across it in a hasty, almost illegible handwriting - one that seemed more like the scrawl of a doctor than a police officer. She tore open the envelope, pulling out several crime scene photographs and pages of detailed reports. As her eyes fell on the gruesome images, she instinctively turned her head away, momentarily repulsed. But, unable to resist the dark fascination that always pulled her in, she forced herself to look again, examining the horrifying scene with a grim intensity.

"Well?" Doyle asked, trying to remain as patient as possible.

"I'll take a look at it." Alex slid the photos and reports back into the envelope, then stood up. "You'll hear from me as soon as I've found something."

"Thank you." Doyle sounded almost euphoric with relief. "You are my saving grace."

II.

THE SMELL OF MENTHOL

The shrill ring of the office phone jolted Alex abruptly from her thoughts, just as she had finally stumbled upon the solution to her problem.

"Harold Lloyd Law Offices, this is Alexandra speaking. How may I assist you?" she answered, her voice delivering the same rehearsed words with the precision of a recording, yet maintaining a warm and professional tone.

"This is Leon Tregennis. Is Mr. Lloyd available? I need to speak with him urgently," came the somewhat clumsy response from the other end of the line.

"Good morning, Mr. Tregennis. May I ask what this is concerning?"

"It's about my sister Beth. Please... I don't know what to do anymore," the man replied, his voice trembling with fear and uncertainty.

"One moment, please. I'll connect you." With practiced ease, Alex pressed the button beside the display. Moments later, her boss, the renowned star attorney Harold Lloyd himself, picked up the receiver. "Leon Tregennis is on line one, Sir," Alex informed him smoothly. "It's about his sister again."

"Thank you," Lloyd replied curtly. "Put him through!"

With a deft motion, Alex placed the receiver back, automatically connecting Leon Tregennis to her boss. She then turned her attention back to her true work - the kind that had long surpassed the realm of a mere hobby.

Spread out before her on the expansive desk was a chaotic array of papers, interspersed with newspaper clippings, police reports, and crime scene photos. Each picture bore the name "Vivienne Sawyer" in bold letters along the bottom - a grim reminder of the victim, who had been brutally mutilated just two days ago.

It's nothing short of a miracle that they were able to identify her at all.

Alex was scanning the gruesome images once more. The woman's teeth had been shattered or violently torn out, making even dental identification impossible.

The only way her identity could have been confirmed was through her DNA, which had been found scattered throughout the crime scene. The fact that they could compare it so quickly meant that a sample of her DNA had already been on record.

Why?

Alex's mind worked quickly, piecing together the puzzle.

Of course!

The answer's obvious.

Just as she reached for her phone to call Inspector Doyle, his name appeared on her screen, as if he had come to the same realization at precisely the same moment. His incoming call lit up her display.

"It was the father," Alex blurted out, skipping any formality, even a greeting. Her abruptness was typical, though she rarely noticed how rude it came across. "Vivienne Sawyer was murdered by Mortimer Sawyer, her own father."

The silence on the other end stretched for a moment, as the caller struggled to process her lightning-fast deduction. "How on earth did you come to that conclusion?" Doyle's voice was tinged with bewilderment, clearly unable to fathom how she had arrived at such a shocking verdict.

"Why was her DNA already in the database?" Alex pressed on, not giving him a chance to answer. "There are, of course, several reasons for that, but two stand out as the most probable in cases like this. Number one: She herself had committed a crime before. Or number two: She was a victim in a previous criminal matter. The first option clearly doesn't apply here, so it must be the latter."

"But why?" Doyle still sounded utterly lost, grappling with her logic.

"You saw the victim at the crime scene yourself, Doyle. Didn't anything strike you as odd? The underside of her left forearm was covered in fine scars. This led me to conclude she was right-handed, though that detail isn't crucial. Those scars - those tiny cuts - are several years old, some even older. The earliest ones likely date back to her childhood. Self-harm like this, Doyle, is common in more than half of the cases linked to domestic abuse." She paused, letting the weight of her words sink in before continuing. "Vivienne Sawyer was an only child. Her mother died when she was young. That leaves only one person - the father - as the source of her suffering. It's likely Mortimer Sawyer abused her, both physically and psychologically. The signs are all there. He's the one who killed her. It's obvious."

Doyle remained silent for a long moment, stunned by her brutal yet methodical breakdown of the truth. "Alright, fine." He exhaled tensely, clearly grappling with the weight of Alex's deductions. "Maybe her father did terrible things to her during her childhood, but that doesn't automatically make him a murderer. I can't just arrest Congressman Sawyer without solid evidence, especially when he's the one pushing so hard to find the real culprit."

"Look more closely at the crime scene photos, Doyle!" Alex snapped, her patience wearing thin. "Vivienne Sawyer was a saleswoman at a small tobacconist's shop, not far from her modest apartment on the outskirts of the city. The reports make it clear - her apartment was sparsely furnished, and she owned very little in terms of clothing, none of it particularly expensive or stylish. So, how do you explain the fact that, on the day she was murdered, she was wearing a designer dress? Just the shoes alone are worth more than two months' rent for her apartment. It's obvious she didn't

27

own other garments like that, and given their value, she wouldn't have worn them casually. She must have had something important planned that day. Either she was going to the press to expose what her father had done to her, or - more likely - she was on her way to see a lawyer, to finally take him to court. Of course, there's a slim chance she was just trying to get a better-paying job in a more formal business setting, but that's not something her father would have known, especially since he claimed they hadn't been in contact for years. That alone suggests something terrible happened between them in the past - why else would Vivienne Sawyer go to such lengths to avoid her only living relative? Whatever her real reason was for wearing such exclusive clothing, her father must have feared the worst. He likely assumed she was about to reveal his abuse, and in his desperation, he saw no other option but to silence her permanently."

"Good heavens, you're quick," Doyle said, clearly impressed as he took a moment to process everything Alex had just laid out.

"I could've solved the case a lot faster if I'd been allowed to inspect the crime scene myself," Alex replied, a hint of resentment in her tone.

"You know that's not possible," Doyle interrupted hastily.

"Of course not. It would never do for anyone to know that you need the help of a 'simple secretary' to solve your cases," she said, her voice dripping with sarcasm. "Now, if I were the great Sherlock Holmes," she added with a derisive snort, "you wouldn't hesitate for a second to invite me to the scene."

"I'm not Lestrade, and I certainly don't have any admiration for that so-called detective."

"You know," she continued, "Holmes and I are not so different."

Doyle raised an eyebrow. "I thought you couldn't stand him?"

"That's true. But isn't it often the case that we despise those who are most like ourselves?"

"In fact, you are like him," Doyle conceded. "The same tangled thoughts running through your head as his."

Alex couldn't help but laugh. "I doubt you have the faintest idea what's going on in Sherlock Holmes' mind, much less what swirls around in mine." She glanced at her watch. "Now, do you have a new case for me, or is there some other reason you're calling during work hours? You know I only have half an hour left here at the office, and I *hate* being interrupted - whether it's in my official work or my unofficial pursuits."

"I still don't understand why you continue working for that lawyer," Doyle mused. "You earn more than enough from your 'side job' to leave him behind. Lloyd's a slimy, miserly fraud. Surely, you don't plan on sticking around much longer?"

"There are far worse people in this world than Harold Lloyd, and you know that better than anyone," Alex shot back. "And let's not forget why I'm really here. Besides, I only work part-time, three days a week. It's hardly a great sacrifice of my time, and, frankly, I enjoy it. Is it such a crime to like what I do?"

"You don't just like it," Doyle countered. "You revel in it. That's a significant difference."

A small, knowing smile crept across her face. Doyle's words had hit closer to the truth than she cared to admit. "Are you worried that one day I might grow tired of simply solving cases and start creating my own by killing people myself?" Her voice was tinged with a peculiar fascination at the thought.

"You wouldn't do something like that," Doyle replied firmly. "I know you too well for that. I just think it's a shame to see you wasting your unique talents on a slimy crook like Lloyd. It's pure squander of your abilities and your time."

"Ah," she said with a grin, "that's only because you don't understand the advantages I can glean from this situation." Her smile faded into something more serious as she heard hurried footsteps echoing down the corridor, approaching fast from around the corner. "I have to go. If you do have a new case for me - and I sincerely hope you do - call me back in half an hour."

She ended the call swiftly, gathered up the scattered documents on her desk, and tucked both her phone and papers into the black leather handbag that lay beneath her desk.

"What are you doing?" a voice interrupted her, and Mr. Lloyd appeared from around the corner, stopping directly in front of her desk. He leaned over, his gaze scrutinizing her closely.

With a small pocket mirror and a bold red lipstick in her hands, Alex sat back in her chair and meticulously traced the outline of her lips, as though she were a film star preparing for her close-up. She watched herself in the mirror, her tone casual yet polished. "Just refreshing my lipstick, Sir. Nothing more."

The lawyer gazed at her, momentarily entranced. "Not a bad idea, Miss Green. Red suits you exceedingly well."

"Thank you, Mr. Lloyd," she purred, her voice laced with a hint of flattery.

He grinned, but quickly reverted to his usual smug expression as he circled around her desk. Perching himself on the wooden surface directly in front of her, he looked down at her with a self-satisfied smirk. "You know you're far more valuable to me than Sidney, don't you?"

Alex met his gaze without a flinch, her expression unreadable as she placed the lipstick down, the atmosphere thick with unspoken tension. "Yes, I know, Sir, and that means a great deal to me," Alexandra replied with a captivating smile. "But Paige is an excellent secretary. Perhaps you shouldn't be so hard on her."

"You're probably right," Lloyd conceded. "Good employees are hard to come by these days. It's a shame you're only part-time here. I'd love to have you in the office full-time, Miss Green. Don't you ever get bored in the afternoons or on the other days without me?"

Alexandra barely managed to stifle a hearty laugh.

If only he knew what I get up to during that time.

30

Even Sherlock Holmes would be envious of some of the cases I've handled.

"Oh, there's always something to keep me busy," she said instead, her voice sweet and light. "Cleaning the apartment, doing laundry, cooking, ironing - the usual domestic things. It all takes time." She felt like a delicate echo of Marilyn Monroe in one of her most glamorous scenes.

"And what about your rare evenings?" Lloyd pressed on, clearly eager to know more. "Are you as busy then as you are during the day?"

"Sometimes," she replied with a coy smile. "But most evenings, I indulge in a fine glass of Chianti and enjoy the magnificent works of Goethe and Schiller - quite exceptional company, wouldn't you agree?"

Lloyd leaned in closer, his gaze lingering with admiration. "You've got excellent taste, Miss Green. I like that."

His desire to inch even closer was palpable, but fortunately for Alexandra, her colleague Paige was notoriously punctual.

The young, petite woman hurried into the office, her long dark-blonde hair tightly braided, and dressed in a sleek navy-blue pant-suit that gave her an air of professionalism. She made her way to her desk, just a few meters from Alexandra's. "Good afternoon, Mr. Lloyd. Hello, Alex," she greeted, her usual uncertainty showing as she nervously tucked a loose curl behind her ear before sitting down.

The moment Lloyd saw her, his demeanor shifted. He stepped back from Alexandra, his expression turning cold as he shot an icy glare at Paige, then walked briskly past her and disappeared into his office without a word.

"Thank you," Alex breathed, relieved. She stood up and quickly made her way over to Paige's desk, leaning against it with a mischievous smile. "So? How was it with David last night? Come on, spill the details!"

31

At the mention of his name, Paige's cheeks flushed crimson with embarrassment. "It was… amazing! He's so kind, so funny, and just unbelievably handsome." She could barely contain her excitement. "I think it might actually turn into something serious."

"Oh, how wonderful!" Alex exclaimed, genuinely happy for her friend. "I'm so glad for you. So, any plans for the next few days?"

"You mean, like another date or something?" Paige hesitated, her smile faltering for a moment. "David's really swamped with work right now, but next week he's got some time off, and he wants to take me away for the weekend."

"Okay, that's good," Alex replied, though she struggled internally to avoid analyzing the man based on the little information she had.

It's odd.

He suddenly has so much work when before he seemed much more available.

Perhaps he's just playing with her.

Or maybe he's genuinely serious.

But if not, he might at least be testing how loyal she is, how much she can handle.

Either way, it wouldn't hurt to pay him a brief visit.

"What's David's last name again?" Alex asked cautiously.

"Moran. His name is David Moran," Paige replied, pulling out her phone to show Alex something.

Moran?

Why does that name leave me with such a bad feeling?

"Here," Paige said, holding out the phone. A photo of a young, handsome man filled the screen. "That's him. Isn't he gorgeous?"

"Yes, very good-looking," Alex remarked, forcing herself to conceal the discomfort gnawing at her. "Where did you two meet? I don't think you ever told me."

"Oh, it was at *The Loop* in Mayfair, during the grand reopening. You really must go sometime. Their cocktails are world-class."

Before Alex could respond, her own phone rang from inside her handbag. Without another word to Paige, she walked back to her desk, rummaging through her bag until she found her phone.

The name *Liz* flashed on the screen.

"Hey," Alex answered, pressing the phone to her ear. "What's up?"

"Great news!" a young woman's voice chimed through the phone. "Guess who has got two tickets to *Carmina Burana* at the Royal Albert Hall tonight?"

"Are you serious?" Alex leapt into the air, her excitement palpable. "When does it start? Where do I need to be?"

"We'll meet at my place at 5:00 p.m. Is that alright with you?"

"Absolutely! But how on earth did you get the tickets? The concert's been sold out for months."

"Let's just say I know someone who knows someone, who owed a favor to a certain influential person in the right circles," Liz replied with a playful tone.

"You're incredible. You know that?"

"Of course I do. See you tonight. Ciao!"

As Alex put her phone away, she was brimming with joy and excitement, her earlier worries completely forgotten. She'd been wanting to go to the Royal Albert Hall for ages, but it had never worked out - until now. Grabbing her coat and bag, she quickly shut down her computer and made for the door. "See you tomorrow," she called to Paige. But before stepping out, she turned back, tossing her red lipstick to her colleague with a mischievous grin. "Here! This'll make dealing with Lloyd a whole lot easier."

"Thanks," Paige said, staring at the vibrant shade of red, then watching as Alex strode out onto the street and disappeared around the corner.

33

As Alex strolled through the streets, her phone rang once more. She didn't need to glance at the display to know who was calling. "Detective Inspector Doyle. Right on time, as always."

"What?" Doyle sounded confused. "I was supposed to... Ah, Alex, you always manage to throw me off balance."

"Sorry, that wasn't my intention," she replied casually as she wandered through central London. "So, what's the case?"

"Elizabeth Tregennis," Doyle answered.

Alex stopped abruptly in her tracks. "Tregennis?"

"Yes."

"Dammit."

"Do you know her?" Doyle asked, his tone slightly awkward.

"Not personally. Her brother's a client of ours."

Through the phone, Doyle could hear the sound of a car horn blaring. "Hey, lady!" a driver shouted through his open window, clearly irritated. "Get your butt off the street!"

"If you don't want the case, just say so," Doyle muttered.

"No, no, it's fine," Alex responded quickly. "Where and how did it happen?"

"In an abandoned warehouse on Dorset Street. She was stabbed thirteen times."

"Thirteen... that's an interesting number," she mused, already deep in thought as she resumed walking. "I'm just two blocks away from Dorset Street. Can I take a look?"

"We've already been through this," Doyle said, his voice tight with frustration.

"Either I get to inspect the crime scene, or you'll have to ask Sherlock Holmes for help instead," Alex replied with equal firmness. "The choice is entirely yours, Inspector." She could hear the hesitation in Doyle's silence, the idea of involving Holmes clearly unappealing to him.

"Fine, you get two minutes," he relented at last, sounding defeated. "Not a second longer."

"That's all I'll need," she responded, quickening her pace, a touch of excitement in her voice. "I'm already here."

Inspector Doyle turned, bewildered, only to find Alex standing behind him, grinning from ear to ear. With a resigned sigh, he slipped his phone into his pocket and stepped toward her. "Try not to smile so conspicuously. You'll give the wrong impression." He lifted the police tape, allowing her to duck beneath it.

Together, they entered the abandoned warehouse. Even in broad daylight, the interior was nearly pitch-dark, as every window had been covered with foil and cardboard. The large, cavernous space was filled with police officers, forensic experts, and other investigators, all combing through the scene.

In the center of the room lay the body of a woman with short, dark, curly hair. She wore a thin, sleeveless black dress that ended just above her knees. Her arms were outstretched, as if she had been crucified, and her entire body was so drenched in blood that it was almost impossible to discern where the thirteen stab wounds were located.

Doyle led Alex right up to the body, close enough for her to examine both the victim and the surrounding area. As Alex scanned the scene, taking in every detail with her sharp eyes, Doyle glanced around nervously, clearly on edge. It was as though he expected someone - someone who absolutely shouldn't see Alex at the scene - to arrive at any moment.

"There's no doubt this is Elizabeth Tregennis?" Alex knelt beside the body, her keen eyes already assessing the scene.

"She's been positively identified," one of the forensic pathologists replied, holding up a plastic evidence bag with the victim's ID inside. The photograph on the card unmistakably matched the lifeless face before them.

"That bastard," Alex muttered under her breath, her mind racing.

"What is it?" Doyle stepped closer, sensing her discovery.

"Look here." Alex glanced briefly at Doyle before pointing to the victim's neck. "He strangled her before stabbing her thirteen times. You can clearly see the impression of a ring on his left index finger."

She stood swiftly, wiping her hands, which had brushed against the blood-soaked floor, with a tissue. "It was Leon Tregennis, her brother."

"How can you be so sure?" the forensic pathologist asked, raising his left hand to show a ring beneath his latex glove. "Plenty of men wear rings on that finger. It could have been me."

"Don't be ridiculous," Alex said sharply, her gaze piercing through the man. "You're left-handed. The murderer was most definitely right-handed - just look at the angle of the stab wounds. They're all slanted from the right. Besides, there's cigarette ash near the body. He was clever enough to take the cigarette butts with him, but he didn't account for the pungent scent of menthol. Leon Tregennis smokes nothing but those vile things."

"How do you know that?" the forensic pathologist asked, his voice tinged with suspicion. "And who the hell are you?"

"That's Alexandra Green," came a voice from behind. A man had just entered the warehouse, stopping just behind Doyle, his presence immediately commanding the attention of the room.

Startled, Doyle spun around. "Lestrade. What are you doing here?"

"This is my jurisdiction, Doyle. You know that."

"Gregson told me you were tied up with another case in Belgravia," Doyle replied, his tone confused.

36

"I was," Lestrade said with a slight edge in his voice. "Until two hours ago. Now, I'm here."

Alex approached the two men, her eyes sharp and unreadable. "Let me guess - Sherlock Holmes helped you."

"No, not this time, Miss Green," Lestrade said, a trace of pride in his voice. "I solved the case without his help."

Alex narrowed her eyes, clearly unconvinced. "I don't believe you."

He's hiding something.

I can see it clearly.

But what?

It must be about Sherlock Holmes.

It's always about him.

Everything ever revolves around that man.

Damn it!

Pull yourself together!

Despite her inner turmoil, Alex kept her expression calm, though her mind raced with suspicion.

"So, you solved a case in Belgravia?" Alex asked, her eyes narrowing as she regained her composure. She scrutinized Lestrade closely. "How did you figure out it was Mrs. Anderson's neighbor? Did you simply ask him, and he confessed on the spot?" She shook her head. "No, I highly doubt that. Correct me if I'm wrong, but you went to Sherlock Holmes. There's a new Chinese restaurant that just opened near Baker Street, not far from 221B. You reek of it - no, you *stink* so strongly of it that anyone with half a brain could put two and two together." She paused, noting how the pungent smell clung faintly to his clothes. "But the scent has started to fade, meaning you were there at least two hours ago, perhaps closer to three. So, you must have gone to him for advice, didn't you? Whether you admit it or not, seeking his counsel is also a form of assistance. So, I'll ask you once more, and I suggest you don't lie to me again: *Did Sherlock Holmes help you?*"

Lestrade hesitated, clearly uncomfortable with the whole exchange. His visit had been intended to one-up Doyle, having caught wind of the rumor that Doyle had enlisted the help of Alexandra Green. But now, his plan had backfired, and it seemed Alex was well aware of it. Finally, with a sigh, he admitted, "Fine, I went to him. He pointed me toward the neighbor." His voice was pained, his pride clearly wounded. "But everything else - I figured out on my own."

"I knew it!" Alex exclaimed, far too pleased with herself, her confidence bubbling over.

Lestrade's discomfort deepened as Alex's sharp deductions cut through his pretense. This wasn't how things were supposed to go, and now, even his own intentions felt exposed under her relentless scrutiny.

"Alex!" Doyle scolded, fixing her with a stern look. "That's enough. Your two minutes are up."

"Very well," she responded coolly. "You already have your culprit. However, his lawyer is excellent - slimy and revolting, yes, but unfortunately, quite good at his job." She brushed past the two men, heading toward the open warehouse doors. "If *he* finds out I was here, you'll have a real problem with me, Lestrade!" she called back before disappearing into the daylight outside.

Lestrade, perplexed, watched her leave, still trying to decipher whom she had meant by *he*. "She could easily be his sister," he muttered, clearly impressed. "In her peculiar eccentricity, she's quite like him."

"Nonsense," Doyle retorted quickly. "Alexandra Green has far more going on upstairs than Sherlock Holmes."

"I'd love to believe that," Lestrade said with a grin. "Maybe they should meet sometime and settle who's the cleverer of the two."

"I don't think that's a good idea," Doyle replied, visibly uneasy. "If those two ever crossed paths, there'd likely be casualties."

"You seem to know Miss Green rather well," Lestrade remarked, his grin widening. "Perhaps *too* well, if you ask me."

"I didn't ask you," Doyle shot back, clearly irritated as he quickly walked away.

Lestrade watched him go, satisfied that he'd struck a nerve. But despite his little victory, he was still left wondering who exactly Alex had referred to. It could have been Sherlock Holmes, his older brother Mycroft, or even Leon Tregennis.

III.

MYCROFT HOLMES

It wasn't until nearly 11:00 p.m. that Alexandra finally returned to her apartment. A little tipsy from a few glasses of wine shared with her friend Liz after the *Carmina Burana* performance, she stumbled through the door and into the hallway, where she lay motionless in the dark for a moment, gathering herself. The blinking red light of her answering machine eventually pulled her from her daze.

With effort, she pushed herself upright, switched on the hallway light, and made her way toward the small dark oak table where the answering machine sat, next to a cheap imitation of an antique vase filled with half-wilted flowers. She pressed the button to play the messages and waited.

After the familiar hum of her standard recorded greeting, Inspector Doyle's voice broke through, sounding unusually nervous and impatient. "I couldn't reach you on your mobile, so I'm trying your landline - but apparently with no success either. Where the hell are you? I need your help. This new case... it's something special. Call me back immediately!"

A sharp beep followed, and the next message played. Doyle again. This time, his voice was even more frantic, his worry palpable.

Alex, still slightly disoriented from the evening's indulgence, felt a pang of concern rising through the fog of her mind.

"Pick up the damn phone!" Doyle's voice rang out, breathless with urgency. "I need you!" He paused, his frustration clear in every word. "If this is about this afternoon, then I'm sorry. I didn't know Lestrade would show up."

40

But you suspected it, didn't you?

Do you really think I didn't notice the way you kept nervously glancing around that warehouse, expecting him to barge in?

You knew he would come - you just hoped I'd be gone by the time he arrived, so you could dispel all those pesky rumors about you and me.

Well, that didn't quite go as planned, did it?

Doyle continued, "Please, Alex. This is important - *really* important. The British government is involved, and without you, I'm done for."

Unmoved, Alex walked past the answering machine, ignoring the message as she strolled down the hallway and into the living room. She tossed her coat onto the couch, paying little attention to Doyle's pleas.

Another message began to play in the background, his voice even more desperate. "Listen!" He nearly bellowed through the speaker as Alex casually poured herself a glass of water and settled onto the couch. "This matter is of the utmost importance. You've been *personally* requested!"

By whom?

Now, Alex's curiosity was piqued.

"Come to 23A Glentworth Street! *Immediately!*" The message ended with a sharp beep, followed by a long stretch of static.

Glancing at her watch, Alex saw the time - 11:27 p.m.

"They're probably asleep by now," she thought, yawning and stretching lazily.

And I should be doing the same.

Despite her fatigue, the weight of the message lingered in the air. Doyle rarely sounded so desperate, and her curiosity, once sparked, was hard to ignore.

But she was way too tired.

Alex rose slowly, her movements sluggish as she trudged toward her bedroom, but she didn't get far. Just moments later, her phone rang - though still set to silent, the vibration reverberated unnervingly in the quiet room.

Damn it!

I just want to sleep.

With a sigh of frustration, Alex turned on her heel and fished her phone out of her right coat pocket. As expected, it was Inspector Doyle, calling for the 37th time that evening.

"Do you have any idea what time it is?" she asked, her voice weary.

"It's 11:29 p.m.," Doyle replied, his irritation evident. "And I've been trying to reach you for over two hours. Where on earth have you been?"

"Carmina Burana," she answered, stifling a yawn as she stretched. "At the Royal Albert Hall. You should really go sometime - they're world-class."

Doyle's sharp breathing crackled through the line. "I hope for your sake you're at home."

"Why?"

"There's a taxi waiting outside your building to take you to Glentworth Street."

Alex moved toward the window, peering down at the street illuminated by the neon glow of the streetlights. Sure enough, a black cab sat idling directly in front of her building, its engine humming.

"Hurry up!" Doyle snapped before hanging up.

For a moment, Alex stood frozen, staring out at the street below. Then, with a resigned sigh, she grabbed her coat, leaving the comfort of her warm apartment and stepping into the chilly London night. Without hesitation, she slid into the waiting taxi, which pulled away from the curb as soon as she shut the door.

The entire ride, which lasted just over 32 minutes, passed in silence. The driver didn't say a word, while the radio played at a low volume, filling the cab with modern disco music - a genre that Alex found entirely unappealing. But she was far too tired to ask the driver to switch stations or turn it off altogether.

By the time they finally arrived at their destination, Alex had dozed off. The driver stepped out and opened her door, giving her a somewhat rough shake to wake her.

She jolted awake, momentarily disoriented, unsure of where she was. Groggily, she stepped out of the vehicle and took a long look at the building before her.

A row of houses, some newly renovated and modern, others old but surprisingly well-preserved, stood before her. The older structures, though aged, seemed meticulously maintained, as if they were polished and restored on a daily basis.

Someone important must live here.

A minister, perhaps?

Or one of the Queen's personal advisors?

Or maybe just a wealthy politician.

Whoever it was, they clearly had money.

But why would someone like that want me?

I'm not that well-known.

And when it comes to personal safety, people instinctively trust a man over a woman - men typically project more protection, more strength.

So, who could this person be?

Or is it a woman?

No!

Even women usually prefer a man in such situations.

Why me, and not Sherlock Holmes?

A growing sense of unease settled in her stomach as she climbed the steps to the front door. She pressed the bell and waited.

After a moment, the door swung open to reveal a man dressed in a sharp black suit, with a white earpiece nestled in his right ear, the wire trailing down his back beneath his jacket. He said nothing, but his expression was serious, almost severe, as he looked at her in silence.

Definitely not your average doorman.

As Alex stepped inside, the man in the black suit immediately shut the door and locked it with a distinct click. He then stood motionless in front of the door, arms crossed, like a tin soldier guarding his post.

Inspector Doyle hurried down the hallway, slightly out of breath, stopping abruptly in front of her. "Finally," he gasped, before turning on his heel. "Come along! Your client is waiting."

My client?

What is this?

Usually, my clients are already dead.

And the dead certainly don't need security.

She followed Doyle down the hall and into a grand living room, accessible through a wide gallery lined with stone busts of historical figures and life-sized statues of nude Greek men. The opulence was staggering.

Alex counted five men in the room, all armed and wired with earpieces - likely agents from either the CIA or the Secret Service. Her eyes then moved to two other figures: one seated in a lavish leather armchair, facing away from her, a glass of Scotch - or perhaps Bourbon - in one hand and a cigarette in the other. The other man stood beside him, similarly with his back to Alex and Doyle. He was tall, gaunt, with short dark hair, and in his right hand, he held a dark-green umbrella with a bamboo handle.

44

"Gentlemen," Doyle said, clearing his throat nervously.

Alex stared at him in astonishment. She had never seen Doyle so rattled.

The seated man stood, turning in unison with the man beside him. Alex's heart sank.

Not him.

Please, not him.

A cold shiver ran down her spine as her eyes widened in shock. She instantly recognized the man with the umbrella - none other than Mycroft Holmes, the embodiment of the British government itself. His expression was as cold and arrogant as ever, the kind that made her want to flee the building on the spot.

"Miss Green, how wonderful that you could join us," said the man beside Mycroft, stepping forward with a warm smile and extending his hand to shake hers.

This just got a whole lot worse.

"You're late," Mycroft chastised, his tone icy. "We've been waiting for some time."

"If I'd known *you* were here, Mr. Holmes, I wouldn't have bothered coming at all," Alex shot back, offering him a venomous smile.

Mycroft narrowed his eyes, visibly surprised by her sharp retort, but said nothing.

"What am I doing here?" Alex turned to Doyle, her patience wearing thin. "If *he's* involved, why do you even need me?" She glanced pointedly at Mycroft. "And what about your brother? Wouldn't he be more suited to handle this?"

"You don't even know what this is about," Mycroft replied, sounding almost wounded. "Besides, the relationship between my younger brother and me can best be described as... difficult."

Difficult?

Alex's brow furrowed in confusion.

No surprise there.

If I had a brother like Mycroft Holmes, I wouldn't like him either.

Mycroft continued, his tone more measured, "It's hardly beneficial to let familial disputes interfere with matters of national importance." He stepped closer, positioning himself beside the other man, and studied Alex with a critical gaze. "I thought you might appreciate the chance to be part of something significant for once."

"As long as either of the Holmes brothers is involved, there's no cause grand enough to warrant my interest," Alex retorted bluntly, her voice dripping with disdain.

Mycroft's pride was clearly wounded, and he wasn't about to let it slide. "So, you'd prefer to remain an unknown, wannabe detective? No recognition, no gratitude, and without the knowledge that you've done something for the greater good of all England? I must say, you disappoint me. I expected more from you."

"And what exactly did you expect?" Alex snapped. "That I'd leap for joy because *you* of all people need my help? I thought you were supposed to be the smart one. So why do you need me?" She huffed irritably. "I don't need your support, and I certainly don't need your charity. Good evening, gentlemen."

She turned sharply on her heel and made for the door that led back into the gallery. But before she could leave, one of the armed men swiftly blocked her path, preventing her from exiting.

"I'm afraid you've misunderstood the situation," Mycroft said, stepping closer. "I'm not *asking* for your help. I'm *ordering* it."

Alex whirled around to face him, her eyes flashing. "You're not my boss. You can't order me to do anything."

"You're a British citizen, just like me," he said coldly. "And as my dear brother is fond of saying - and he's not entirely wrong - I *am* the British government. So, you will do what I tell you!" His voice rang out, filled with authority and impatience.

"Or what?" Alex shot back, her voice defiant. "You'll arrest me?"

"Something like that," Mycroft responded, his tone softening just slightly.

Alex frowned, confusion crossing her face.

Unfazed, Mycroft continued, "You entered a crime scene without proper authorization. That's illegal."

"Your brother does that all the time."

"You are not my brother," he replied with steely calm. Then, almost as an afterthought, he muttered, "Thank God."

What's that supposed to mean?

Why is he glad I'm not his brother?

Does that mean he actually likes me?

More than his own brother?

Well, that wouldn't be hard - he doesn't seem to like Sherlock much at all.

This is just intimidation.

Nothing more.

Thank goodness.

Feeling a touch of relief, Alex exhaled quietly. "Alright," she said, her voice now calm and measured. "Why am I here?"

"Because of me," said the unfamiliar man behind Mycroft, stepping forward along with Inspector Doyle.

"This is Congressman Stephen Shepard," Mycroft introduced him curtly.

Doyle handed Alex a sheet of paper, its surface covered with letters cut from various newspapers, all stuck together to form words, sealed in a clear plastic evidence bag.

Seriously?

How terribly old-fashioned.

And, frankly, dull.

47

With little interest, Alex took the obvious ransom note and read the message aloud: "'Stephen Shepard will meet his end, but before that, 0104009 104036 101257053.'" She squinted at it in confusion. "What? What is this supposed to mean?"

Now that's interesting.

Definitely not old-fashioned after all.

But a puzzle like this... it's beyond me.

Doyle began, "We were hoping that you-"

"No, no, no," she interrupted hastily, shaking her head. "I'm no codebreaker or mathematician."

"Couldn't it be some kind of binary code or something?" Shepard asked, his voice subdued.

"Binary codes are made up of only ones and zeroes," both Alex and Mycroft responded at the exact same moment. Their eyes met, equally surprised by the synchronization, and for a brief moment, they stared at each other in silence.

"It's clear the sequence either refers to a name or a specific date," Alex continued, piecing her thoughts together. "But I'm not the right person to crack it."

Before she could say anything further, Mycroft snatched the note from her hands, flipped it over, and handed it back without a word.

> *"You can't live for everyone,*
> *especially not for those*
> *with whom you don't want*
> *to live.*
> *Sweet sleep!*
> *pure joy,*
> *we sink and cease*
> *to be.*
> *unbidden,*

48

unasked
when pain
is unrestrained,
You come like
the circle of
inner harmonies flows freely,
for, and most willing
You untie the knots
and wrapped in pleasant madness
of strict thoughts,
blend all the images
of joy
oh my..."

Alex looked around at the three men, her expression question-ing. "That's Goethe," she said without hesitation. "But why?"

"You have an excellent knowledge of Goethe's works, far bet-ter than anyone I know," Mycroft replied, watching her closely. "Are you saying none of this makes sense to you?"

Alex thought for a moment. "Sleep is merely a metaphor for death here - the final release, the end, however you want to inter-pret it. But you don't need me to figure that out. The more im-portant question is, who is this message truly intended for?" She paused, considering the puzzle. "The sentences are jumbled, but even more than that, the words themselves are arranged in a very unusual order. What you have here are two completely separate quotes from Goethe, unrelated except for their common author." She turned her sharp gaze to Doyle. "Can I take this with me? I'd like to study it more closely."

"Unfortunately, no. It's evidence."

Undeterred, Alex walked over to a small side table near the leather chair, laying the sheet of paper, still in its plastic covering, flat upon it. She took out her phone and snapped a photo of both sides.

Returning the paper to Doyle, she then addressed the congressman. "For now, you can relax, Mr. Shepard. The poem is clearly not intended for you. Until the person whose name I also can't decipher just yet is dead - or whatever that cryptic message refers to - you're not in any immediate danger." She let out an involuntary yawn, a sign of her exhaustion. She wasn't used to being up this late. "Now, gentlemen, if you'll excuse me. I wish you all a good night." With that, she turned her back on the men and made her way toward the exit.

This time, none of the armed agents dared to block her path.

However, Mycroft wasn't so easily deterred. He followed her into the hallway, and just before she reached the front door, he gently - though as firmly as the situation allowed - took hold of her arm, stopping her. "The reference to Goethe isn't a coincidence," he said, his tone pressing.

Alex looked at Mycroft, slightly disoriented, sensing something unexpected in his voice - was it concern? Affection? "What are you getting at?"

"Whoever sent this knows you, Miss Green," Mycroft replied, his tone heavy with implication.

Alex laughed, unimpressed. "Your brother, Mr. Holmes, is as much a fan of Goethe's works as I am. This might not be about me at all - it could easily be about him. In the end, isn't everything always about Sherlock Holmes?" She exaggerated the statement with dramatic flair.

Unconsciously, Mycroft's grip on her wrist tightened slightly, as though he didn't even realize it. "This has nothing to do with my brother. Sherlock has his own demons to deal with."

Alex pulled her wrist free from his grasp, not without effort. "Moriarty is dead."

"How can you be so sure?" Mycroft asked, his voice tinged with suspicion. "Even *he* isn't entirely certain."

"*He*? Your brother?" Alex scoffed, growing more irritated. "I always thought he was supposed to be clever, but it seems intelligence is being confused with madness these days." She scrutinized Mycroft closely, hoping to discern his true intentions - why he had followed her, why he seemed so unsettled.

He's hiding something.

Not just from me, but from everyone.

What is it?

Yet Mycroft Holmes was like a locked book, his face revealing nothing, his body language a model of restraint.

He's very good.

"Good night, Mr. Holmes," Alex finally said, turning toward the door. Her curiosity nagged at her, but her exhaustion won out.

As the man from earlier opened the front door for her, Mycroft called after Alex in haste, "Be careful, Miss Green! You're walking on very thin ice, and it could crack at any moment."

Alex paused for a second, but didn't turn back to face him. She let his words hang in the air, considering them briefly before striding out of the building. To her relief, the taxi that had brought her there was still waiting outside.

The driver leaned casually against the front passenger door, puffing on what looked to be his seventh cigarette, as evidenced by the pile of discarded butts beneath his feet.

"Please take me home," Alex pleaded, her exhaustion weighing heavily on her.

He stubbed out his cigarette and opened the back door for her. As she slid into the car, she caught sight of Mycroft standing at the entrance of the building, watching her leave.

Their eyes met briefly, and for the first time, Mycroft's expression revealed something more - something vulnerable. It was as if the impenetrable wall he always kept around himself had crumbled, showing a glimpse of his true self.

He's worried - genuinely worried.

About me?

Why?

Damn it.

He's making it difficult to hate him.

He's nothing like his brother... but I still can't allow myself to like him.

No!

Finally, the driver slid into his seat, sparing Alex from Mycroft's unsettlingly human gaze.

Why does he carry that umbrella everywhere?

It hasn't rained for days, and there's no forecast for bad weather anytime soon.

Mycroft Holmes is indeed an extraordinarily strange man.

And yet, despite her best efforts, he fascinated her.

During the thirty-minute ride home, Alex's thoughts were consumed by Mycroft Holmes, though she wished they wouldn't be. The more she resisted thinking about him, the stronger the urge became to unravel the mystery surrounding him.

He's definitely hiding something.

And I'm going to find out what it is.

IV.

GOETHE AND IRON MAN

A little after 2:00 a.m., Alexandra trudged exhaustedly through the stairwell and entered her apartment. She was so drained that she didn't even make it to her bedroom. Instead, she collapsed onto the couch like a sack of potatoes, her body giving way to fatigue as she shut her eyes.

Strange.

Something's off.

Why is it so cold in here?

Her eyes fluttered open briefly, scanning the room. That's when she noticed - the large living room window was wide open.

What?

In an instant, Alex was fully awake. She bolted upright, her heart pounding. She rushed to the side and flicked the light on, her hand trembling. The sudden brightness made her squint as the glare overwhelmed her tired eyes. Once her vision adjusted, she began scanning the room in a mix of fear and confusion.

Then she heard it - the unmistakable sound of running water coming from the bathroom, as if someone were taking a shower.

I must be dreaming.

But the sound was unmistakably real, beyond any doubt.

Fear surged through her, swift and electric. No longer hesitating, she dashed to the kitchen, yanking open a drawer and pulling out the largest, sharpest knife she owned. Clutching it tightly in front of her, hands shaking, she moved toward the bathroom, each step slow and deliberate, trying to make as little noise as possible.

Intruder caught showering?

What a ridiculous headline.

53

No one will believe me.

I barely believe it myself.

As she neared the closed bathroom door, her pulse quickened, thudding loudly in her ears. She forced herself to focus on what lay ahead, mentally preparing for whatever - or whoever - was behind that door.

You've got this.

You've survived worse.

Come on!

Do it!

She gripped the knife tighter, ready for whatever awaited her on the other side. With a forceful yank, Alex flung the unlocked door open and leapt into the bathroom. "Don't move!" she shouted.

A young woman gasped in shock, letting out a piercing scream. In her panic, she slipped on the slick porcelain floor of the shower, crashing backward and hitting her head hard against the tiled wall in the corner.

"Liz?" Alex lowered the knife, her face contorting in disbelief. "What the hell are you doing here?"

"I'm so sorry," Liz mumbled, still dazed from the fall. "I must've lost my apartment keys somewhere at the bar."

"So, you just break into my place?"

"I knocked, and I tried calling you, but you didn't answer," Liz explained, grabbing a towel from the shower wall and wrapping it around herself, clearly embarrassed. "I didn't mean to scare you." She gingerly stepped out of the shower, her face flushed with shame.

"How did you even get in here?" Alex demanded, her eyes narrowing suspiciously.

"The window was open."

Really?

Could that be true?

Suddenly, she remembered.

Oh!

Yes, she's right.

I had only pulled it closed but didn't lock it.

Completely drained from the adrenaline and confusion, Alex turned and walked back into the living room. She placed the knife on the kitchen counter before collapsing onto the couch, utterly exhausted.

Liz followed her in small, hurried steps. "I'm really, really sorry," she repeated, her voice filled with remorse.

"It's fine," Alex muttered, too tired to muster any more anger.

Liz looked at her friend with concern, clearly sensing something was wrong. "What happened? Where were you all this time?" Liz, brimming with curiosity, walked over to the window and shut it properly. "I dropped you off at home around 11. Why are you only getting back now?" She moved to sit beside Alex, her worry growing. "You look like you've seen a ghost."

Oh, you have no idea...

Liz's face suddenly paled. "Was it because of me? I really didn't mean to frighten you."

Alex rubbed her weary eyes and turned to Liz. "No, it wasn't just because of you - though you *did* scare me half to death. But honestly, it was this Holmes who frightened me even more."

Liz's eyes suddenly widened with excitement. "Which Holmes are you talking about? Sherlock? Oh, he's *so* charming!"

No, damn it!

It wasn't Sherlock Holmes!

Why must everything always be about him?

Alex shot her friend a stern look, instantly wiping the infatuated grin off Liz's face.

There are others in that family who give me nightmares...

"Okay," Liz said, blinking in confusion. "Spill it! What happened?"

"You've heard of Mycroft Holmes, Sherlock's older brother, haven't you?"

"Wait." Liz's expression shifted from curiosity to disgust as her eyes widened in shock. "You were with *him*?" she asked, her tone dripping with distaste for the man. "What were you doing?"

"No, I wasn't *with* him. I..." Alex hesitated.

Can I even tell her?

What if it puts her in danger?

No, that's ridiculous.

But Mycroft seems to think this could be connected to me.

And, as much as I hate to admit it, he's an incredibly sharp man.

He knows exactly what he's talking about.

So... could he be right?

"Alex?" Liz's voice broke through her thoughts, concern evident in her tone. "Are you alright? You're acting really strange."

Okay.

I have to tell her.

I trust her.

I just hope I'm not making a mistake.

"Do you trust me?" Alex asked, fixing her friend with a stern gaze.

Liz chuckled lightly. "Yeah, of course."

"I'm serious," Alex insisted, her tone firm. "Do you trust me?"

Liz, sensing the gravity of the situation, did her best to match Alex's seriousness. "Yes, I trust you completely."

Alex hesitated for a moment, uncertainty clouding her thoughts. Then she took a deep breath and said, "For the past five years, I've been working with the Scotland Yard as a sort of a private detective."

"What?" Liz stared at her, utterly shocked. "Are you serious?"

Didn't I just say that?

Alex remained outwardly composed, the look on her face answering Liz's question with a clear, emphatic *yes*. But before she could continue, the unmistakable scent of Chinese food wafted through the air. She shot Liz a suspicious look. "You've been back on Baker Street, haven't you?"

Liz's eyes widened in surprise. "How do you know that?"

"The Chinese restaurant." Alex pointed at Liz's still unwashed hair.

"Oh, damn," Liz muttered, immediately realizing how she'd given herself away. "Now I smell it too."

Alex scrutinized her closely. "What were you doing there?"

"Nothing!" Liz protested.

The young secretary shook her head, letting it drop slightly in exhaustion. "Honestly, it's a bit creepy that you're still chasing after Dr. Watson, especially considering his wife hasn't been gone that long. And, besides, he's far too old for you."

"I'm sorry," Liz said, turning her gaze away from Alex. "I can't help it." Then she looked back, her eyes sincere. "Mockery does not drive away love."

Alex rolled her eyes and stood up. As she walked toward the kitchen, she muttered, "It must be serious if you're quoting Goethe at nearly 3:00 o'clock in the morning." But before she could even finish the sentence, she stopped dead in her tracks, her mind racing back to Mycroft's cryptic words.

The reference to Goethe is no coincidence.

Goethe?

Why Goethe?

And how does Mycroft Holmes even know about my love for Johann Wolfgang von Goethe?

Of course.

When you're practically the British government, you know everything.

A cold wave of fear washed over her, freezing her both inside and out.

Does he know the other things?

Does he know the truth about me?

Could he... help me?

The exhaustion that clung to her made it impossible to think clearly. Her mind, fogged by fatigue, struggled to form a coherent answer. Deciding it wasn't worth losing more sleep over, she turned to Liz. "You can sleep on the couch. There are pillows and blankets underneath." With a heavy yawn, Alex trudged toward the hallway. "Good night." She lumbered off to her bedroom, her steps sluggish, her mind still faintly buzzing with unanswered questions about Sherlock Holmes' enigmatic brother.

After far too short a night, it took Alexandra a while to fully return to the present. Still groggy, she sat up in bed, pushing her long dark hair out of her face as she cradled her pounding head.

What have I gotten myself into?

She grabbed her phone and glanced at the display, already showing three missed calls from Inspector Doyle.

I'm starting to think he might actually be interested in me.

Frowning, she climbed out of bed, her eyes still fixed on the phone in her hand. After only two steps, she tripped over her shoes and fell forward, sprawling onto the floor. Her fingers accidentally brushed the phone's screen, opening the photo gallery. There, staring back at her, were the images she had taken the night before.

Goethe!

Slowly, she pushed herself up, her gaze settling on the puzzling poem scribbled on the back of the blackmail letter. She flipped through the photos, studying the cryptic message on the other side.

What do these numbers mean?

And why do I feel like the answer has been staring me in the face this whole time?

Just then, the bedroom door swung open, and Liz entered, carrying a plate of deliciously fragrant pancakes. "Good morning, sleepyhead," she chirped, far too energetic for this hour. "Hope you're hungry!"

"Are those pancakes?"

"Yes, I thought it was the least I could do as an apology," Liz said, her voice tinged with guilt.

Alex grinned, delighted by the gesture. "Consider yourself completely forgiven, honestly." She eagerly followed Liz into the living room, where the breakfast table was already set, every detail meticulously arranged. As Liz fussed over her, serving everything with care, Alex wasted no time diving into the pancakes with a ravenous appetite.

"So?" Liz asked, sitting down on the opposite side of the table. "What was that whole thing with Mycroft Holmes last night? What's his connection to you and the Scotland Yard?"

"Like I said, I do some work for the Scotland Yard on the side," Alex replied, her voice muffled as she chewed contentedly. "Mostly solving so-called 'unsolvable' murder cases."

"Like Sherlock?" Liz's eyes widened in fascination.

"Yes, like Sherlock," Alex muttered, clearly less than thrilled by the comparison.

If I had gotten a penny for every time someone said that...

"Why didn't you ever tell me?" Liz asked, her expression turning serious. "You've basically been lying to me for five years."

"I didn't lie to you," Alex corrected, setting her fork down. "I just didn't tell you everything. It was for your own protection."

Liz narrowed her eyes, scrutinizing her friend with suspicion.

"Don't give me that look!" Alex snapped, irritated. "Do you have any idea how many murderers I've helped put behind bars over the last five years? And trust me, every single one of them would love nothing more than to get back at me someday."

Liz's face paled at the thought.

"But let's not dwell on that. Please." Alex took a long, fortifying sip of her black coffee. "As for Mycroft Holmes, even I'm not entirely sure what his role is in all this. What's clear is that he's incredibly influential within the British government - an immensely powerful man. But last night, I wasn't meeting with him directly. I was with Congressman Stephen Shepard." She pulled out her phone and showed Liz the photos of the blackmail letter. "This was the reason I was there."

"So, Goethe, then," Liz remarked after a while, stating the obvious. "But why Goethe, for heaven's sake?"

"I haven't the faintest idea," Alex responded, her voice heavy with frustration.

Liz stood up, looking a little uneasy. "You do realize this has *something* to do with you, right?"

"Oh, it's just a coincidence," Alex muttered dismissively.

"I wouldn't be so sure," Liz replied, moving toward the stove. "What if the blackmail letter isn't really meant for Congressman Shepard, but for *you*?" She grabbed a damp cloth and began meticulously wiping the stains off the counter. Pausing for a moment, she glanced back at Alex, who had been staring at her in confusion. "You should consider getting police protection."

Alex nearly choked on a large piece of pancake, coughing violently at the mere thought. "Don't be ridiculous!"

"I'm not being ridiculous!" Liz returned to the table, her eyes stern with concern. "I just don't want anything to happen to you."

Before Alex could reply, her phone rang. Without glancing at the display, she answered in an irritated tone. "What on earth do

60

you want, Doyle? Can't this wait until later? It's six in the morning!"

"This is not Inspector Doyle, Miss Green," came a deep, resonant voice on the other end of the line. "And no, it cannot wait."

"Who is this?" Alex asked, bewildered.

"My name is Sherlock Holmes."

Oh, dear...

Alex's hand went numb, and the fork she was holding clattered onto the plate with a sharp crash. "What do *you* want from me?"

"That depends entirely on what *you* want from my brother," the voice on the other end replied sternly. "Why did you meet with him last night?"

Alex rolled her eyes in irritation. "Why don't you ask him yourself? Or have the two of you stopped talking to each other?"

"Who is it?" Liz asked, her curiosity practically bursting at the seams.

Suddenly, a mischievous idea sprang into Alex's mind. A sly smile curled on her lips as she said, "Sherlock Holmes," and, without hesitation, handed the phone to Liz. "It's for you."

Liz's face lit up as if she had just won the lottery. She grabbed the phone with trembling hands and pressed it to her ear. "Hello, Mr. Holmes?" she stammered, her voice filled with awe. "I'm your biggest fan. The way you solved *A Study in Scarlet* was simply magnificent!"

Alex leaned back, thoroughly entertained, watching Liz gush over the phone. But after a moment of indulgence, she stood up and walked to the hallway, grabbing her coat. "I'll see you later," she called to her friend, who was too absorbed in bombarding her idol with admiration to respond. "You can keep my phone for today."

With a cheeky grin still lingering on her face, Alex slipped out the door and left the apartment, savoring her small, playful victory.

On her way to work, Alex passed by an old phone booth on a street teeming with people. Just as she walked by, the phone inside started ringing.

Alex stopped in her tracks and glanced back.

Seriously?

Is this some kind of joke?

For a moment, she considered ignoring it and continued walking. She didn't notice the elderly man behind her who stepped into the phone booth and answered the call. As she was still within earshot, the man leaned out of the booth and called, "Alexandra Green?"

Alex froze, startled, and turned around hesitantly, eyeing the old man.

"A very urgent call for you," he said with a gap-toothed grin, revealing his remaining yellowed, neglected teeth. "It's the government."

Her brow furrowed as she considered simply walking away, pretending she hadn't heard him.

"Seems important," the old man added, extending the receiver toward her.

Shaking her head in annoyance, Alex begrudgingly returned to the phone booth. She snatched the receiver and brought it to her ear. "What on earth do you want, Mr. Holmes?" she asked coldly, fully aware that the caller could only be Mycroft Holmes himself.

"First, I would appreciate a bit more courtesy from you, Miss Green," came Mycroft's voice, cold and condescending. "Second, I'd be grateful if you could refrain from bothering my brother in the future. Third, and most importantly, I'm quite eager to know if you've made any progress on deciphering the message."

Alex, boiling with anger, took a deep breath. "How I speak to you is entirely my business," she snapped. "And don't think for a second that I enjoy talking to someone as revolting as you. You should be thankful I'm speaking to you at all. As for your brother, I've done nothing to him. If he claims otherwise, he's either lying or twisting the facts." Her voice grew louder with each word, her rage mounting. Several passersby turned to stare at her, their confused glances going unnoticed in her blind fury. "And I only got the message about six hours ago! Not even Sherlock Holmes could crack that code in such a short time. If I'm moving too slowly for your liking, then why don't you give the damn letter to *your brother* and leave me in peace!"

Mycroft chuckled softly, clearly amused by her outburst. It only fueled her rage further. "I don't understand why you're so hostile toward me, Miss Green. After all, we're on the same side - you, me, and Sherlock."

"We are *not* on the same side," Alex shouted into the phone, her voice trembling with fury. "You're a greedy bastard who exploits his own family! Why else would your brother refuse to speak with you? And Sherlock? He's an uptight, peculiar overgrown child who would rather shoot holes in his walls out of boredom than do something remotely useful!"

"Please, leave my brother out of this," Mycroft responded, his voice infuriatingly calm. "Though I must admit, it's fascinating that you call me a bastard while you are on your way to meet someone far worse right now. I'm not a bad person, you should know that."

"I'm sure Hannibal Lecter would say exactly the same," Alex retorted, though she felt her anger cooling slightly.

"What have I done to you that makes you despise me so much?" Mycroft asked, his tone steady.

Good question.

Next question.

He was right. What had he actually done? Why did she hate him so much? It wasn't Mycroft who people constantly compared her to - it was his immature little brother, Sherlock.

Mycroft Holmes hasn't done anything to me.

Oh no, don't start liking him now.

Pull yourself together!

"Are you still there?"

"Yes," Alex replied, now thoroughly confused. "Look, I'm sorry I yelled at you. But with less than three hours of sleep, it's hard to be pleasant."

"You still haven't answered my question," Mycroft remarked, unfazed.

He's impossible!

"I really need to go now, or I'll be late for work," Alex said curtly. "I'll let you know as soon as I find anything. You'll be the first to hear." With that, she hung up the phone and hurried out of the booth, her nerves on edge.

Her whole body was trembling as she sped down the street.

Why am I shaking?

What is he doing to me?

I think I'm losing my mind.

Yes, that's it.

I'm going mad.

Completely unsettled, Alex sprinted forward, her thoughts in turmoil. She loathed feeling unsure of herself - it was a rare and unwelcome sensation. Confused and disoriented, she suddenly darted across the busy street, charging over the crosswalk without paying attention to the traffic light, which was still glaring red.

The screech of brakes, the blare of a car horn, and the furious shouting of the driver, who hurled insults at her, snapped Alex back – violently - to the past.

Damn it.

Not again.

Frozen, trembling from head to toe in front of the halted car, Alex's mind was transported to a memory so vivid, it felt like reality. She couldn't move.

Before her eyes, she saw a boy - a long-forgotten childhood friend - who had mysteriously disappeared when he was about six years old. He was running, just as she remembered him from that distant day. The bustling street before her transformed into a field overgrown with tall grass, and there he was, racing across it, wearing a golden-yellow helmet far too large for him and a red-and-yellow suit of cardboard armor that encased his small frame.

Iron Man.

Suddenly, a man yanked her forcefully by the arm, dragging her off the street. "Are you suicidal?" he cried out, his voice filled with shock.

"Victor," was all Alex could manage to say, her voice barely a whisper.

The man froze at the sound of that name, staring at her in disbelief, as though she had just uttered something profoundly unsettling. "Are you alright?" he asked after a long pause. "Hello? Can you hear me?" He shook her, and not very gently.

At last, Alex snapped back to the present. When she saw the man in front of her, she instinctively recoiled in surprise - it was Dr. John Watson, the very person who had just dragged her off the street. "What the hell!" she exclaimed, flustered. "Are you following me?"

"Who is Victor?" Watson asked, his voice calm and measured.

"Nobody," Alex replied, still confused and disoriented.

Iron Man.

Who is that?

"What do you want from me?" she asked, her mind spinning.

"For starters, a 'thank you' would be nice," Watson said, raising an eyebrow.

Alex frowned. "For what?"

"Do you even realize what just happened?" Dr. Watson asked, his tone filled with concern.

"Oh, yes. The man my best friend has a crush on just interrupted me from recalling an important memory from my childhood."

"What?" He stared at her, baffled for a moment. "Actually," he continued, regaining his composure, "you ran through a red light like someone with a death wish, completely out of it." He paused, as if lost in thought. "So, my stalker is your friend," he muttered, pacing in place. "I should have known she was connected to you."

"Wait, do you know me?" Alex asked, incredulous.

"Who doesn't?" Watson replied, sounding a bit offended. "Sherlock is always talking about you. Apparently, you've somehow impressed him."

Somehow?

Alex turned abruptly and began walking down the sidewalk. When Watson hurried to catch up with her, she quipped, "Your friend really needs to learn how to give a proper compliment."

"Oh, I doubt he intended it as a compliment," Watson replied with a dry smirk.

Alex shot him a fleeting glance before quickening her pace - she was already running late. "Thanks for your help, Dr. Watson. And a word of advice: don't let my friend know you've spotted her. She's incredibly shy and would never dare approach you in person. Goodbye," she called back as she rushed off down the street.

Watson stood there, watching her retreating figure, breathing heavily.

Who the hell is Iron Man?

And what does he have to do with Victor?

Just before 7:00 a.m., Alex finally arrived at the law firm. She hurried inside, flicked on the lights, and collapsed into her chair, breathing heavily.

Damn it, Liz still has my phone with the photos.

Without wasting a second, she picked up the office phone and dialed her own mobile number, waiting impatiently for her friend to answer.

"Hey, did you know that Doyle's been calling you nonstop?" Liz said the moment she picked up. "Oh, and Sherlock's brother also wanted to talk to you urgently. Seems like you're quite the hot commodity these days."

"Listen, if anyone else calls, *do not* answer. I don't care who it is - unless it's me. Got it?"

"What's going on with you? You're not usually this weird. Mycroft Holmes must've really gotten under your skin last night."

"Cut it out!" Alex snapped, her tone sharp. "You have no idea what we talked about."

"Well, I've picked up on a few things by now," Liz replied slyly. "But what's the deal with that letter? Have you managed to figure anything out with those numbers?"

"Not yet. That's actually why I'm calling. Can you email me the two photos? Send them to the firm."

"Of course," Liz said cheerfully. "I really hope you can make sense of that mess. Because honestly, I have no idea how those Goethe quotes connect to the coded message."

"You can't live for everyone, especially not for those with whom you don't want to live," Alex muttered under her breath, pacing back and forth across her office floor. She had been repeating the quote endlessly, but it brought her no closer to solving the puzzle. Just as an idea struck her - that perhaps the numbers on the other side of the message could somehow be integrated into the Goethe

67

quote - her boss, Harold Lloyd, burst out of his office, storming toward her.

"What on earth are you doing?" he demanded, staring at her with confusion as she stood in the middle of the room, gazing up at the ceiling. "Don't you have work to do?"

"Please, just look!" Alex responded sweetly, pointing shakily toward the lamp above. Only when Lloyd drew nearer and looked up as well did she continue, "There! Do you see that black thing? It's a spider. I'm terribly sorry, Mr. Lloyd, but as long as that ghastly creature is in the same room as me, I simply *cannot* concentrate."

"Typical woman," Lloyd muttered, shaking his head in frustration. He grumbled to himself as he exited the office, leaving for his early morning appointment.

Only once he was out of sight did Alex return to her desk, where the two printed out photos of the blackmail letter were spread across the surface. She had gone to great lengths to prevent Lloyd from coming anywhere near her workspace - if he had seen the images, it would have raised far too many questions, questions she had no desire to answer.

"What's missing here?" Alex murmured to herself, standing before the copies of the letter, her brow furrowed in concentration.

"A doorbell, I'd say," came a deep, resonant voice from the doorway. Alex looked up, startled, to see a man who had just entered the room unnoticed and now stood only a few steps away from her.

"What are you doing here?" Alex demanded, disbelief flickering across her face as she processed the fact that Sherlock Holmes himself had just shown up at her boss's law firm. "First your brother, then your lapdog, and now you? What on earth do you want from me?"

"Dr. Watson is not my lapdog," Sherlock replied, his tone frigid. "He is my *highly* loyal associate."

"He's your lapdog," Alex insisted, leaning back with folded arms. "He follows you everywhere. If you jumped off a cliff, he'd do the same."

"Not *exactly* the same," Sherlock corrected in his typical know-it-all manner. "First, he'd attempt to talk me out of it, likely engaging in a prolonged discussion. Should I persist, he'd curse himself and then jump at least two meters farther."

Alex clearly had no patience for this man. She sank back into her chair, her expression icy. "What do you want?"

"Who is Victor?" Sherlock asked abruptly, his sharp gaze locked on her, studying her reaction.

In an instant, Alex shot up from her seat, her face twisting with unrestrained fury. "Get out!" she hissed, pointing to the door. "Now!"

"So, it's someone who clearly means a great deal to you," Sherlock mused, as if speaking to himself while he began to pace the room. "A friend? No. Family, then?" He paused, turning to look at her with piercing intensity. "Victor is your brother, isn't he? Odd. The Alexandra Green I know has no siblings."

He continued to move thoughtfully through the office, but Alex's expression was now one of rigid, silent anger. Sherlock's deductions, though chillingly precise, had begun to scratch at something buried, something she wasn't prepared to confront.

"Victor is *not* my brother! And if you don't leave right now, I'll call the police!" Alex snapped, her voice sharp with fury.

"What are you hiding? What's the big, dark secret that no one is allowed to know? Is that why you despise my brother and me so much?" Sherlock's calm yet cutting voice probed deeper, pushing her toward the edge.

That was enough. Alex stormed around her desk, grabbing Sherlock by the arm and forcefully shoving him toward the door. "I never want to see you again - *anywhere*! Is that clear?"

"It'll take more than that to intimidate me," Sherlock replied coolly, unfazed by her outburst.

"Perhaps your brother, then?" Alex shot back with venom.

Sherlock froze, his face betraying a brief moment of vulnerability. That slight hesitation told Alex everything she needed to know - she had just struck a nerve.

Without another word, she spun on her heel and walked back into her office, leaving him standing in the doorway.

Sherlock, however, remained where he was, his gaze lingering on her retreating figure as he tried to untangle the web she had spun around herself. "She's good," he muttered to himself before finally turning and walking away, his mind already whirring with new questions.

V.

M LIKE ...

"This is how a day off should be spent," Elizabeth Markle - known to most as Liz - murmured as she lounged on the couch in her best friend's apartment. She was absorbed in an old book by Sir Arthur Conan Doyle, the title *The End of the World* scrawled in bold red letters against a grey background. Liz flipped through the pages, pausing to admire the intricate illustrations with clear delight.

Alex's phone lay on the oval coffee table in front of her. Though the ringer was off, the incessant vibrating hadn't stopped since she'd arrived.

Just as Liz turned to a new chapter, another call came through. The phone buzzed loudly against the glass surface, startling her. She jumped slightly and leaned forward to glance at the display. "Strange," she muttered, furrowing her brow. "The number isn't saved." She shrugged. "Oh well, I'm not supposed to answer her calls anyway."

Settling back into the couch, Liz's attention drifted to something else - a crumpled, old photograph that had slipped out of the book and landed on her lap. It must have been tucked between the pages, hidden until now. Curiosity piqued, she picked up the photo and examined it more closely.

On the partially yellowed photograph, two children could be seen. A little girl with long, dark brown braids and freckles, clutching a fabric doll shaped like a light-blue hippopotamus, and a boy, who couldn't have been more than two years older than the girl. He had wild red curls and a mischievous face full of the same bright freckles. In his left hand, he proudly held a wooden toy sword, which rested awkwardly across his lap, likely too big and too heavy for him to manage. On the back of the photo, two names

71

were scrawled. The first was still legible, and Liz easily read it as *Margaret*. The second name, however, had faded so much that only a *V* was clear, with perhaps an *I* if she squinted and let her imagination fill in the blanks. The rest was too smudged, but Liz guessed it might have said *Victor*.

"Who are they?" Liz wondered aloud, examining the smiling faces of the children once more. She didn't recognize them, but the photo seemed over twenty years old. Still, she couldn't shake the feeling that she knew the girl - *must* have known her.

Driven by a hunch, Liz suddenly leapt from the couch and began rifling through every shelf and drawer in the living room, not entirely sure what she was looking for but determined to find something.

"If I had a secret, where would I hide it so that no one could ever find it?" she muttered to herself, freezing mid-step as the answer hit her. "Of course. The bedroom."

Feeling like Sherlock Holmes himself chasing down a red-hot lead, Liz made a beeline for her best friend's bedroom. The thrill of discovery coursed through her, as if she were about to unlock a mystery that had long been buried.

Without a second thought for Alex's privacy, Liz rummaged through every drawer and cabinet, driven by curiosity. Finally, crouched before the wardrobe, she found something: a false bottom hidden beneath a pile of neatly folded T-shirts.

"This is so exciting!" she exclaimed, her enthusiasm untempered by the moral implications of her snooping. She pried open the hidden compartment with no hesitation, blinded by the thrill of discovery. What she pulled out, however, caused her breath to catch in her throat - a worn, light-blue stuffed hippopotamus, its fabric threadbare and patched in several places. "Oh, Alex, what have you done?" Liz whispered in shock, only now realizing that the little girl in the photograph had to be her best friend. But if that was Alex, then who was Margaret? And the boy? *Who is Victor?*

72

Her mind racing, Liz continued to dig through the secret compartment, hoping to uncover more clues. To her surprise, there was indeed more. She pulled out several crinkled drawings, clearly done in watercolors. The pictures were childish but poignant, depicting two small children - a boy with a wooden sword and a girl holding the very same light-blue stuffed hippopotamus.

On the final picture, however, the scene shifted: the familiar boy and girl were there, but now they were joined by two more boys, roughly the same age, with dark, curly hair. One of them was stout, with a round belly, while the other held a large hammer and wore a red cape. In the background, distant from the other children, stood another figure - a girl with two dark braids, her expression so dark and menacing that Liz felt an involuntary shiver run down her spine just looking at her.

Beside the children was a grand house, almost like a castle, engulfed in flames. Crooked gravestones lined the yard before it. In the bottom-right corner of the drawing, in elegant, flowing script, were the words *Margaret* and *Abbey House.* The handwriting was far too delicate and precise to belong to a child - it must have been written by an adult, likely a woman.

"What is this?" Liz muttered, her heart pounding in her chest. *Who is Margaret? And what does Abbey House have to do with Alex?* She stared at the haunting drawing, knowing that she had just unearthed a mystery far more complicated than she had anticipated.

"Abbey House?" Liz muttered aloud, her brow furrowed in thought. "Why does that name sound so familiar?"

A sudden wave of panic hit her - after all, it was already quarter past twelve, and Alex could return from work at any moment. Hastily, Liz snapped photos of the drawings and the stuffed animal with her own phone, then quickly stowed everything back into its hiding place, praying that nothing looked out of order. She rushed back to the living room, took a photo of the old, yellowed photograph as well, before slipping it back between the pages of the book and returning the volume to its original place on the shelf.

Settling back onto the couch, Liz could no longer relax. Her nerves were frayed, and the dread of Alex discovering her snooping was eating away at her. To distract herself, she pulled out her phone and began searching for *Abbey House* online.

What she found sent a chill down her spine. The search results were filled with disturbing articles and shocking images that made her stomach drop.

Just then, the front door creaked open.

"I'm home," Alex called from the hallway as she closed the door behind her. But instead of making her way into the living room as usual, she froze mid-step, her voice growing tense. "You went through my apartment, didn't you?" Her irritation was palpable.

"I'm sorry," Liz admitted, guilt written all over her face as Alex walked in and stared at her intently. "I was hoping you'd hidden a secret stash of cigarettes somewhere."

"I quit three years ago," Alex replied sharply, still clearly annoyed. "And so did you."

"I know," Liz sighed, "but I can't think straight anymore."

Alex crossed her arms, her piercing gaze not letting up. "That doesn't explain why you thought rifling through my things was a good idea."

Then she shook her head in frustration and made her way to the kitchen. She paused before one of the hanging cabinets, opened it, and reached behind a set of old coffee cups that she despised but kept on display for her aunt's sake. With a sigh, she pulled out a half-empty pack of cigarettes, which she promptly tossed to Liz.

"You're a lifesaver, you know that?" Liz exclaimed gleefully, dashing out to the balcony with the pack clutched in her hands.

"Smoking kills," Alex muttered as she followed her out, handing Liz a lighter to help her light up the much-desired cigarette.

Liz, lighting her cigarette, then offered the pack to Alex, silently hoping she'd join her. Alex hesitated for a moment before relenting. "Ah, what the hell," she said, taking one for herself and lighting it up. She took a long drag and exhaled a cloud of smoke with visible relief. "After the day I've had, I need this."

As the two leaned against the balcony railing, arms resting on the cool metal, Alex continued, "If only you knew the kind of day I've had."

"Well, spill it already!" Liz urged her impatiently.

"On the way to the office, I ran into Dr. Watson."

Liz's eyes widened in disbelief, causing her to choke slightly on the cigarette smoke. "What? Wait - seriously? What did he say?" she asked between coughs, barely able to contain her excitement.

Alex cast her mind back over the day's strange encounters. "Apparently, he knows me, and so does Sherlock. In fact, it turns out that Sherlock holds me in higher regard than I'd have thought. And if that wasn't bizarre enough, Sherlock Holmes himself showed up at my office."

"What? Sherlock Holmes, *in person*?" Liz was practically beside herself with curiosity. "And what did he want from you?"

Alex waved her hand dismissively, taking another drag. "Oh, it's a long, complicated story that honestly isn't worth telling."

Liz, unsure, debated whether to share her own discovery, but hesitated. To do so would reveal she hadn't really been searching for cigarettes at all. It would mean admitting that she'd snooped through Alex's apartment, and that wasn't something she was ready to confess just yet. Instead, she settled for silence, nervously flicking the ash off her cigarette.

Alex shot her a side glance, sensing that Liz was hiding something but deciding not to press her on it - for now. After all, she had enough mysteries to unravel without adding her best friend's strange behavior to the list.

"And how was your day?" Alex asked, clearly exhausted.

"Compared to yours? Pretty dull, I'd say. Even your phone had more excitement than I did - it was ringing non-stop."

"Let me guess, Inspector Doyle?" Alex raised an eyebrow.

"Yeah, him too. Mycroft Holmes called as well, and there was also an unknown number," Liz replied, shrugging.

"Oh!" Alex exclaimed as if something had just clicked in her mind. "That unknown number probably was the lost-and-found office. I asked them to call if your apartment keys turned up any-where."

Liz sighed, her guilt showing. "I totally forgot about that. Hon-estly, what would I do without you?"

"Probably sleep on the street, or maybe break into someone else's place to shower." Alex glanced at Liz, a smirk forming on her lips. "Speaking of which, how *did* you manage to get in through that tilted window?"

Grinning mischievously, Liz pulled out a roughly one-meter-long cord from her pocket and waved it in front of Alex. "Simple. You just tie a loop at the end, drop it onto the window handle, push the window shut tight, and then use the cord to pull the handle down. Voilà! You're in."

Alex chuckled, impressed. "Looks like you've had some prac-tice with that," she said, stubbing out her cigarette. "Come on, let's go pick up your keys." She turned and made her way back into the living room, heading toward the hallway.

"Don't forget your phone!" Liz called after her, shutting the balcony door behind them. She grabbed Alex's phone from the side table and followed her friend out of the apartment. Together, they made their way out into the bustling streets of London.

It was already dark by the time Alexandra had said her goodbyes to Elizabeth and started her walk back home. The streets of London had quieted down, the usual crowds now thinned, leaving behind an almost idyllic, romantic atmosphere, as the soft glow from the streetlamps bathed the sidewalks in a dim light. But suddenly, her attention was drawn to a tall, slender man, dressed in a long, dark coat. He carried an umbrella in one hand and a phone in the other, pressed to his ear. The color of the umbrella was too shadowed by the dusk to be sure, yet there was no mistaking who he was.

Mycroft Holmes.

What a coincidence.

Before he could spot her, Alex quickly slipped into a narrow side alley, moving with as much discretion as possible, and waited until he passed.

"I don't care who it is," Mycroft's voice cut sharply through the quiet night air as he barked into his phone. "Get me the file, and I'll decide myself whether it's necessary to intervene or not."

Pulling her coat collar up and keeping her head low, Alex silently crossed the street, sticking to the shadows, where the streetlights didn't reach. She followed Mycroft from the darkness, careful to remain unseen.

"You seem to forget who you're talking to," Mycroft snapped impatiently into his phone. "The decision is entirely mine. This is a personal matter." He snorted, clearly irritated. "Then explain that to him yourself!" he ordered, his tone even more exasperated. "If Alexandra Green says he's not in immediate danger, then that's exactly how it is. No questions." There was a brief pause as Mycroft listened to the response on the other end of the line. His hand, trembling slightly, wiped across his forehead as though clearing away invisible sweat. "Just do as I say!" he finished with finality, before ending the call and slipping his phone into his coat pocket as he turned the corner.

Alex quickened her pace, her footsteps nearly silent as she trailed him, her mind racing with questions. What was that call about? And more importantly - why had her name been mentioned?

After Mycroft disappeared into a grand house, a stately building that appeared to be his own residence, Alexandra came to a halt, watching until the heavy door slammed shut behind him with a resounding echo. She was about to turn back, her curiosity momentarily satisfied, when she felt a sudden, vice-like grip on her body.

Before she could react, a strong, muscular arm wrapped around her waist from behind, pulling her against an unseen attacker. Simultaneously, a rough hand clamped tightly over her mouth, silencing any chance of a scream. A cold, sharp object pressed against her neck - then pierced it.

As the chilling sensation of liquid surged into her veins, Alex's mind raced. Her thoughts spun wildly between panic and analysis. It was clear: someone had injected her with something. Whether it was a deadly poison or merely a sedative, she couldn't tell.

Her vision blurred, the world around her dissolving into darkness.

Just before she succumbed to the overwhelming drowsiness, one final thought crystallized in her mind - she would soon find out the truth. That is, if she ever woke up.

A low, throbbing hum was the first thing Alexandra became aware of. Her head pounded fiercely, each pulse like the echo of a heavy blow. Her temple throbbed, and for several moments, all she could see was overwhelming blackness. Slowly, painfully, her vision adjusted to the sharp glare of a single exposed lightbulb hanging directly above her.

"Where am I?" she mumbled, dazed, unaware that she had spoken the words aloud.

"What do you think?" came the cold reply from a man standing directly in front of her. His voice was sharp, clipped, and his hair was cut short, almost military in its precision.

Alex forced herself to focus, glancing around the room. She was tied to a chair, her wrists bound tightly behind her back. The dim, oppressive room had no windows - only heavy, nearly black curtains concealing any sign of the outside world. The only source of light was the naked bulb swaying slightly from the ceiling above her.

"Who are you?" she managed to ask, her voice hoarse as her vision continued to clear.

The man leaned in closer, so close she could smell the stale whiskey and cheap cigars on his breath. His face was rough, shadowed, and unwelcoming. "You should've stayed at home," he growled, his words like cold steel. "This is far too big for someone like you."

Alex blinked, trying to clear the fog in her mind. "I was just out for a walk," she said, her voice surprisingly steady despite the terror rising within her.

The man's reaction was immediate. His hand shot forward, gripping her throat with crushing force while his other hand produced a small, gleaming blade. The cold steel pressed against the soft skin of her neck, sending an icy shiver down her spine.

"Don't lie to me," he hissed, his face inches from hers. "I know the truth. And I suggest you start cooperating."

"What do you want from me?" Her senses started sharpening with the adrenaline now coursing through her body.

"You have no idea who you're dealing with," he replied, his voice low and dangerous. His grip on her throat tightened ever so slightly, just enough to remind her of how fragile her position was. The blade pressed a little closer, the cold edge a sharp reminder of her mortality.

Alex's mind raced, analyzing the situation. She was caught, trapped, and dangerously close to a man who clearly had no qualms about harming her. But what was he after?

"You don't either," Alex retorted, her voice sharp, though her pulse had steadied. Her gaze, now clear and calculated, slid down the man's muscular, tattoo-covered arms. Every inch of exposed skin from his wrists to his neck was inked in ominous black patterns. Her eyes locked onto the throbbing artery in his neck, subtly measuring his pulse.

He's not nervous.

His heart rate is elevated, sure, but not enough to suggest fear or anxiety.

No, this man was something far more dangerous.

He's calm in this situation.

Too calm.

Alex quickly pieced it together - he was used to this. The kind of man who's done this before.

An assassin.

Her eyes flicked back to his face, hard and unreadable. Yes, she was sure of it now.

But why someone like him?

What does he want from me?

Was she just in the wrong place at the wrong time? Could it really be random?

No.

The universe isn't that lazy.

"What do you want from me?" she asked again, her tone level. "Who are you working for?"

"Who I work for isn't your concern," he growled, his voice low and dangerous. "But I'll tell you what I want." He leaned in closer, his face mere inches from hers. "There are certain matters you'd do well to keep that clever little head of yours far away from."

"You're planning to kill the MP, Shepard," Alex said, her words firing out with sudden clarity. "You've been following him. That's why you were there, right?"

"You've no idea what's really at play here," the man sneered, inching closer until his breath was warm against her face. "Shepard's nothing but bait. A pawn to lure me to my real target."

"Which I clearly am not, or I'd already be dead."

The man squinted slightly, watching Alex with a hint of surprise.

"You're obviously a professional," she continued, her voice steady despite the tension in the room. "Drawing this out, toying with me - because that's all this is to you - isn't something you'd do with your actual targets. So, what is it that you really want?"

"Isn't it obvious?" His tone held a hint of disappointment, as if her sharpness had finally faltered. "You see so much in the smallest detail, Miss Green, but you're missing what's right in front of you. By now, you should know exactly what I want."

Mycroft.

"Dammit." The expletive slipped from her lips, her realization far from satisfying. Her face tightened, clearly reflecting how little she liked the conclusion she'd drawn.

"Ah, now you live up to your reputation." The man's smile was slow, dark amusement gleaming in his eyes.

"What reputation?" Alex's brow furrowed, her tone sharpened. "I'm just a secretary."

The man laughed, clearly entertained. "A simple secretary who somehow manages to outshine even the famous detective Sherlock Holmes."

81

"Then you fear me more than you fear him?" Alex asked, her sarcasm barely veiled. "That might be the best compliment I've ever received, considering it's well known that his older brother is the smarter of the two." Her tone shifted slightly, more calculating now. "I assume your opinion is based solely on the fact that *I* was the one who followed Mycroft Holmes, not Sherlock. Because, let's face it, the great detective barely cares about his brother's affairs. The fact that you know my name tells me you know far more about me than you're willing to admit."

The man's grin widened. "Sharp, indeed. But even the sharpest blades can be dulled."

Alex felt the weight of his words settle over her, cold and heavy. She was deep in something bigger than she'd anticipated, and it was clear this man, whoever he was, intended to make sure she felt every bit of that weight.

"All well and good," the man said darkly, his tone dripping with menace as his eyes bored into Alex. "But let's finally get down to business. I don't have all night."

"Business?" Alex scoffed, her gaze icy. "I don't negotiate with criminals."

"You might want to reconsider that stance, Miss Green," he retorted, a sinister edge to his voice. "You might end up regretting it." He cleared his throat and took a few steps back, dragging a narrow chair from the side of the room and placing it directly in front of her. Sitting down, he crossed one leg over the other and leaned back, exuding the calm arrogance of someone in complete control. "Shepard's death is inevitable. There's nothing you or anyone else can do to stop it. Not even Sherlock Holmes could prevent it, especially not in his... current condition."

His condition?

What is he talking about?

Why does everything always circle back to that damn detective?

82

I am not Sherlock Holmes.

And what does he mean by 'his condition'?

Sherlock's health hasn't changed - has it?

The man's grin widened, a twisted pleasure crossing his face. "Shepard's fate is sealed. Whether he wants it or not. But it's Mycroft Holmes," he said with a gleam in his eye, "whose death will be delivered by my hand. Ah, I've waited so long for this. His name has been on my list for quite some time, and the moment is finally here."

Alex's eyes narrowed. "Why are you telling me this?"

Why doesn't he just kill me and be done with it?

"I could kill you, of course," the man mused, leaning in with a predatory smile, "but unfortunately, I'm not allowed to. Not yet." His voice dropped lower, almost playful. "Consider yourself lucky, Miss Green. However, cross me again, and your name will most certainly make its way onto that same list."

His grin widened into something grotesque, almost inhuman. "I'm sure you're wondering why I've gone through all this trouble. Why the elaborate setup just to catch you in my little web? Honestly, I didn't think you'd actually follow him. But it turns out my employer knows you quite well."

Alex's blood ran cold.

Mycroft.

The name echoed in her mind, the pieces of this disturbing puzzle clicking together.

This wasn't about Shepard at all.

It was about Mycroft - and me.

"Get to the point!" Alex snapped, her patience now thoroughly worn thin. Any lingering fear had dissolved, replaced by a restlessness that simmered under the surface.

"Always the same with women," the man sneered, a disgusted look crossing his face. "Faster! Harder! Louder! That's all you ever want." He licked his lips with a disturbing slowness, stepping closer to her with a predator's grace. "But it's the feeling that matters, isn't it?" His voice dropped to a whisper as his hand trailed along her cheek, cold and deliberate, before slipping down to her throat. In an instant, his grip tightened like a vice around her neck.

Alex gasped for air, her lungs screaming as a burning pain shot through her chest, radiating outward. She could feel her pulse pounding against his cruel fingers.

The man crouched down, his face inches from hers. "I want you to stay away from Mycroft Holmes," he growled, his voice low but commanding. "He's mine. Mine alone. And if you cross me again, you're dead. Do you understand?"

Alex's vision blurred, black spots creeping at the edges. She tried to speak, to answer, but all that escaped her lips was a strangled whimper.

"What?" he mocked, his smile widening, clearly savoring her suffering. He tightened his grip for another agonizing moment, watching the life drain from her eyes before he finally loosened his hold. He leaned back, staring into her face with an unsettling calm. "Care to repeat that?"

Alex gulped down air desperately, her body trembling as she forced out a breathy, pained whisper. "I understand."

The man's grin stretched wider, as though her submission fed some dark pleasure within him. He leaned in even closer, his breath hot and foul against her ear. "Good girl," he whispered. "As a reward, I'll give you the first letter of my name."

A dramatic pause hung in the air between them, thick with menace.

"M," he whispered softly, savoring the moment.

He straightened up and turned his back on her, as though the entire encounter had been nothing more than a game.

M?

Moriarty?

84

No, that couldn't be. Moriarty was dead. Dead and buried. She had no doubt about that.

Moran?

No, that didn't seem right either. But who?

The puzzle gnawed at her, even as her body fought to recover from the brutal attack.

Alex's mind was a storm of confusion. Every thought that crossed her felt like it was pulling her deeper into a dark maze, twisting her perception, leaving her vulnerable to the chaotic game her own mind seemed to be playing against her.

The man, still grinning that twisted smile of his, turned back toward her. This time, he held a syringe in his hand, the needle gleaming under the dim light like the fangs of a serpent. His voice was a cold whisper, dripping with menace. "You understand, of course, that going to the police is out of the question. If they even catch a whisper of what I'm planning, it'll be too late - for him... and for you. So, if we do meet again," his grin widened, eyes gleaming with sadistic promise, "I'll make sure to tear your heart out with my bare hands."

His dark, guttural laugh filled the room as he approached her slowly, the syringe in his hand reflecting her fading hope.

The world around Alex began to blur, her senses slipping away. She tried to focus, tried to think, but it was as if she were sinking into a pit of shadows, each breath dragging her deeper into unconsciousness. She could no longer process what was happening, everything blending into an indistinct haze.

The last thing she felt was the sharp prick of the needle against her skin. Then, nothing.

Alex suddenly found herself in a strange, liminal space - a world between life and death, a dimension she had grown uncomfortably familiar with. She sat in a dark red leather armchair, the room around her resembling a gothic library. Dusty bookshelves, crammed with volumes of every size and shape, formed rows that partitioned the space into small, isolated chambers.

Moran?

Moriarty?

No... that can't be right.

That would be too simple.

But then, what does the "M" stand for?

Without warning, Alex stood up from the armchair as if nothing had happened. She felt unusually light, almost weightless, as if her body were hollow, floating in this eerie dreamscape. She moved purposefully through the library, weaving between towering shelves, until she reached a staircase that spiraled downward into a shadowy basement. It was as though she knew exactly where to go, as if some unseen force was guiding her.

The marble steps beneath her feet were veined with deep crimson, and the air in the basement was stale, thick with the scent of neglect. She felt a creeping unease.

How is this possible?

How can I smell the air and feel the stone beneath me in a dream?

It's so real - so disturbingly real.

At the far end of the dimly lit chamber stood a long filing cabinet, made of cold, industrial steel. Alex approached it, her heart pounding in a way that felt both real and surreal. She opened one of the drawers and rifled through the tightly packed folders, each one marked with letters and numbers.

There it is.

M.

Her hand hesitated for a split second before she pulled out a thick file - thicker than any of the others - and laid it on top of the filing cabinet. With a slow, deliberate motion, she ran her fingers over the beige, worn cover. Then, with a deep breath, she opened it.

This is it.

The truth lay before her.

A photograph was the first thing to greet her, showing a man whose face was eerily similar to her captor's, though he appeared older, more weathered by time. Beneath the photograph, the name was scrawled in neat, almost clinical handwriting.

Thomas Montaigne.

The pieces began to fall into place, but the revelation only deepened her dread. Everything was becoming more convoluted, more dangerous. As she flipped through the pages of Montaigne's file, reading the horrific details of his life - his brutal rise to power, his violent nature - her stomach turned with disgust.

What a vile man.

She couldn't take it anymore. With a sudden, angry motion, she slammed the file shut. The noise echoed unnaturally, and as if the world around her couldn't bear the weight of her discovery, everything went dark.

The library, the basement, the file - all of it vanished into a suffocating black void.

And Alex felt herself falling, spiraling downward into an abyss, unsure if she would ever wake from this nightmare.

VI.

THE TRAP

Like a startled deer, Liz sprinted down Baker Street in the early morning, her destination clear in her mind: 221B. Breathless, she came to an abrupt halt before the iconic dark green door, gasping for air after running all the way from her apartment without a single pause.

She hesitated for only a moment before pressing down the brass handle, stepping into the dimly lit stairwell that smelled faintly of dust and pipe smoke. A hauntingly beautiful violin piece floated down from the upper floor, filling the narrow space with an almost ethereal melancholy. As much as her legs trembled from the sprint, her heart raced with dread. John Watson and Sherlock Holmes - she was about to face them both. But there was no other option. No matter how terrified she was, she had to go through with it.

"Good day," came a voice, startling her. An elderly woman stepped into the hallway from a nearby room, her eyes landing on Liz's disheveled appearance. "Can I help you, dear?"

"Is Sherlock Holmes here?" Liz stammered, barely able to catch her breath.

"Oh! A client!" The elderly lady exclaimed with unusual delight. "I'm Mrs. Hudson, the landlady. Sherlock's upstairs. Come along, I'll take you to him." Without waiting for a response, the sprightly old woman bustled up the stairs, knocking eagerly on a closed door.

Liz followed her, each step up the narrow staircase feeling like a step toward her doom. She stood beside Mrs. Hudson, trying to steady her nerves, when the older woman pushed open the door, and the beautiful violin music abruptly ceased.

"Who is it?" asked a man, his back to them, his voice cold and precise. He slowly lowered his violin, though he did not yet turn to face them.

"A new client!" Mrs. Hudson replied, practically beaming.

The man turned then, and it was unmistakably Sherlock Holmes.

Liz's heart pounded so hard it threatened to burst from her chest. Running seemed like a very appealing - no, necessary - escape at that moment.

"Sit down," Sherlock said, pulling a chair into the center of the room and gesturing for her to sit. "Before you faint from sheer terror."

Her cheeks flushed with embarrassment, and she prayed he wouldn't think too poorly of her. Trembling from head to toe, Liz sat on the chair as instructed. Sherlock took his place opposite her, lounging in his familiar brown leather armchair, crossing his legs with practiced ease. His sharp eyes studied her with that unnerving intensity only Sherlock Holmes possessed.

"Would you like some tea?" Mrs. Hudson's sudden offer jolted Liz out of her petrified silence.

She nodded quickly. "Yes, please. That would be lovely."

Mrs. Hudson bustled off to the kitchen, filling the kettle and leaving Liz alone with Sherlock, who continued to scrutinize her, his head cocked slightly to one side, as though she were a puzzle he was piecing together.

"Hm," Sherlock mused aloud, his brow furrowing. "I've seen you before, haven't I? Aren't you the one who always follows John around?"

Liz's heart stopped. Panic flared in her eyes. Without a second thought, she leapt from the chair and bolted for the door, suddenly realizing how foolish it was to come here in the first place.

But Sherlock was faster. In an instant, he was in front of her, blocking her path with that infuriatingly calm demeanor. "I wouldn't recommend fleeing," he said quietly, though the command in his voice was unmistakable. "Running from me only delays the inevitable."

Mrs. Hudson walked closer to them, holding a steaming cup of fruit tea in her hand. "Here, dear," she offered with a kind smile, pressing the cup into Liz's trembling hands.

"So, you are Elizabeth Markle, John's stalker in the flesh," Sherlock concluded, his voice dripping with dry amusement, deducing everything he needed to from her overly obvious reaction.

With the warm cup in her hands, Liz slowly turned back with him, while Sherlock sat down again.

He grinned, clearly enjoying her discomfort. "Dr. Watson isn't here, Miss Markle. So, you can rest easy." He straightened in his chair, the amusement in his voice vanishing, replaced by a more curious tone. "Now, I am far more intrigued as to why you're here. You would never dare come unless it was truly important. Too frightened for that, aren't you? So, what is it?"

With shaky legs, Liz reluctantly shuffled back to the lonely chair in the middle of the room, sinking into it as though her knees might give out beneath her. She clutched the teacup with both hands, as if it were the only thing keeping her grounded. "It's about my friend... Alex. She's my best friend," she began hesitantly, casting worried glances toward Sherlock. "I can't reach her. I've tried everything, but it's like she's vanished into thin air."

"Maybe she simply wanted some peace and quiet," Sherlock said dismissively, leaning back in his chair again, clearly losing interest in the conversation. "People do that."

"No," Liz shook her head, anxiety lacing her voice. "That's not like her at all. Alex is always reachable, no matter what. And she should've been at home, but she wasn't. I... I just wish she hadn't gotten involved." She sighed heavily, the weight of her worry almost tangible.

Sherlock's eyes flickered with a spark of interest. "Involved in what, exactly?"

"Stephen Shepard, the Member of Parliament - he received a threatening letter," Liz explained, her voice trembling slightly.

Sherlock narrowed his eyes, a flicker of confusion passing over his sharp features. "What does your friend have to do with that?"

Liz hesitated for a moment, unsure if she should divulge such sensitive information. After all, her friend Alex was essentially Sherlock's competitor. But then she reasoned that it was for Alex's own good. "Alex was brought in by the Scotland Yard to assist with the case. Sometimes she helps them solve cases when they hit a dead end."

Sherlock sat up straighter, his expression one of surprise. "Alexandra Green," he repeated, letting the name linger in the air as if the very sound of it held some hidden significance. He paused for a moment, then met Liz's gaze with sharp intensity. "Do you have the threatening letter?"

"No," Liz responded, shaking her head almost too fervently. But quickly, she pulled out her phone and offered it to him. "But I do have some photos." She stood there, anxious, watching as Sherlock examined the images of the letter, the very ones Alex had taken.

"Goethe," Sherlock murmured, his eyes never leaving the screen. He studied the photos in silence, his mind rapidly processing the details. After what felt like an eternity, he finally looked up at Liz. "I'm afraid this message wasn't meant for Stephen Shepard at all - it was meant for your friend."

Liz stared at him, horrified. "What makes you say that?"

"There are only three people in all of London widely known for their intense devotion to Johann Wolfgang von Goethe's works, people who know most of his poems by heart. Those three are my

91

brother Mycroft, myself... and your friend, Alexandra Green. I'd even wager she's more intimately familiar with Goethe's extensive literature than Mycroft and I combined. Therefore, it's clear this isn't about Shepard at all. And, as I feared, my brother is somehow involved."

Liz's breath caught in her throat. "Can you do anything to help her?" she asked, desperation leaking into her voice.

Sherlock rose to his feet, his demeanor as cold and calculating as ever. "Not yet," he said curtly, pressing Liz's phone back into her hand. "This is not just any case. Your friend is caught in something much larger than she knows, and I fear it's only just beginning."

His expression was unreadable as he pulled out his own mobile and took several measured steps to the side. He quickly dialed his brother's number, his fingers moving with practiced precision. The line rang once, then twice, but no answer. Undeterred, he tried again. Still nothing.

Annoyance flickered briefly across his face, but it was quickly replaced by a flash of inspiration. He turned sharply towards Liz, his gaze piercing. "Where does your friend live?"

"Great Ormond Street, Number 8," Liz replied, her voice tinged with uncertainty.

Sherlock's mind raced as he processed the information. "Stay here," he ordered briskly, already moving towards the door. "I may not be able to contact Mycroft, but that won't stop me from finding out what's going on."

As he exited, the door shutting behind him with a soft click, Liz was left standing there, clutching her phone and feeling an ominous weight pressing down on her.

The day after her abduction - at least, Alex hoped it had only been a single night - she slowly regained consciousness. She found herself lying on her back on the couch, disoriented and groggy. As she struggled to sit up, one burning question echoed in her mind: How had she made it back to her apartment? She couldn't recall a single detail, try as she might.

Still feeling woozy, she staggered across the living room, her stomach churning with each unsteady step. Without warning, nausea overcame her, and she rushed to the bathroom, collapsing over the toilet to vomit violently. With her hands pressing against her throbbing temples, she slumped onto the cold tile floor, a pitiful wreck, trying to piece together the events of the previous day.

Then, suddenly, her phone rang - its sound deafening to her fragile state, like a cacophony of trumpets, horns, and church bells crashing in her skull. Each ring echoed in her head, amplifying her discomfort.

"I'm coming," she croaked, crawling back to the living room on all fours. She reached for her phone, lying abandoned on the floor next to the couch, and answered it, switching to speaker mode before collapsing onto the rug. "What do you want, Doyle?" she asked, her voice weak and ragged.

"Are you... drunk?" the Inspector's voice sounded startled. "You sound terrible."

I wish that were the case.

"Sorry, I've had... quite the night," Alex mumbled, feeling the weight of exhaustion settle into her bones.

"I can only hope you learned something from it," Doyle retorted, his tone both frustrated and accusatory.

You have no idea...

Alex forced herself upright, cradling her aching head in her hands. "What do you need?" she asked, doing her best to keep her voice steady.

"Have you not seen the news yet?" Doyle's voice sharpened. "It's all over the channels this morning."

Intrigued but still groggy, Alex crawled toward the television and turned it on. The screen flickered to life, displaying a live report of a bombing at a judicial building in Glentworth Street. As the camera panned across the chaotic scene, Alex recognized the street instantly.

It was the very place where she had last seen Mycroft Holmes.

"Shepard," Alex whispered, her voice thick with shock as she stared at the nightmarish images of the obliterated building on her television screen. "What happened? How is this even possible?"

"The explosion happened two doors south of Shepard's residence," Doyle explained gravely. "The Member of Parliament is unharmed. It looks like this was some sort of warning."

"A warning? For whom?"

"For you, Alex," Doyle's voice was firm, almost unnervingly certain. "It's clear as day. I need you to come to the station immediately. You must be placed under police protection."

"Don't be ridiculous," Alex scoffed, grabbing her phone as she struggled to stand upright. "If this really was meant for me, I'd be dead already. There's more to this, something we're missing. Where's Mycroft? I need to speak to him."

"That's not an option," Doyle responded, his tone turning icy. "Mycroft's abroad for the day. He left explicit orders not to be disturbed under any circumstances. And he made it abundantly clear that you, in particular, are to stay away from him."

"Can't you see that all of this is connected to him somehow?" Alex's voice quivered with frustration. "I *have* to talk to him."

"Orders are orders," Doyle snapped. "Besides, Mycroft was very insistent that you stay out of the Shepard case from this moment forward. He doesn't want you involved."

Alex's mind raced back to her encounter with Montaigne the night before. "It's too late for that now, and Mycroft knows it," she muttered under her breath.

"Get to the station. *Now*," Doyle's tone left no room for argument.

"I'm not exactly feeling great," Alex retorted, her voice strained and weak. "I think I need to throw up again before I go anywhere. Maybe after that."

"Fine," Doyle replied, his frustration barely contained. "I'm sending a team over. Just to be sure you're safe."

"I don't need a babysitter," Alex muttered, thoroughly unamused. "It's going to take a lot more than this to put me in the ground." Without waiting for a response, she hung up, tossing her phone onto the couch before sinking down beside it, exhausted.

Damn it!

I have to warn Mycroft.

He needs to know what Montaigne is planning.

I can't let him kill him.

But how?

Her mind raced, but it was no use. The wave of nausea hit her hard, cutting through her thoughts like a knife. She barely had time to register what was happening before she sprinted back to the bathroom, her body betraying her desperate need for control.

It took barely 25 minutes before someone knocked at her door.

Doyle's men are surprisingly fast.

Alex slowly pulled herself off the bathroom floor and went to the sink.

Another knock echoed through the apartment, more insistent this time.

"Just a moment!" she called, washing her hands, rinsing her mouth, and quickly fixing her hair. She stepped into the hallway and hesitated at the door.

A third knock, this time sharp and impatient, reverberated through the wood.

That's not Doyle's men.

Her heart raced. Instinctively, she moved closer and peeked through the peephole.

That damn bastard!

Fury boiled up inside her as she realized who was standing on the other side. Without thinking, she yanked the door open. "What the hell are you doing here?" she snapped, her eyes blazing.

The man standing in front of her grinned, tilting his head slightly so his face was fully visible beneath the odd grey hat he was wearing. "I thought you'd be happy to see me," he said, sounding far too sure of himself.

Alex crossed her arms and stepped aside as the man strolled in uninvited. "Do I *look* happy?" she muttered.

"Depends on how you define happiness," he replied, settling himself on her couch as if he owned the place.

Alex rolled her eyes, slammed the door shut, and followed him into the living room. Standing over him with her arms still crossed, she asked bluntly, "What do you want?"

"You look terrible," he observed without the slightest hesitation. "What happened to you?"

Before she could even think of a biting retort, a sudden, uncomfortable thought crossed her mind - one she hadn't expected. She let out a quiet breath, sat down next to him on the couch, and fixed him with a pleading look. "I need your help," she said, her voice soft but steady. She paused for a moment, surprised by how easily the words had come out. "It's about your brother."

96

"Mycroft's affairs are none of my concern," Sherlock said defiantly, wrinkling his nose. "If he needs my help, he can ask me himself. I don't appreciate you being sent to do his bidding."

"I never said Mycroft needed your help," Alex retorted quickly. "I said *I* need your help, Sherlock!"

Sherlock's eyes widened in surprise. "It must be a matter of life and death if *you* are asking for *my* help." He grinned slyly. "What's this about?"

Just as Alex was about to explain the situation with Montaigne, a different question leaped to the forefront of her mind. "Wait a second. Why are you even here? What do you want from me?"

"Despite your apparent hallucinatory episode, your mind still functions remarkably well," Sherlock said, leaning back and crossing his legs. "What do you think I'm here for? After all, aren't you a famously notorious genius? Surely this deduction shouldn't be too difficult for you."

Alex cradled her aching head in her hands.

Is he serious right now?

Why can't he just tell me straight, like a normal person?

Of course, if he were a normal person, he wouldn't be Sherlock Holmes.

He'd be, well, anyone else.

"What's the matter?" Sherlock asked, watching her intently. "Is this beyond your intellectual grasp? Disappointing. I thought you were more capable than that."

"Be quiet!" Alex snapped, rising from the couch. "I'm thinking." She began pacing the living room, arms crossed, her mind racing.

Why is he here?

Could he know about Montaigne?

Did he see the message and decode it?

Is he here to rub it in my face, to show me I'm nowhere near as brilliant as he is?

No, Sherlock didn't need to prove that to anyone. He already believed it, didn't he? He wouldn't gain anything by questioning her abilities - he was fully aware she didn't see him as a rival, so it wouldn't benefit anyone for him to try to undermine her intelligence.

What then?

What could possibly be the real reason behind Sherlock Holmes standing in her living room, after she explicitly told him never to seek her out again? And how did he even know where she lived?

Liz!

Suddenly, her heart sank, and she spun around to face Sherlock. "Where is she?"

"She's fine," Sherlock replied, clearly impressed by Alex's swift deduction. "She's in Baker Street at the moment. Mrs. Hudson, my landlady, is looking after her."

"So, Liz sent you here?" Alex asked, frowning.

"Your friend was deeply worried about you, Miss Green. If it had been anyone else, I wouldn't have taken the case."

"Case?" Alex blinked, confused. "What case?"

"Yours." Sherlock stood up and walked to the center of the room, stopping just a few feet from her. "Where were you last night? What happened to you?"

Alex turned away from him, biting her lip. "I can't tell you that."

"Then I can't help you." Sherlock replied coolly, and without hesitation, he turned to leave the living room.

"Wait!" Alex rushed after him, grabbing his arm just as he was about to reach the door. "What do you know about a man named Thomas Montaigne?"

98

Sherlock froze, his eyes widening in shock and alarm. "Montaigne? He's a despicable man with a frighteningly high skill set. Primarily works as a contract killer for wealthy businessmen who want someone conveniently removed from their path. What on earth do you have to do with him?"

"He wants to kill Mycroft," she blurted out, the words tumbling from her mouth before she could stop them. Yet, she didn't regret telling him the truth. "He plans to murder him. And soon."

"How do you know that? I doubt Montaigne would simply tell you his intentions," Sherlock replied skeptically.

"But he did," Alex said, giving him a moment to digest the weight of her words. "Last night, I saw your brother while I was on my way home. It was a coincidence, but he didn't see me, so I followed him. I wanted to find out what he was hiding from me. What happened after that is a blur... as if someone drugged me. It was Montaigne. He's the one who kidnapped me."

Sherlock's usual mask of detachment faltered for a brief second. "Montaigne," he muttered to himself, clearly processing the gravity of the situation. "He doesn't make idle threats. If he's after Mycroft, it's serious."

"That's what I'm trying to tell you!" Alex's voice rose in frustration. "He told me straight to my face that Mycroft is his next target. He... he could strike at any moment, Sherlock."

The detective's gaze sharpened, his mind already whirring at lightning speed. "Then we don't have much time." His tone was deadly serious, all traces of his earlier sarcasm gone. "If Montaigne has set his sights on Mycroft, this isn't just a game anymore. We need to act, now. But... Why would he do that?" Sherlock asked, his tone sharper now.

"Honestly, I have no idea," Alex admitted, still shaken. "I thought he was going to kill me, but he said he wasn't allowed to. His employer forbade it, and apparently, I'm not on his list. But

99

Mycroft's name is right at the top. If no one intervenes, Montaigne will soon be able to cross it off for good."

"You've been ordered not to tell Scotland Yard, haven't you?" Sherlock didn't wait for her answer before continuing. "Instead, you tried contacting my brother."

"How do you know that?" Alex asked, taken aback by his perceptiveness.

Sherlock gave her a thin smile as he pulled her phone from his coat pocket and handed it to her. "You really should lock your phone, or at the very least, not leave it lying around in my reach while you're distracted on the couch."

Alex stared at her phone in disbelief, then glanced back up at him.

"Why Mycroft?" he asked, the question lingering between them.

"I don't know. Montaigne didn't explain that part," she replied, frustration creeping into her voice. Suddenly, a thought struck her. She reached into her handbag and pulled out the prints of the blackmail letter, handing them over to Sherlock. "Look at this. What do you make of it?"

Sherlock took the sheets, his eyes narrowing as he studied the cryptic message again. He remained silent for several moments, piecing together the clues in his mind, before speaking again.

"You can't live for everyone,
especially not for those
with whom you don't want
to live.
Sweet sleep!
pure joy,
we sink and cease
to be.

100

unbidden,
unasked
when pain
is unrestrained,
You come like
the circle of
inner harmonies flows freely,
for, and most willing
You untie the knots
and wrapped in pleasant madness
of strict thoughts,
blend all the images
of joy
oh my..."

"Interesting," he muttered, more to himself than to her. "This is no ordinary threat." He glanced up, his expression unreadable, but his mind was clearly racing. "There's a pattern here, but it's incomplete. We're missing something crucial." His gaze fell back to the letter, scanning it intently. "And it's not just about Mycroft. Whoever's behind this is playing a much deeper game."

On the reverse side of the letter, beside the poem, were the numbers from the front. Alex had circled specific letters next to each number, revealing a clear and ominous message.

0104009 104036 101257053
0E0I00D T0S0UM T0FORC0YM

"Mycroft must die," Sherlock read aloud, more intrigued than shocked by the hidden message. "Good," he remarked, surprisingly upbeat, as though the puzzle had brought him some unexpected delight. "I'll help you."

"And how exactly do you plan to do that?" Alex asked, eyeing him skeptically.

"How good are you at disguises?" Sherlock responded, a mischievous glint in his eyes.

"Why?" Alex was baffled by the sudden shift in conversation.

"Your apartment is being watched by the Scotland Yard," Sherlock explained nonchalantly, as if it were the most obvious thing in the world. "They arrived just after I came upstairs. They didn't see me, and we can't have them seeing you either. It would complicate things." He grinned, clearly energized by the thrill of the situation. "So, let's not waste any time."

Alex stared at him, still processing the sudden turn of events. But Sherlock was already on his feet, pacing with an eager restlessness. "You're not seriously suggesting we sneak past the police?" she asked.

"Precisely." He flashed her a look, as if the answer were obvious. "Now, let's find you something inconspicuous. You'll need a complete change of appearance."

Her head spinning from the rapid development, Alex couldn't help but smirk, despite the chaos of it all. "You're insane."

"Perhaps," Sherlock replied, the grin never leaving his face. "But insanity gets results."

Alex crept through the dark streets of London, cloaked in an oversized, shabby coat, with a false beard and an equally fake wig, heading straight for Mycroft Holmes' house.

This is a mistake!
A damn mistake!
But I have to warn him.

As she approached the burgundy-brick house, a small front garden led to a narrow, cobblestone path that wound toward the front door, up a few steps in the middle. Instead of heading for the front entrance, she climbed up the fire escape on the side, making her way to the first floor. There, she found a narrow ledge-like balcony with several tall windows that offered a glimpse into an unlit, shadowy hallway inside. Once out of sight, Alex shed her ridiculous, but effective, disguise.

And now?

Am I seriously going to break in?

Maybe I should just ring the doorbell like a normal person.

Just as she was about to turn back and descend the fire escape, she heard a loud crash from within the building. It sounded like something large and heavy - a statue, perhaps - had toppled and shattered.

Damn it!

Montaigne is already inside.

There was no turning back now. Without a second thought, Alex edged along the balcony until she reached a window with broken glass scattered on the sill.

I'm going to regret this.

I just know it.

But I don't have a choice.

With her stomach churning with unease, she slipped through the broken window, landing on the floor amid the glass shards, which crunched under her weight. Rising cautiously, she placed her hand on the floor to steady herself, only to realize too late that it was directly into the sharp fragments of glass scattered every-where. A deep, stinging cut shot through her palm, followed by a pulsing warmth as blood began to flow. But Alex barely registered the injury - she didn't have time to care.

She scanned the dark corridor, moving swiftly but quietly, her fingers tracing the wall as she advanced, desperate to avoid running

103

straight into Montaigne's trap, but determined to reach Mycroft before it was too late.

Then, everything happened in a flash.

A hard blow struck her from behind, sending her crashing to the floor in an instant.

Alex had no idea how long she had been unconscious, lying in the hallway. When she finally awoke again, her head pounded with a relentless throbbing, and the metallic taste of adrenaline lingered on her tongue. Slowly, she pushed herself into a corner, her mind clinging to any semblance of clarity. But one thing was immediately certain: she was no longer alone.

Muted footsteps echoed softly down the hall, measured and deliberate. They were coming straight for her. Instinctively, Alex pressed herself deeper into the shadows, holding her breath. The figure passed by without noticing her, and in a flash of desperate courage, she leapt from her hiding spot and tackled the intruder to the ground. Her movements were driven by survival, not skill, yet somehow, by sheer luck, she managed to wrestle the gun from his grasp and turn it on him. Standing in the middle of the hallway, armed and trembling, a brief surge of power coursed through her - but only for a fleeting second.

Suddenly, the entire corridor flooded with harsh, blinding light. Alex recoiled, shielding her eyes from the brightness with her free hand. As her vision adjusted, she saw armed men in black uniforms rushing towards her from all directions, encircling her like wolves cornering their prey.

Her heart pounded as she looked down at the man she had just overpowered, expecting to see Montaigne. But it wasn't him. To her horror, it was Mycroft Holmes. He groaned in pain, struggling to sit up. The realization hit her like a blow to the gut, and her face turned deathly pale.

"Arrest her at once!" Mycroft's voice was like a cold blade, cutting through the air with precision. Two security officers advanced swiftly, wrenching the gun from her grasp and snapping handcuffs onto her wrists with practiced ease. The suddenness of it all left Alex feeling utterly powerless, lost in a maelstrom of chaos she could no longer control.

"This is a misunderstanding!" she stammered, panic rising in her throat as the throbbing pain in her bloodied hand intensified. Her head spun, and her thoughts blurred.

"A misunderstanding?" Mycroft's eyes burned with fury and disappointment. His gaze flicked to the shattered window and the trail of blood on the floor - clear evidence of her forced entry. "You broke into my home, smashed a window, assaulted me, and disarmed me with my own weapon. For a man in my position, this could not be more severe."

"For someone who practically *is* the British government, you're surprisingly easy to disarm and overpower - by a woman, no less," Alex retorted, her voice dripping with defiance, completely unaware of the gravity of her situation. She was still dazed, likely from the blood loss.

Mycroft stepped closer, his imposing figure towering over her as his cold gaze bore into her. "Attempted murder of a government official is a serious offense, Miss Green. You, of all people, should know better."

Alex's eyes flashed with stubborn resolve. "If I had actually tried to kill you, you'd already be dead," she muttered, her tone unapologetic.

Mycroft's jaw tightened as he turned away, his patience clearly worn thin. "Take her to Newgate," he commanded the guards, his voice laced with finality. His movements were slower than usual, no doubt a result of the blows Alex had landed on him. Without another glance at her, he disappeared down the corridor, vanishing around the corner.

Panic seized Alex as she realized what was happening. "This is a mistake!" she shouted after him, her voice desperate and filled with fear. "Ask your brother! Talk to Sherlock! He'll tell you the truth!"

But Mycroft didn't turn back. The security officers tightened their grip on her, dragging her toward the exit despite her futile attempts to resist.

Newgate Prison, a name long synonymous with infamy, had always held a place of dark renown in English history, though it had ceased to officially exist for some time. Commissioned by King Henry II in 1188 at the city gate of Newgate, it had been significantly expanded in 1236. Even in its early days, the prison had served various grim purposes, chief among them the incarceration of the condemned awaiting execution.

How fitting.

Not that Newgate had always been entirely escape-proof. The infamous thief, Jack Sheppard, had managed to break out three times before finally meeting his end at the gallows in 1724.

The original prison was eventually torn down, making way for a new and even more imposing structure. Built between 1770 and 1778, its menacing facade of rough-hewn stone stood as a deterrent to all who gazed upon it, looming next to the Old Bailey, the Central Criminal Court of London. And now, Alex found herself locked away in one of its cold, unforgiving cells.

Who would have thought I'd one day share quarters with the likes of the pirate William Kidd?

A uniformed officer, armed and stern, approached her cell with a tray. On it sat a piece of stale bread and a bowl of dark green, vaguely soup-like liquid. He stopped outside her cell door without a word.

Alex leapt to her feet. "I want to make a phone call. Please."

"No," the officer replied curtly, sliding the tray through the narrow opening at the base of the door.

"Please," Alex implored, her voice tinged with desperation. "It's my right!"

The officer didn't so much as glance back, continuing his unhurried march down the stone corridor.

"Damn it!" Alex cursed, kicking the door in frustration. The pain shot up her leg immediately, throbbing with intensity, but it was nothing compared to the helplessness gnawing at her. She cast a disdainful glance at the tray of meagre rations and pushed it away with a grimace. Resigned, she sank onto the hard cot, the cold metal biting through her clothes.

"What am I supposed to do now?" she murmured, burying her face in her hands, elbows resting heavily on her knees. There seemed to be no way out of this nightmare.

As Alex prepared to lie down, she once again heard footsteps echoing down the corridor. But this time, it wasn't just one person. She listened intently, her senses on edge.

The door to her cell unlocked and swung open. Two prison guards stood in the doorway, while two more stepped inside. They halted in front of her.

"You have a visitor," one of them said, snapping a pair of handcuffs onto her wrists with the help of his colleague. They gripped her arms firmly, dragging her out of the cramped cell and into the corridor, where they marched her forward. After a short

107

walk, they stopped outside a small room, its large windows allowing a clear view from all sides of whatever transpired within.

The door swung open, and Alex stepped inside. She stopped cold when she saw Sherlock Holmes seated at the lone table in the center of the room. Reluctantly, she sat across from him, her eyes flicking toward the two guards who remained stationed near the door, watching her with suspicion.

"Please tell me you've spoken to your brother, and I can go home," Alex pleaded, her voice dripping with desperation.

Sherlock shook his head, his expression was unchanged. "I'm sorry."

"You're *sorry*?" Alex shot to her feet, her fury boiling over. "Because of *you*, I'm stuck in here, even though I was trying to help your brother! And all you have to say is that you're sorry?" Her voice rose with every word, laced with outrage.

"Sit down!" barked the guards, their hands hovering near their batons, ready to act at a moment's notice.

Alex inhaled deeply, reining in her temper, and begrudgingly did as she was told.

"What happened was never intended," Sherlock continued, his voice calm but with a hint of empathy she rarely heard from him. "But it's for your own good."

"What are you talking about?" Alex snapped, her frustration evident. "Montaigne wants to kill *your* brother, not me. I told you that!"

"The message was meant for you," Sherlock said, his tone firm yet revealing nothing beyond his usual cold logic. "The blackmail letter to the MP," Sherlock clarified. "It was designed to draw *your* attention, knowing that only you could solve the riddle within."

"That's nonsense!" Alex scoffed, twisting her cuffed wrists uncomfortably. "I solved it by chance. Besides, Montaigne told me directly what he plans to do."

108

"My brother is safe," Sherlock replied, taking a measured breath. "It's nearly impossible for anyone to get close enough to him to do any harm."

"That's not true," Alex countered firmly. "I was able to slip into his house without being seen."

"Of course," Sherlock replied, his grin mischievous. "Only because you had my help."

"But someone else was already there before me," Alex added. Sherlock's startled expression told her that he hadn't known this, nor had anyone else. "I didn't break the window." She glanced down at her bandaged hand. "It was already shattered when I climbed up the fire escape. And shortly after, someone knocked me unconscious. That's all I really remember."

"Other than the fact that you hit my brother," Sherlock said with a dry smirk.

"Don't tell me you're feeling sorry for him now."

Sherlock laughed, genuinely amused. "No, thank God, we're not quite at that stage."

Alex couldn't help but smile, despite the fact that she usually disliked family squabbles. But in this case, she was willing to make an exception. "Can you get me out of here?" she asked, her tone suddenly serious.

"Not yet," Sherlock replied. "For now, it's actually safer for you to remain here."

"And what happens then? What if Montaigne *does* manage to kill your brother? What if he succeeds? Am I still in danger after that? I haven't done anything to..." She suddenly fell silent, as Montaigne's chilling words echoed in her mind.

I could kill you, of course, but unfortunately, I'm not allowed to. Not yet.

The memory of Montaigne's threat stuck in her thoughts like a thorn.

109

"You're right," Alex blurted out, interrupting Sherlock before he could respond. "This has something to do with me. But it's not just me - Mycroft is involved somehow. But how?"

"What do you and my brother have in common?" Sherlock asked, his eyes narrowing as if he were finally beginning to piece together the puzzle.

"You," Alex whispered, her eyes widening in sudden realization. "You, Sherlock."

Sherlock's own eyes widened in shock, and for a brief moment, he almost fell backward off his chair.

Leaning in over the table, Alex lowered her voice to a whisper. "Please, talk to your brother. Maybe he knows more. There *has* to be more to this - we both know that. And be careful. If this involves you as well, then you're in as much danger as I am."

"Time's up," one of the guards said, his voice stern as he pointed to the clock hanging above the door.

"Speak to Mycroft!" Alex urged sharply as she rose from her chair. Before Sherlock could reply, the two guards moved in, escorting her back to her cell.

As the door closed behind her, the weight of her warning hung heavily in the air.

VII.

MARGARET TREVOR

For more than three days, Elizabeth Markle had done nothing but obsessively stare at the photos of the blackmail letter. She had, like Alex before her, printed out both images and pinned them to a board in front of her. Beside the photos, she had scrawled the names *Margaret* and *Victor*, as well as the words *Abbey House* and *Iron Man*, all written in green marker over the small photos of the two children and the drawings Liz had discovered in Alex's apartment.

Over and over, her eyes flitted between the images and the words, searching for a plausible connection, but the solution remained maddeningly elusive. Driven by a last flicker of hope, she grabbed her phone and searched the internet for newspaper articles about *Abbey House*, scouring the text for any name that might stand out. What she found, however, was something entirely different.

Frozen in shock, she stared at the name glowing on her screen.

Holmes.

"Abbey House was the Holmes family's estate?" she whispered to herself, realizing she had just stumbled onto a critical clue.

Liz hurriedly stuffed all the photos into her bag, grabbed her coat, and dashed out of her apartment. Like a woman possessed, she ran through the streets of London, trying to figure out her next move, but the truth was, she had no idea where exactly she was headed. All she knew was that she had to go northwest.

By sheer coincidence, she stumbled near a black taxi just as a tall, slender man in a dark suit, holding a dark green umbrella, was about to step inside.

"Mycroft!" she screamed, panic lacing her voice as she hurried toward him.

The man recoiled in shock and looked at her warily. "Who are you?"

As Liz approached, breathless, she said, "You're in danger."

"What? What are you talking about?" he asked, clearly perturbed.

"You and your brother - both of you are in danger!" she panted, pulling the photos from her handbag.

Mycroft's eyes narrowed with suspicion, but as he flipped through the photos, a glint of disdain softening into alarm, his face turned pale as he reached the last image - the photograph of the two small children. Fear flickered in his normally unreadable expression. "Victor," he muttered under his breath, the name slipping out involuntarily. It was as if he couldn't believe he was holding a picture of that child. His eyes, now cold and calculating, turned toward Liz. "Where did you get this photo?"

"From Alex," Liz replied. "She had it tucked away in one of her books. She probably forgot it was even there. The drawing was hidden in a secret compartment in her wardrobe, along with the blue hippo."

As Mycroft examined the picture of the stuffed toy, memories flooded his mind. "Margaret," he said quietly, lost in thought.

"You know the girl?" Liz asked, her voice tinged with both curiosity and dread.

Mycroft remained silent for a moment, his mind clearly racing as he grappled with memories long buried. Then, with an air of authority and urgency, he turned toward her, his expression darkening. "The boy too," Mycroft replied with a heavy sadness in his voice. "He was Sherlock's first best friend. And Margaret was his younger sister."

"What happened?" Liz could tell from the deepening shadows in Mycroft's gaze that something terrible must have occurred.

112

Before answering, Mycroft ushered her into the taxi, which pulled away without him needing to give any instructions. "Victor drowned in a well near our old estate."

"Abbey House, right?"

Mycroft gave a weak nod, his posture sagging under the weight of the memory.

"And what happened to the girl?" Liz pressed, her curiosity now mixed with a growing sense of dread.

The mention of Margaret seemed to chill Mycroft to his very core. His complexion paled, and he looked as though he'd just seen a ghost. "I can't tell you that," he said, his voice distant, as if he were trapped within the prison of his own memories.

"Oh, but you *will* tell me!" Liz snapped, her frustration flaring at his evasiveness. She locked eyes with him, her fierce gaze cutting through his usual armor of arrogance and self-assurance, causing it to melt away like ice under a scorching sun. "Come on! Speak! This has everything to do with Alex, and you know it. You're hiding something, and I want the truth - *now*!"

"Margaret is dead," Mycroft managed to say, each word seemingly dredged up from a well of agony he could no longer suppress. Those three words, simple as they were, caused a visible crack in his typically stoic demeanor. "She died shortly after Victor disappeared."

"How?" Liz's voice softened considerably, touched by the raw grief she saw in him. She hadn't expected him to suffer so deeply when speaking of the girl.

"She always refused to come to Abbey House to visit us," Mycroft continued, his tone slow and laden with sorrow. "Margaret said she was too frightened of the place. But on the day of her death, she was there. I saw her." As the memories of that day flooded back, the bitterness of the loss became almost unbearable for him. "She was looking for him. Her brother. She searched

113

everywhere. And eventually, she came to Abbey House. *'You took him from me. It's your fault he's gone,'* she yelled at us."

Mycroft paused, his expression haunted, as if reliving her words made him realize, perhaps for the first time, that there had been truth in her accusations. "It was the last time any of us saw her alive."

His voice faltered, leaving an oppressive silence hanging between them as the taxi continued to roll through the dim streets of London.

"What happened?" Liz repeated, her patience wearing thin as Mycroft still hadn't given her a clear answer. "How did she die?"

"I don't know," Mycroft replied, exhaling heavily as he leaned back into the taxi seat. "I was just a child when it happened. I didn't want to know how."

Liz snorted, her frustration growing. It baffled her that Mycroft didn't seem to recognize just how strange the entire situation was. "You never wondered? Never questioned how it could have happened?"

Mycroft's gaze locked onto hers, his eyes glassy, reddened. "Every single day," he said quietly.

Liz studied him, her initial irritation fading. The anguish in his voice told her that Margaret had not been just another figure from his past. She mattered.

"Margaret was... unique. Fascinating. Special," Mycroft began, and a faint, wistful smile touched his lips. "Intellectually, she was every bit my brother's and my equal. No, she surpassed us both by far. In fact, it was because of Margaret that her brother first met Sherlock." His smile quickly faded, and his expression darkened. "Which, in the end, cost him his life. And hers." He sighed deeply. "None of us had many friends. We were always... peculiar. Strange. People thought we weren't normal. Sherlock had Victor. And I... I had Margaret."

"The girl was your friend?" Liz's eyes widened in surprise, and a twinge of disbelief flickered across her face. She couldn't picture Mycroft Holmes - a man who seemed so distant, so unreachable - actually having something as ordinary as a friend.

"Yes," Mycroft replied, the words laced with pain. "She was the only person in the world who truly understood me. Margaret and I were kindred spirits - more than that, really."

A sudden thought flashed in Liz's mind, bold and improbable. "What if she's still alive?"

Mycroft's eyes snapped to hers, his irritation immediate. "Stop the car!" he barked at the driver. The taxi swerved to the side of the road and halted. Mycroft leaned in closer to Liz, his voice low and laced with a barely contained fury. "If she were alive, I would know it. Now, get out!" His voice was sharp, wounded by the very idea.

"You may be clever, Mycroft, but you're blind to what's right in front of you," Liz said calmly, stepping out of the taxi.

Just as she was about to close the door, Mycroft's hand shot out, gripping her wrist with unexpected force. He pulled her back, his face inches from hers, his voice a venomous whisper. "You have no idea what you're talking about," he hissed, before letting her go.

"And neither do you," Liz retorted, slamming the door shut before walking away, frustration gnawing at her. "Damn it," she muttered under her breath. "I'm no closer to figuring this out."

The taxi merged back into traffic, its taillights disappearing down the street. Mycroft sat in the back seat, brooding, the words Liz had thrown at him replaying in his mind. The more he dwelled on it, the more uneasy he became. As the puzzle pieces began shifting in his thoughts, he came to an unsettling realization: perhaps she wasn't entirely wrong. His plans changed abruptly. He would revisit the old case files of Margaret Trevor, files he had buried long ago, along with the painful memories.

115

Lying on the hard bed with her knees bent, Alex stared blankly at the ceiling. There was nothing remarkable or interesting about it - just thick, old concrete walls, dull and gray. On the sides, marks had been scratched in by previous inmates, presumably counting the days of their imprisonment.

Alex counted, reaching 382. She rolled her eyes.

382 days.

That's a damn eternity.

I've only been here five hours, and it already feels like half a year.

How am I supposed to endure this without losing my mind?

Her thoughts were abruptly interrupted by the sound of hurried footsteps approaching down the corridor. Although the prospect of a visitor offered a welcome break from her monotonous imprisonment, she remained lying on the bed, her eyes fixed on the dreary ceiling above.

"Well, I see you've already made yourself comfortable," said a voice that had become far too familiar to her.

Alex jolted upright and walked to the cell door. Peering through the bars, she could hardly believe her eyes. Mycroft Holmes himself stood before her.

"I'd offer you a cup of tea, but I seem to have run out of hot water," she replied, her tone dripping with disdain as she glared at him.

"Sharp as always," Mycroft responded, giving her a practiced, insincere smile. He gave a quick nod to the guards accompanying him, and they left without hesitation. Once they were alone, Mycroft stepped closer, his expression turning serious. "Have you nothing to say to me?"

"I'm not apologizing," Alex said coldly, "especially not for saving your life."

Mycroft chuckled, amused by what he clearly saw as her misguided view of the situation. "You knocked me out. Have you forgotten that? In what universe does that translate to saving someone's life?"

"I didn't break the window," she retorted, her tone suddenly serious, her eyes reflecting a hardened resolve. "Someone was there before me. You have to believe me."

"I do," Mycroft replied, his voice unexpectedly softened, tinged with something like warmth - and gratitude.

Alex stared at the man, utterly confused. His sudden kindness disoriented her. This wasn't the Mycroft she knew - cold, distant, the infamous 'Ice Man.'

I should hate him.

After all, it's his fault I'm in here.

But I can't.

Why not?

What is it about this man that keeps me from hating him?

"There was a man on the surveillance footage," Mycroft began, interrupting her thoughts. "He entered my house just twenty minutes before you did, and he disappeared shortly after you followed him."

"That was Montaigne," Alex blurted out before she could stop herself.

Mycroft's face turned ghostly pale in an instant. "Thomas Montaigne?" He seemed to be hoping, desperately, that he had misheard her.

Alex nodded. "You know him?"

"All too well," Mycroft replied, the fear stark in his eyes, a rare and unsettling sight. Without another word, he stepped back from the cell door and motioned for the guards to approach. "Get Miss

117

Green out of here!" His voice was sharp, commanding - so much so that the guards didn't dare question the order.

The guards immediately obeyed, unlocking the door without hesitation.

"We have much to discuss," Mycroft said, looking at Alex as she stepped out, reluctant but determined. They began walking down the corridor, with the guards trailing them.

"Am I free now?" Alex asked, her confusion deepening.

Mycroft allowed a faint, almost imperceptible smile. "For the moment, yes."

"What do you mean by 'for the moment'?" she asked, frowning.

"You're not entirely free, Miss Green," Mycroft clarified. "While your innocence is no longer in question, I can't simply let you go. You're now in danger as well."

Alex snorted, irritated. "What a load of nonsense."

As they exited the building, the cool air of the London street hitting her face, Mycroft stopped and gave her a measured look.

"Goethe," he said, delivering the word with the practiced superiority of someone who always knew better, casting her that familiar I-know-something-you-don't glance.

At that very moment, a sleek black limousine with tinted windows pulled up beside them. Mycroft's personal car. He moved to the rear door, holding it open for Alex with a grace that carried an air of finality.

Alex hesitated, eyeing the door cautiously. Was this really a good idea? Yet, as she looked back at Mycroft's steely gaze, it was clear - there was no room for argument. His eyes left no space for escape.

Reluctantly, she climbed inside.

Mycroft followed her into the limousine, taking a seat beside Alex as the car smoothly began its journey.

"Goethe, of all things," Alex muttered aloud, casting a sidelong glance at the man next to her. "What's your plan now? Where are you taking me?"

"To a safe house," Mycroft replied calmly.

"And what about you? Montaigne's target is you, isn't it?" she asked, her voice laced with suspicion.

"I'm coming with you," he said, his tone matter-of-fact.

What?

Mycroft Holmes and I under the same roof?

This is a disaster waiting to happen.

Why is he doing this?

Why is he suddenly so concerned about me?

This isn't like him.

Mycroft doesn't care about feelings... or does he?

Why is he confusing me so much?

What's happening to me... to him?

"Don't worry," Mycroft's voice cut through her chaotic thoughts, "the property is vast enough for the both of us. If you prefer, you can take the south wing all to yourself, and I will make do with the north."

Alex didn't respond. She turned her gaze to the window, watching the London streets roll by in silence.

What am I supposed to do now?

Maybe staying in prison would've been better than this.

After a long pause, Mycroft's voice broke the stillness again, but this time, it had changed, softened. "Who is Victor?"

Alex turned to face him. "You've spoken with your brother, haven't you?"

"And with Dr. Watson," Mycroft added, a faint smile pulling at his lips. "Did I truly distract you so much that you walked into traffic while the light was red?"

119

Alex quickly averted her gaze, unable to withstand the intensity of his piercing blue eyes, which seemed capable of unearthing her every thought.

"Who is Victor?" he asked again, but this time with more insistence.

"A friend," Alex murmured, struggling to pull fragments of long-buried memories to the surface. Memories she had purposely tried to forget. "Victor was... one of my friends. Or maybe he was my only friend," she added, speaking more to herself now. She shook her head, confusion clouding her face. "I don't know anymore. It was all so long ago. But I remember... I didn't have many friends as a child."

"Why not?"

Alex turned her gaze back to Mycroft. "How many friends did you have in your childhood?"

"Only one," he replied, lowering his head in sorrow. The memory of Margaret was still a wound that refused to heal, a wound that felt as fresh as the day it had been inflicted. "She was... something special."

"She?" Alex's eyes widened with curiosity.

Mycroft nodded, the weight of her name pressing down on him. "Margaret." He sighed heavily, as if merely speaking her name drove a dagger into his heart. "She was Victor's sister. Did you know her?"

"No." Alex shook her head, her response firm and unambiguous. It was clear to Mycroft that she was telling the truth. "I didn't even know Victor had a sister." She hesitated for a moment, her curiosity battling with her reluctance to pry, but in the end, she couldn't resist. "What happened to her?"

"I don't know," Mycroft admitted, his voice thick with grief. "No one does. Margaret disappeared just days after Victor. She was never found."

"After?" Alex sensed something hidden in his tone. "Why do you say 'after'? Did you find Victor? Where is he?" Her voice grew sharper with each question, frustration boiling beneath her calm facade. "What did you do to him? Where is Victor?"

"He's dead." Mycroft's voice broke under the weight of his words. It was not easy for him to say, but he owed her the truth—she had been honest with him, as much as her memory allowed. "He's been dead for over twenty years. He drowned in a well near Abbey House."

"Abbey House," Alex echoed absently, as if the name unlocked something buried deep in her mind. "Iron Man." Suddenly, a wave of panic washed over her, crashing into her like a storm. "I have to get out! Stop the car! Now!" She thrashed wildly, her eyes wide with terror, as if the walls of the car were closing in on her, suffocating her. The spacious backseat of the limousine suddenly felt claustrophobically small. "I need to get out!" Her breath came in short, desperate gasps.

Mycroft, sensing the urgency in her voice, immediately signaled the driver to pull over. The car hadn't even fully stopped when he flung the door open, and Alex bolted out, stumbling into the street. Instinctively, Mycroft followed her.

But Alex didn't get far. After only a few staggering steps, her legs gave out, and she collapsed.

In the last second, Mycroft caught her, cradling her in his arms before she could hit the ground. He held her close, her slender form limp against him. The sudden intimacy of the moment startled him. He had never been so close to anyone like this - never allowed himself to be. Yet here he was, holding her, feeling the warmth of her body against his. A strange sensation coursed through him, one that shook him to his core.

He was not used to feeling anything.

This... this was new.

And it disturbed him that he was capable of such emotions. Mycroft Holmes, the man who prided himself on his cold rationality, found himself unmoored by something as simple as holding a woman in his arms. He had always believed that emotions like affection and love made one weak, vulnerable. But now, in this fleeting moment, he felt the opposite. He felt stronger than ever before. Yet the fact that it was Alex, unconscious in his arms, who brought this out in him filled him with an unsettling worry.

He had only ever felt this depth of concern for one other person - his brother, Sherlock. And before that, Margaret. The thought unsettled him even more, especially when Liz's earlier words echoed in his mind. Perhaps Margaret truly was still alive.

The more Mycroft looked down at Alex, the more that nagging thought grew, until it became almost undeniable: Elizabeth Markle's suspicions might not be as far-fetched as they seemed.

Dusk had already fallen by the time Alex finally awoke. The faint aroma of freshly brewed fruit tea had stirred her from her slumber. She slowly sat up, her eyes widening in surprise as she took in her surroundings. The room she found herself in was exquisitely furnished with antique pieces made of dark cedar wood, each one intricately carved with delicate patterns. The ceiling was unusually high, adorned with elaborate rosettes and ornate designs.

Incredible.

This place must have cost a fortune.

Still a bit groggy, Alex rose to her feet and staggered toward the door. The moment her hand touched the brass handle, memories of the past few days came flooding back. Like a fast-paced montage, the events played out in her mind, growing more unsettling with each vivid recollection.

Iron Man.

That was the last thing she could distinctly remember.

Who is that?

Unsure of what might lie beyond the door, she opened it a crack and cautiously peered into the hallway. She stepped out onto a long corridor lined with dark wallpaper and elegant wooden paneling that reached up to her shoulders. Portraits of various dignitaries, likely figures of high political rank, hung on both sides, though none of the faces were familiar to her. Between the portraits, every few meters, stood tall vases filled with flowers, busts of elderly men, and life-sized suits of armor arranged neatly against the walls.

Alex moved quietly to the end of the hallway, where a broad staircase with a carved wooden banister greeted her. She glanced down but saw no one.

If no one's here, why do I smell freshly brewed tea?

Leaning on the banister for support, she descended the stairs and ventured onward, her curiosity pulling her into the adjacent room. It was a grand study, centered around a large fireplace made of red brick, where a fire crackled warmly, casting a soft, soothing light across the room. The heat radiated gently, creating an inviting atmosphere. Along all four walls stood towering bookshelves made of nearly black wood, each one brimming with books that reached up toward the lofty ceiling.

In the middle of the room were two large, dark brown leather armchairs, both facing the fireplace. Between them sat a small, round side table. A long Oriental rug, with soft, muted colors, stretched across the floor, its intricate patterns perfectly complementing the beige wallpaper and the dark cedar wood accents of the room.

Alex's breath caught in her throat for a moment. The room felt like something out of another time - both luxurious and foreboding, as though the very walls held secrets whispered by the flickering firelight.

What is this place?

"Good evening," said Mycroft, seated in one of the leather armchairs, a delicate teacup in hand. He glanced over the wide backrest of the chair, his eyes scanning Alex from head to toe, as though dissecting her for faults invisible to the average observer. "Tea?" he offered, setting down his own cup before pouring a steaming, rose-colored liquid from a porcelain teapot into a second cup beside him.

Alex watched, intrigued. For a man who so often seemed devoid of emotion, Mycroft now appeared almost... warm. At least, for the moment.

It's just tea.

Don't get carried away.

He's Mycroft Holmes, for heaven's sake.

Anyone can pour tea - it doesn't make him a better man.

Still, when he extended the cup toward her, his smile was so unexpectedly gentle and disarming that it only deepened her confusion.

Why is he being so kind?

He has no reason to be.

He should despise me, like he despises everyone else.

So, why doesn't he?

What makes me different?

Despite her hesitation, Alex accepted the cup with a small, appreciative smile, allowing its warmth to seep into her cold fingers.

"Please, sit," Mycroft gestured toward the empty armchair beside him, as if it had been placed there specifically for her. His manner was polite, almost deferential, which made her nerves twitch even more.

He's done nothing to me.

Not really.

But then, like a blow to the chest, she remembered their phone conversation from a few days prior. *"What have I done that makes you despise me so much?"* he had asked.

Nothing.

Absolutely nothing.

With deliberate care, Alex lowered herself into the chair, which proved even more comfortable than it appeared. After a moment's silence, she ventured, "You knew Victor, didn't you? And Margaret, his sister? How?"

Mycroft raised his cup to his lips, sipping thoughtfully before replying. "Victor was Sherlock's closest friend. They were inseparable. Played together every day."

"What did they play?" Alex pressed, her tone earnest. She needed answers, particularly about the enigmatic "Iron Man."

Mycroft sighed slightly, as though the question were beneath him. "What children usually play. Tag. Hide and seek. The usual games," he replied with a hint of impatience, clearly not understanding the weight of her inquiry.

"Superheroes?" Alex locked eyes with him. "Did they ever play superheroes?"

That, at last, seemed to strike a chord. Mycroft's gaze flickered, betraying a moment of hesitation before he set his cup down. His previously cool demeanor shifted, just slightly. But enough.

"Oh yes, many times. Sherlock was always Thor, wearing that ridiculous red-and-blue sweater he adored. And Victor..." His voice trailed off.

"Iron Man," Alex finished, her own voice trembling as the pieces began to fall into place. The color drained from her face, and her entire body began to shake. Suddenly, the once-fragmented

125

memories began to align, creating a picture so hauntingly clear it left her breathless.

In her mind's eye, she could see the two boys playing vividly - Sherlock, with his dark, curly hair and wide, innocent eyes, and Victor, his red, wild curls barely contained by the oversized super-hero helmet, his freckled face glowing with childlike joy.

Her hands trembled so violently that she nearly dropped her teacup, but Mycroft, quick as ever, rose from his seat and caught it. He placed the cup safely on the table, then knelt before her, gently clasping her trembling hands in his. His touch was careful, unchar-acteristically gentle, as though he feared she might shatter like porcelain. "Are you alright?" he asked, his tone filled with an unexpected warmth.

Alex couldn't speak. She was overwhelmed, trapped between a tidal wave of emotion and the unexpected tenderness of Mycroft's proximity. The way he looked at her, so intently, with concern instead of cold calculation - it made everything worse, made her feel as though the delicate control she'd fought so hard to maintain was crumbling.

Tears stung the back of her eyes, but she swallowed them down.

No. I will not cry.

Not in front of him.

She clenched her jaw, determined not to let Mycroft Holmes see her fall apart. He couldn't know just how close she was to breaking - he must never know.

"What are you remembering?" Mycroft's voice was quieter now, his thumbs tracing gentle circles over her knuckles in an attempt to soothe her. "What are you afraid of?"

I can't tell him.

No, I can't.

Not when I don't even know the truth myself.

What if I'm wrong?

126

What if my memories are deceiving me?

What if nothing I've seen is real?

Her thoughts swirled into a confused, frantic haze. She couldn't bear the weight of it - the uncertainty, the fear that gripped her so tightly it was suffocating.

"Please," Mycroft implored softly, his voice almost a whisper. He looked into her eyes, his gaze piercing yet strangely gentle. "I cannot help you if you don't talk to me."

For the first time, Alex saw something raw, something human in the man who was so often called a cold and unfeeling puppet-master. In that moment, Mycroft wasn't the untouchable figure of power she'd known - he was simply a man, asking for a truth that only she could give.

"I've forgotten most of my childhood," Alex began hesitantly, her voice soft, almost as if she was speaking to herself rather than Mycroft. "When I was about four or five, I had a terrible car accident. So much of what happened before that is just... gone. But recently, after reading about a young boy who was kidnapped in the papers, things started coming back to me, little by little. I can see Victor so clearly, as if he's standing right in front of me. He was so full of life, so happy, as if nothing bad had ever happened. And now I can see Sherlock too, holding that ridiculous homemade hammer of his. Both of them were wearing rubber boots," she added absently, her gaze drifting past Mycroft. "It was supposed to rain that day, or so the weather report had said, but the sun was shining the whole time." Alex let out a soft, amused chuckle, caught up in the fragments of memories. "Thor," she muttered, almost to herself. "I laughed at him, you know? 'You're supposed to be so brilliant, and that's the best you could come up with - *Thor*?' I said to him. Sherlock was so hurt, I could tell. I was awful to him. Just horrible. Honestly, it's a miracle I even had one friend." She looked at Mycroft now, her expression suddenly serious. "I was always a strange child. In school, everyone hated me. But it didn't really bother me. They were all so slow, so behind.

127

They didn't understand me. They called me 'stupid goat' and other names, even though I was smarter than all of them combined." She sighed heavily. "Friends... what are they good for anyway?"

Mycroft's gaze softened slightly, his own thoughts drawn to the past. "I only ever had one friend too," he said quietly. "No one was like her. No one could compare. She grasped things so quickly, far faster than anyone else. Even Sherlock's intelligence seemed pale next to hers, and she was much younger than he was."

"Margaret," Alex whispered, as if reading his thoughts. She said the name aloud, hoping it would stir something deeper, some long-buried recognition, but nothing surfaced. It remained unfamiliar to her, despite its weight in Mycroft's voice.

For a brief moment, their eyes locked. A shared silence fell between them, stretching out, strange yet oddly compelling. Neither of them moved. The tension in the air was palpable, heavy with something unspoken. Time seemed to slow as they lingered in that moment, neither quite knowing what to do next. Mycroft reached out and brushed his hand softly across her cheek. The touch was tentative, almost delicate. He leaned in slightly, closing the space between them, until he was so near that he could feel the warmth of her breath, shallow and quick, against his skin.

Just as his lips were about to meet hers, his phone rang sharply from his pocket, shattering the delicate spell that had fallen over them.

The moment was gone, as quickly as it had come, leaving only silence and awkwardness in its wake.

Mycroft jerked away abruptly, fumbling in his pocket as he moved a few steps to the side. He answered the call with a look of barely contained irritation. "Yes, this is Holmes speaking. ... No ... Can this not wait until tomorr-" He was cut off mid-sentence, and his scowl deepened. "I don't care..."

Alex could barely make out the rest of his conversation. Her mind was swirling in confusion, thoughts colliding with each other like chaotic waves.

Did he just try to kiss me?

Is this real?

The most emotionally distant man on the planet almost kissed me?

How is that even possible?

And why didn't I stop him?

Do I... want him to kiss me?

But I hardly know him...

Or do I?

Those eyes of his - they speak of something deeper, something that feels familiar, as if I've known him my whole life.

Well, I knew Sherlock back then, didn't I?

So why can't I remember Mycroft?

And who is this Margaret?

Shouldn't he want to kiss her instead?

This man is driving me insane.

For that alone, I should hate him - but I can't.

I like him.

Damn it.

It's true - I like Mycroft Holmes.

"Will you be alright on your own for a few hours?" Mycroft's voice cut through her spiraling thoughts, startling her. He was standing behind her, pocketing his phone. His tone was tense, his expression strained. "I have something to take care of. It won't take long."

"It's fine," Alex replied, forcing a smile.

He's acting as if nothing happened between us.

Typical.

129

Did it mean nothing to him?

Was there even something between us?

Did I imagine it all?

Of course.

Mycroft Holmes is far too cold-hearted to feel anything remotely resembling love.

He's the Ice Man - through and through.

"I'm sure I'll manage without getting too bored," she added, her tone light but detached.

"If you need anything - or if you're hungry - Mr. Wiggins is in the kitchen. He'll do his best to accommodate you."

"Thank you," Alex said, her voice clipped. She could see the discomfort etched into his posture, the way he seemed almost eager to escape the situation. Despite how much his indifference stung, she refused to let him see the pain it caused. Her gaze turned icy, and she looked away.

Just leave already.

An apology hovered on Mycroft's lips, but he couldn't bring himself to utter it. As if some internal switch had flipped, the charming man from moments earlier transformed back into the cold, unfeeling figure the world knew all too well. He sniffed, rolled his eyes slightly, and with a brisk, prideful stride, he exited the room.

In that moment, it was impossible to tell who felt more hurt.

I need to get out of here!

Anger simmered within Alex. She wanted nothing more than to storm out, to run - but she didn't even know where she was.

I'm probably in the middle of nowhere.

Somewhere so remote that if Mycroft decided to kill me, no one would hear me scream for miles.

130

But instead of fleeing, Alex chose to stay. She reached for the now lukewarm cup of tea and took a slow, deliberate sip, her eyes fixed on the crackling flames in the fireplace.

It was late at night when Mycroft finally returned. He moved quietly, but Alex, who was always a light sleeper, had noticed his presence long before he even entered the room, where the fire in the hearth had long since died out.

"You're late," Alex said the moment Mycroft made to turn around and leave. She stood up, her eyes fixed on him with a mixture of accusation and suspicion. "Where have you been?" She had spent the entire evening in the chair, thinking about what the man had truly been up to.

Mycroft stared at her, perplexed. "Is something the matter?"

"Where were you?" Alex repeated with insistence, her gaze sharp and demanding.

"What's wrong with you?" he asked, shocked by the sudden fury in her voice. He clearly hadn't anticipated her anger. Had he done something wrong?

Alex stepped closer, pointing at him as if accusing him in a courtroom. "You bastard!" she shouted, her voice rising in a fury that startled even her. "It was all an act, wasn't it? You pulled out one of my hairs, and to cover it up, you tried to kiss me!" Without warning, she slapped him hard across the face. "What did you do with it? Where have you been?"

Mycroft winced, rubbing his stinging cheek, his face a mask of confusion. "You need to lie down, Miss Green," he said in his usual cold, detached tone. "You're spouting nonsense."

131

"Don't deny it!" Alex's arms flailed as she fumed. "You were at Scotland Yard. Admit it! I can smell Inspector Doyle's obnoxious aftershave from a mile away. What were you doing there?"

"Calm yourself!" Mycroft, now visibly unsettled, took a step back. He wasn't accustomed to being confronted like this, especially not by a woman - one he held in such regard, no less. This situation was spiraling out of control, and yet there was something about her perceptiveness that intrigued him. "Yes, I was at Scotland Yard," he admitted cautiously. "But it wasn't because of you. It was about my brother. This isn't the first time I've had to intervene for Sherlock. I assure you, this has nothing to do with you."

Alex exhaled deeply, slowly regaining her composure. His sincerity seemed undeniable, and his explanation had a ring of truth to it.

Or he's an extraordinarily skilled liar.

What is happening to me?

"I'm sorry," she said quietly, her voice breaking, tears threatening to spill from her eyes. "It's just too much. I can't take this anymore." And with that, the dam broke, and she began to sob uncontrollably.

Mycroft hesitated only for a moment before stepping closer and gently wrapping his arm around her, pulling her into a careful embrace. "It's alright," he whispered, his voice uncharacteristically soft, holding her with surprising tenderness.

Alex wiped her tears, managing a small, fragile smile. "I should go to bed now. Good night, Mr. Holmes."

"Good night," Mycroft replied, watching as she left the room and ascended the stairs to the upper floor. He let out a relieved sigh as he turned to leave the room himself. But then, the soft chime of his phone stopped him in his tracks. He pulled it out and glanced at the message.

132

Test was positive. You were right. Regards, Doyle, Mycroft read, and his heart sank. Despite having expected this result, the confirmation filled him with dread.

"She is her," he muttered to himself, his voice heavy with foreboding. "She really is." Now fully alert, he dialed his brother's number and waited for Sherlock to pick up.

"Sherlock," Mycroft began, his voice steeled but betraying the weight he carried. "I need your help." The admission was painfully difficult for him to make, but he knew it was the truth. Only Sherlock could understand what he was grappling with now. "Do you remember Margaret Trevor?"

"How could I ever forget her?" Sherlock's voice came through the phone, a mix of irritation and something more nostalgic. "She insulted me, Mycroft. She insulted me when she was four years old, and it still stings to this day. But why ask about her now? She's been dead for ages."

Mycroft hesitated.

"Mycroft?" Sherlock pressed.

"She's alive. Margaret Trevor is alive," Mycroft said, his voice strained with the weight of the revelation. "She has always been."

Sherlock's breath caught in his throat. "Where is she?" he asked, horrified, the shock in his voice unmistakable.

"You would never believe me," Mycroft replied, his tone heavy with both regret and certainty.

133

VIII.

HIPPO

The following morning, Alex trudged down the stairs, feeling the weight of exhaustion from the previous night. She found Mycroft seated in the living room at a long, polished table, holding a cup of tea in one hand and his phone in the other. He was in the midst of a heated conversation with someone who clearly irritated him. When Alex entered the room, his gaze shifted to her, though his voice remained sharp.

"Handle it, Ryder!" Mycroft barked into the phone. "This is absolutely not my problem... The Prime Minister won't be pleased, and you know it... As I've already said, it's *your* problem." He ended the call abruptly and placed the phone beside him on the table.

Noticing Alex awkwardly stepping further into the room, he quickly rose from his seat, greeting her with a surprisingly warm smile. "Good morning, Miss Green."

"Good morning, Mr. Holmes," Alex replied. Her eyes caught a faint reddish mark on his cheek - a reminder of the slap she'd given him the night before. A pang of guilt washed over her, and she nervously cast her eyes down to the floor.

Mycroft noticed and offered a slight smile, clearly unused to seeing anyone embarrassed in his presence. "Mr. Wiggins has prepared a small breakfast for you. I do hope you'll have something to eat. After all, breakfast is the most important meal of the day."

Alex returned his smile, albeit sheepishly. "You're right." She took a seat next to him at the table. "I don't usually eat much. Food

134

tends to distract me when I need to focus. But, today, I'll make an exception."

Before Mycroft could respond, Mr. Wiggins entered the room, balancing a large silver tray laden with an impressive spread of delicacies, which he neatly arranged in front of Alex. The sight of the lavish breakfast made her mouth water. "Tea or coffee, Miss?" Wiggins asked in a respectful tone, looking almost reverent in his formal attire.

"Tea please."

Wiggins nodded swiftly and left to fetch the tea.

I feel like royalty.

I could get used to this.

As she began to tear apart a buttery croissant, her gaze shifted towards Mycroft, who had already buried himself in a newspaper. She debated whether to address what had happened the night before, the strange tension between them, and ultimately decided she couldn't leave it unspoken.

"I'm really sorry about last night," Alex said hesitantly, breaking the silence. Mycroft lowered his newspaper and fixed her with a calm, inquisitive look, encouraging her to continue. "I didn't mean to slap you, truly. It's just... I - I have a hard time..."

"Trusting people?" Mycroft finished for her, his gaze steady but gentle.

Alex nodded slowly.

"That's perfectly understandable," he replied, studying her closely. "If I were in your position, I doubt I would react any differently."

"My position?" Alex furrowed her brow. "What do you mean by that?"

"You've forgotten much of your childhood and spent years unaware of your true past. Now, as fragments of it start returning to you, it's only natural that you'd struggle with trust."

What?

What is he talking about?

Victor?

Does he know more than I do?

Why can't I remember?

What's happening to me?

"I just wish it were easier," Alex murmured, frustration laced in her voice as her thoughts spiraled.

Mr. Wiggins re-entered the room, carrying a teapot and a fresh cup, which he gently placed in front of her.

"It will get easier," Mycroft said, his voice steady but distant, before returning to the newspaper in his hands.

Alex stared at the steaming tea for a moment, her mind clouded with confusion. Then she began to dig into the lavish breakfast spread before her. But she didn't get very far. Only a few minutes later, her phone rang. She retrieved it from her pocket and answered the call, all the while feeling the piercing gaze of Mycroft upon her. He was half-reading his newspaper, half-watching her with quiet intensity.

"Hey, Liz," Alex said, visibly relieved to hear her friend's voice. "Yeah, I'm fine... No, I'm not at home... I don't really know where I am exactly... Please, calm down! I'm in a safe place, I promise." She cast a quick glance at Mycroft. "Wait, what?" she suddenly gasped, her voice rising in shock, causing Mycroft to glance up, startled. "You're where? Why on earth are you...?" Alex's face paled instantly. "Who told you that? How the hell do you know about Victor?" She sprang to her feet, her expression frantic.

Mycroft, now fully alert, set the newspaper aside and watched her nervously, fearing that Liz might have revealed too much.

"No, that can't be true. That's a lie. Doyle's lying... I said he's lying!" Alex's voice trembled with desperation. "How long have you known me? Have I ever lied to you?... Don't bring that up, that doesn't count. I'm serious this time!... So, who do you believe?

Him or me?" She closed her eyes and took a deep breath. "Fine. I'll call you later. Bye." Alex ended the call and spun around, glaring at Mycroft with fury. "What the hell have you done?"

Mycroft simply shrugged, trying to feign ignorance.

"My best friend thinks I'm *dead*!" she yelled, her anger boiling over. "What did you tell her? What were you really doing last night?"

Mycroft hesitated. He wanted to tell her everything, to come clean, but he knew it wouldn't help. The truth would only hurt her more. So, he remained silent, though every fiber of his being fought against it.

"Say something! Talk to me! What have you done?" Alex's voice cracked with emotion. His silence, his refusal to engage, only fueled her fury.

And to think, I even apologized to him.

I hate him.

"Fine. If you won't talk, I'm leaving." She stormed toward the door.

Caught off guard, Mycroft hurried after her, grabbing her arm just before she reached the grand entrance hall. "You're not going anywhere, Miss Green. That's an order! If you step out of that door, you're as good as dead."

"From what I've been told, I've already been dead for over twenty years," Alex shot back, hurt flashing in her eyes. She studied his face, searching for answers. "Why won't you tell me what happened back then? You know something. Why are you keeping it from me?"

"Your friend is simply misinformed. That's all," Mycroft tried to placate her. "Please, trust me."

"Never," she snapped, ripping her arm free from his grip. "I'd like to take you up on your offer from yesterday now. Stay away from me!" Without waiting for a response, she turned and stormed up the stairs to the upper floor.

137

Mycroft stood there, frozen, watching her retreat. He didn't know what to do. He couldn't tell her the truth - she wouldn't believe him anyway. Unless, of course, he got a little help.

As the thought took shape, the doorbell rang, as though fate itself was answering his unspoken request.

Startled, Mycroft rushed to the door and opened it.

It was none other than Sherlock, who had come to see his brother at the break of dawn.

"Have you told her yet?" Sherlock asked as he stepped inside the grand building. Just then, the sound of a door being slammed in anger echoed from upstairs, causing Sherlock to smirk. "So, not yet. How much longer are you going to keep the truth from her?"

"You know better than anyone that she'd never believe it," Mycroft replied grimly.

"Does she remember anything at all?"

"Thor and Iron Man," Mycroft said quietly.

"Thor," Sherlock muttered with a slight smile, recalling the memories. But then his expression darkened with a tinge of sadness. "She was rather cruel to me. Just like you. Perhaps that's why the two of you got along so well."

Mycroft, now visibly uneasy, hurried his brother into the sitting room. "What did you find out?"

Sherlock joined him at the table, his sharp eyes glancing over the remnants of a breakfast buffet that had barely been touched. "Well," he began, a calculating look on his face. "How serious are you?"

Mycroft looked puzzled. "Serious about what?"

"About her, of course." Sherlock raised an eyebrow. "Come on, Mycroft. It's glaringly obvious she means something to you. This is the finest of all your estates, handpicked to impress her. And this extravagant breakfast - who wouldn't be tempted to throw their arms around you and cry, 'I love you, Mycroft'?"

138

Mycroft shook his head a little too defensively. "I chose this house because it's the most secure of all. And as you can plainly see, she hardly touched the breakfast. She despises eating just as much as we do."

Sherlock's teasing smile faded, replaced by a cold, serious expression. "So, there's no doubt that it's really her?"

"No doubt," Mycroft said, his voice heavy. The mere thought of Margaret still weighed on him, even now that he knew she had been alive all this time. "So, what were you able to find out about her?"

"Not nearly enough," Sherlock admitted, his fingers drumming lightly on the table. "But the real Alexandra Green has been dead for almost 38 years. She was Margaret's grandmother. The driver of the car that caused the accident back then was Julius Moran. He and his brother Sebastian supposedly died at the scene of the crash - at least that's what the police report says. But I doubt very much that they're actually dead."

Mycroft's eyes widened slightly in alarm. He knew that Sherlock's suspicions usually led to dangerous pursuits.

"Lestrade is having their graves dug up as we speak," Sherlock said with a glint of excitement in his eyes, clearly relishing the unfolding mystery. "We'll see what they find. It should only take about half an hour before we know for sure." He poured himself some tea into one of the clean cups, steam still rising from the pot, and took a leisurely sip. "But I'll leave it entirely to you to tell her the truth."

Sherlock's words hung in the air, leaving Mycroft to wrestle with the enormity of the secret he still hadn't revealed.

"Mr. Wiggins!" Mycroft's voice rang out through the hallway.

It took a moment, but soon the butler appeared, looking slightly startled when he spotted Sherlock. "Oh, good morning, sir! Is there something I can get for you?"

"My brother won't be staying long," Mycroft interrupted in his usual cold manner. "Fetch Miss Green. Inform her that I will tell her everything."

The butler blinked, visibly confused, but gave a quick nod before turning on his heel and hurrying away.

"Well then," Sherlock said, draining the last of his tea. "Good luck with that, dear brother." He stood, already moving toward the door.

Mycroft hurried after him. "Where are you going, Sherlock?"

"You can handle this on your own. I'll let you know as soon as Lestrade calls," Sherlock replied with a casual wave of his hand.

"Sherlock, I'm asking you - don't act like a child!" Mycroft's frustration was evident in his voice.

In an instant, Sherlock spun around, his sharp eyes flashing. "If you've forgotten how delightful she was to me as a child, perhaps I should refresh your memory." He tugged up the sleeve of his right arm, revealing the unmistakable bite marks just below his elbow. "Your beloved friend bit me."

Mycroft stared at the old scars, memories of the past flooding back. "That was entirely your fault," he said, as if trying to brush off the incident.

"My fault?" Sherlock scoffed, pulling his sleeve back down. "You provoked her."

"That's not true. She was merely defending me," Mycroft replied, a rare smile almost tugging at the corner of his lips.

"Successfully," Sherlock muttered, already walking away.

Before Mycroft could respond, Mr. Wiggins burst down the stairs like a man possessed. "Mr. Holmes! Mr. Holmes!" he shouted, breathless as he skidded to a halt before the two brothers. "She's gone, sir! Miss Green - she's fled! Jumped out the window."

Mycroft and Sherlock exchanged a brief, tense look before bolting toward the door, both of them hoping to catch up with her before it was too late.

140

"Alex!" they shouted, their voices echoing across the estate as they sprinted across the grounds, but there was no sign of the young woman anywhere.

She had vanished without a trace.

Even though she could clearly hear the two men calling after her, Alex didn't stop for a single moment.

Keep shouting, you fools.

I won't let you deceive me.

If they wouldn't tell her the truth, then she'd have to uncover it herself, no matter the cost. Alex slowed her pace, now swiftly walking along the empty road, and pulled out her phone. She dialed her friend's number.

"Hey," she said, trying to keep her voice as calm as possible, though her heart was pounding. "Could you do me a favor and come pick me up?"

"Hey, of course. Where are you?"

"Well... that's the tricky part. I'm not entirely sure. All I know is I'm somewhere outside the city."

"Great. That narrows it down," Liz replied sarcastically.

"Yeah, I know. Hang on - wait a second. There's a sign up ahead." Alex jogged toward the nearby road sign. "I'm near Barnet College."

"Barnet College? That's in Southgate! How the hell did you end up there?" Liz asked, clearly baffled.

"Mycroft Holmes," Alex replied, her tone sharp with frustration. "He's got some sort of mansion out here. He calls it a 'safe house.'"

Liz practically exploded at the sound of his name. "Mycroft again! What the hell is going on between you two? Why are you constantly with him?"

"This is only the second time! Calm down!" Alex tried to soothe her friend's obvious annoyance. "He was just trying to help me."

"Then why are you running away?" Liz shot back, her contempt for Mycroft all too clear.

"I'll explain everything later, okay? Just come get me, please."

"Fine. Wait for me at the college. I'll figure out how to get there."

"Thanks. See you soon." Alex hung up and slipped her phone back into her pocket. She wasn't far from the college now, though she could still see Mycroft's estate in the distance, looming over the landscape like an unsettling shadow. As she walked, a deep sense of unease gnawed at her. She hadn't wanted to leave him like this - so abruptly, so full of doubt - but she felt she had no other choice.

The truth was all that mattered.

It was the last thing her mother had told her before she passed away. Those words echoed in Alex's mind as she pushed forward, determined to find the answers she so desperately needed.

A few hours later, Liz finally arrived in Southgate, only to find Alex sitting on the curb, looking like a forlorn shadow of herself, lost in her own thoughts. Liz had to honk to get her attention - otherwise, she might have spent the entire day waiting for Alex to even notice her presence.

Startled, Alex leapt up and hurried into the car. The first thing she managed to say was, "Thank you," before throwing her arms around her friend's neck in a tight embrace. "You're my savior."

"It's nothing, really," Liz smiled as she pulled the car away from the curb. "Now, spill it. Why the hell is Inspector Doyle claiming you're dead?"

"I have no idea. That's exactly what I need to find out. And more importantly, I have to uncover the truth about Margaret Trevor."

Liz felt a cold shiver run down her spine. She feared Alex might have realized that she had gone through her apartment.

"What's wrong?" Alex immediately noticed her friend's uneasy reaction.

"Please, don't be mad," Liz pleaded, her voice filled with dread.

Alex turned to her, suspicion in her eyes. "What did you do?" Her expression quickly turned to one of alarm. "You weren't actually looking for my cigarettes, were you?"

"I'm so sorry," Liz muttered, guilt flooding her voice.

Alex's temper flared instantly. "What the hell is wrong with you? First, you break into my apartment, and then you go snooping around. Can I trust no one anymore?"

"You *can* trust me. Honestly. I didn't mean any harm," Liz said, her guilt now so overwhelming it made focusing on the road difficult.

"Then just tell me already, before you crash us into a tree! What did you find? I doubt I have anything to hide, but let's hear it!"

"I found an old photograph tucked inside one of your books - *The End of the World* by Arthur Conan Doyle, if I'm remembering correctly. It was of two little children, a boy and a girl, and their names were written on the back."

143

"Margaret and Victor," Alex murmured, both surprised and confused.

"You know the photo, then? Who are they?"

Alex shook her head. "No, I don't recognize the photo. I just guessed. I only know Victor." She sighed heavily, staring out the window. "He was my best friend when we were kids. He lived nearby, but he was always at the Holmes family estate, playing with Sherlock. I rarely went there - every time I was at that place, I felt this overwhelming fear. But I can't remember why."

"Probably the fear of Mycroft," Liz quipped, trying desperately to lighten the somber mood with a laugh.

But Alex didn't laugh. She gazed out of the window, deep in thought. Oddly enough, she didn't find the comment amusing at all. "No, I wasn't afraid of him. Even though I can't fully remember him, I know for sure I never feared Mycroft. Never." She turned back to Liz, her expression grave. "It was something else. Maybe it has something to do with the car accident."

"What car accident?"

"Shortly after Victor disappeared, my mother and I were involved in a terrible accident while she was driving me home. It was pouring rain that day, and it was already late, twilight setting in. Another car crashed into us head-on." Alex sighed in frustration. "That's all I remember. Much of what happened after, or even before that day, has been lost to me because of the accident."

"If you can't remember, how did that photo end up in one of your books?" Liz was clearly struggling to make sense of it all.

"Most of those books belonged to my mother. She must've hidden it there. Probably forgot about it herself."

"And what about the false bottom in your wardrobe?"

"You were in my bedroom?" Alex snapped angrily. But her anger quickly subsided, as her mind was preoccupied with what Liz had said. She began to recall something she'd long since buried. "All the furniture - except for my bed - belonged to my mother.

144

When her health worsened and she had to move into a care facility, she left everything to me. Since I'd only just arrived in London and didn't own a single piece of furniture, I took hers, seeing as they were mine anyway. But I know nothing about a hidden compartment in the wardrobe. I tend to wear the same few things, so I hardly ever use it." She eyed Liz sharply. "What did you find in there?"

"Drawings. A child's drawings, signed with the name Margaret. And... a light blue stuffed hippopotamus."

"Hippo," Alex murmured aloud, the name leaping back into her memory with startling ease. She recognized that stuffed toy all too well.

How could I have forgotten about Hippo?

"My favorite toy." Alex smiled wistfully. "Hippo was my best friend for the longest time, until I..." Her voice faltered, trembling.

"Alex? What is it?"

"Until I met Mycroft." It hit her like a blow to the head - sudden and sharp. She remembered the day she first met Mycroft Holmes. "We... we were friends. Best friends, even?"

Liz shot her a horrified look. She couldn't quite believe that someone like Mycroft Holmes could have *any* friends. But it seemed Liz already knew parts of the story, including the existence of Margaret. "He was right."

"Who?" Alex asked, thoroughly confused.

"Mycroft," Liz replied. "He said Margaret was his best friend, his soulmate." She took a deep breath. "Alex, that's you."

"What? No," Alex cried out, utterly bewildered. "That can't be. I'm not Margaret. I'm *me*."

"Are you really sure about that?"

Alex's confidence crumbled, replaced by a wave of uncertainty and desperation.

No.

Not anymore.

Maybe she's right.

Maybe Mycroft is right.

Who am I?

"Can you just take me home?" she asked, her voice drained of all energy.

"Of course. And when we get there, you'll see for yourself what I found. Maybe it'll help you remember."

Alex was adrift, lost in a sea of confusion. She stared out of the window, her thoughts swirling as the scenery outside rushed by in a blur. Then, out of nowhere, she started laughing.

"What's going on with you?" Liz asked, concerned.

"He was round as a ball," Alex said, barely able to contain her amusement. "Mycroft. He was *so* fat."

"What?" Liz's disbelief was palpable. "But he's a stick now!"

"He wasn't back then," Alex laughed harder, the memory overtaking her, and soon Liz found herself laughing too, unable to resist the contagious humor.

As if on cue, Mycroft called Alex right at that moment. It was as though he'd sensed the two women talking about him.

Alex took a deep breath, struggling to compose herself before answering the phone. "Mr. Holmes, I'm sorry for running off like that. Please don't be mad at me! I had to do it. Staying locked up with you wasn't going to help me get the answers I need about my past. I just want to know what really happened."

"Miss Green, I assure you, that's my goal as well, but don't for a moment think I was pleased with your little escape. You gave me quite a fright."

"I already told you, I'm sorry!" Alex was grinning again, the image of a younger, rounder Mycroft still vivid in her mind. "At least try to see the bright side."

"What, pray tell, is the bright side?" Mycroft's tone was cold, completely failing to grasp what could possibly be amusing.

"You look much better now than you did back then," Alex quipped before quickly hanging up the phone. She and Liz immediately burst into uncontrollable laughter.

How could I have forgotten that?

Sherlock used to tease him endlessly about it.

I bet he still drops hints about Mycroft's weight even now.

Though biting Sherlock again might not be the best idea.

Does he still have the scar?

He bled so much.

It felt good to laugh and to feel pieces of her childhood falling back into place, even if Alex still wasn't entirely sure who she truly was. The memories were returning, bit by bit, and with them, the mystery of her past began to unfold.

Finally arriving back at her small yet cozy apartment, Alex made a beeline for her bedroom. Liz, meanwhile, hesitated in the hallway before slowly wandering towards the living room. It didn't take Alex long to find what she was looking for. With a strange, long-forgotten sense of nostalgia, she pulled out the old watercolor drawings and her beloved stuffed toy.

I thought I had lost you.

She clutched the pale blue hippo tightly in her arms, and, as if a switch had been flipped, the memory of the first time she met Mycroft Holmes came rushing back:

147

"Leave the girl alone!" Mycroft's voice rang out with an unexpected courage as he confronted a group of boys who had circled around young Alex, throwing schoolbooks, sticks, and stones at her.

When the bullies spotted the chubby boy standing defiantly before them, they burst into mocking laughter.

"What do you want, you fat elephant?"

"Leave her alone! She hasn't done anything to you." Mycroft stood his ground, though his knees were trembling like jelly beneath him.

The group didn't hesitate. They charged at Mycroft, shoving him harshly to the ground.

"No!" Alex screamed in horror, her face showing clear guilt as the stranger - this boy who was trying to help her - was now being beaten in her place. "Stop it!" Furious, she grabbed a fist-sized rock from the ground and hurled it at the boys.

To her own shock, the stone struck one of them square in the forehead, drawing blood. The injured boy yelped and ran off, sobbing like a baby.

Mycroft, with a swift kick, managed to drive another attacker away, sending him fleeing.

Between them, Alex and Mycroft soon scattered the rest of the group without much effort.

Once the boys were gone, Alex rushed to Mycroft's side and helped him up. "Thank you," she said, offering him a kind, grateful smile.

Blushing fiercely, Mycroft couldn't hide the embarrassment that flushed his pale cheeks. It was clear that no girl had ever smiled at him before. "I'm Mycroft," he mumbled, still shy and unsure.

"Margaret," Alex replied instinctively, as the memory echoed through her mind.

Back in the present, she sat on the edge of her bed, holding the stuffed hippo, her mind reeling from the flood of long-buried memories. Everything felt so vivid, so painfully clear - the laughter, the fight, the kindness exchanged in a brief moment that somehow forged a lifelong bond.

Margaret?

That name had slipped out of her, as if it had always been hers.

I am Margaret.

Truly.

"Alex! Come here quickly!" Liz called from the living room, her voice laced with unusual nervousness.

Snapping out of her thoughts, Alex jumped up and hurried to her friend, her mind racing as she tried to piece together the tangled threads of memory and identity. When she reached the living room, she found Liz kneeling on the floor, her gaze fixed under the dining table.

"What is that?" Liz pointed at something beneath the table.

Alex moved closer, her heart pounding. She bent down and saw it - a small, black, rectangular device with several wires snaking out of it. A faint ticking noise filled the air. On the front of the device, a display showed red, blinking numbers.

00:25

Damn it!

"Get out! Now!" Alex shouted, yanking Liz with such force that they nearly tripped over each other as they bolted from the room. They raced down the stairs, their footsteps echoing in panicked rhythm, and burst out onto the street. But they didn't stop. They kept running, sprinting as far as they could, desperately trying to escape what they both knew was coming.

Just as they reached a safer distance, a deafening explosion rocked the air, shattering the stillness of the street. The blast wave hit them with terrifying force, flinging both women across the road and into the bushes.

149

Everything went quiet for a moment, save for the ringing in Alex's ears as debris rained down around them.

IX.

SCOTCH

The news of the bomb in Great Ormond Street spread like wildfire through the media, reaching every corner of the globe within minutes. Mycroft Holmes, on his way to the Parliament at that very moment, received the dreadful message via phone from one of his aides. The shock nearly took his breath away.

"Any casualties?" Mycroft asked, though he dreaded the answer. Still, he needed to know for certain.

"No, sir," came the response. "But several injured."

"Which hospital?"

"St. Barth's, sir."

Without a second thought, Mycroft ended the call and leaned forward to address his driver. "Take me to St. Barth's immediately!"

Before he could settle back, his phone rang again. Irritation flickered across his face as he answered. "What is it?"

"Have you heard the news?" It was Sherlock.

"What do you think?" Mycroft's tone was clipped.

"Good. Saves me the effort of wasting time explaining it to you," Sherlock continued, his voice brisk. "But I've got more intel. There were no remains of Julius or Sebastian Moran in the family graves. If they're really dead, which I doubt, they've been buried elsewhere. But that, of course, makes no sense. I'm convinced they're still alive - perhaps pulling the strings behind Montaigne or even the explosion."

"Since when did you start dealing in mere speculation?" Mycroft asked, perplexed. "That seems far too convenient, don't you think?"

"Fine. If you've got a better theory, feel free to enlighten me," Sherlock replied, a hint of impatience creeping into his voice.

Rolling his eyes, Mycroft responded sharply, "I don't have time for your games, little brother. Duty calls." With that, he ended the call and slipped the phone back into his coat pocket.

As the car sped toward the hospital, Mycroft's mind raced. Montaigne, the Moran brothers, the bomb - all of it was part of a tangled web he needed to unravel quickly. Too many lives were at stake, and this time, the danger felt all too personal.

Liz lay in a hospital room with a broken leg, two bruised ribs, and multiple abrasions, though the other two beds beside her remained empty. Alex, who had escaped with only minor cuts and bruises, sat at the edge of the bed, watching her friend with deep concern. "I'm so sorry," she said, guilt weighing on her voice.

"You have nothing to be sorry for," Liz replied, her tone light. "If I hadn't been in the apartment, you wouldn't have even noticed the bomb. In a way, I saved your life."

Alex's eyes widened in surprise. "You're right. Thank you." Her expression quickly darkened again. "But everything's gone. All the photos, the memories... even Hippo. Who knows what other secrets my mother left behind."

"It is tragic," Liz agreed, shifting uncomfortably. "She must have hidden all those things for a reason, hoping you'd eventually find them and remember your past."

"That must mean something happened back then that I wasn't supposed to forget."

"Indeed," came Mycroft's voice, cutting through the room like a blade. He stood suddenly in the doorway, having appeared without warning. His hands were empty, save for his ever-present dark-green umbrella - no flowers, no chocolates.

How rude.

Startled by his presence, Alex stepped back from the bed, keeping a cautious distance.

"We need to talk," he said, his tone leaving no room for argument, his gaze fixed sternly on Alex.

"Fine. Talk," she shot back, her voice sharp.

Mycroft raised an eyebrow, his face clouded with displeasure. "I was thinking of a place more... private."

"Anything you have to say to me, Liz can hear too. I have no secrets from her," Alex replied, her patience wavering. She added quietly, "At least, not knowingly."

It was clear Mycroft wasn't pleased with Liz's presence. Her inclusion made him uneasy - something he rarely felt and certainly never enjoyed. "What is the last thing you remember?" he asked, his brow furrowed.

"The car accident, I think," Alex responded slowly, her eyes turning inward as she tried to recall. Mycroft, with a slight nod, urged her to continue. He wanted every detail. "It was raining, and it was already dark. My mother was driving me home after I'd spent the whole day searching for Victor."

The memory hit her like a sudden gust of wind, the voice of her younger self echoing in her mind: *You took him from me. It's your fault he's gone.*

"The road was clear, and then this car came speeding up behind us. 'Why won't they just pass already?' my mother had shouted. The headlights blinded us. Then they overtook us."

"They?" Mycroft interjected, his voice laced with intensity.

"Yes, there were two men in the car. I remember the passenger staring at me, like he knew me. Just before they passed, they swerved left and forced us off the road. There was a loud crash and..."

153

Alex shuddered involuntarily, the memory of the pain flooding her mind. "And then everything went black."

Mycroft resisted the urge to comfort the distraught woman before him. It felt far too foreign, especially with Liz in the room, watching. He wasn't accustomed to displays of affection, particularly not in such personal circumstances.

"I can't remember anything else," Alex said, wiping the tears from her face. She looked up at him with a mixture of confusion and sorrow. "But I remembered Hippo... and you. Do you recall how you tried to protect me from that group of boys?"

A rare, soft smile crept across Mycroft's usually stoic face. That memory, even for him, held a warmth he couldn't deny. "It was one of the best days of my life," he admitted quietly, "even though it ended with me on the ground, getting thoroughly beaten."

Alex smiled too, albeit faintly, and in that moment, she felt a rush of affection for Mycroft, a flood of old, deeply buried feelings surging to the surface, sweeping her mind and heart with a sense of familiarity she hadn't known in years.

But Mycroft's expression soon darkened. "Now, unfortunately, to the bad news," he said gravely. "The two men who were thought to have died all those years ago - they're still alive."

Alex's face drained of color, and she instinctively stepped back, shaken by the revelation. "How is that possible? Are they the ones responsible for the bomb? Are they connected to Montaigne?"

"It's a possibility," Mycroft conceded, "but I find it unlikely."

"What are their names?" Alex asked, her voice tense.

"Julius and Sebastian Moran."

"Moran?" Alex's shock deepened, her breath catching in her throat. "Did one of them have a son named David? Was there a boy in the car?"

Mycroft frowned, clearly taken aback by the question. "Why do you ask?"

"That's Paige's boyfriend - David Moran. Damn it!" Alex began pacing the room, her thoughts racing. "I knew I'd heard that name before. I need to call Paige. I have to warn her."

Before she could dash past Mycroft and out of the room, he stepped in her way, gently but firmly stopping her. "There's no mention of a boy in the reports from the accident."

Alex lifted her gaze to meet his, her eyes filled with a growing sense of dread. "Do you really think all of this is just a coincidence? Paige is in danger, Mycroft. Moran's coming for her."

"You have no proof of that," Mycroft said, his voice calm yet unyielding.

"Alex, calm down," Liz interjected from the bed, her voice strained with pain. "You need to think about yourself for a moment, not Paige. She'll be fine."

"You don't know her," Alex argued, her frustration rising. "Paige is clumsy, always in the wrong place at the wrong time. She's an easy target for anyone trying to get to me."

"As long as we don't know *why* someone would want to hurt you," Mycroft said, his tone measured but stern, "running off blindly won't help. It might be exactly what Moran wants - luring you straight into a trap."

Alex halted, her mind battling between fear for Paige and the unsettling truth Mycroft had just spoken. Every instinct told her to act, to protect her friend, but Mycroft's words lingered, forcing her to reconsider.

No!

I must help her.

"Should I just leave Paige to her fate?" Alex asked in despair. "I couldn't live with the weight of knowing that someone else died because of me."

Mycroft remained silent, loosening his grip on her arm. His face grew pale, as if he were recalling something dreadful from his past.

Alex stared at him, bewildered.

What's going on with him?

What is he hiding?

Why do I have this terrible feeling that he's killed someone?

Damn it, I don't have time for this.

I need to warn Paige.

Without another word, Alex turned and bolted out of the room, slamming the door behind her, leaving only Mycroft and Liz in the quiet hospital room.

"Is it true?" Liz suddenly asked, her voice soft but filled with urgency. "Is Alex really Margaret? Is she?"

Mycroft nodded, unable to speak. The weight of the truth pressed heavily on him. He didn't dare say it aloud, afraid that putting it into words might shatter the fragile reality he was clinging to, like a dream dissipating into thin air.

"Shouldn't you tell her?" Liz pressed. "She deserves the truth."

"She has to discover it herself," Mycroft replied, swallowing the bitter ache in his throat. "She wouldn't believe me, even if I told her."

Before Liz could respond, the door flew open again, and Alex stumbled back into the room, her eyes brimming with tears. Desperation twisted her expression. "She's not answering," she gasped, her voice trembling. "Paige never does that. She's always reachable, even at 2 a.m. - something's wrong."

"I'll contact Scotland Yard," Mycroft said, already pulling out his phone.

"I have to get to her," Alex pleaded, her voice thick with anxiety.

"Lestrade, it's Mycroft Holmes," he said into the phone. "I need a favor. I need the address of Paige..." He paused, glancing at Alex, as he didn't know her full name.

"Sidney," Alex quickly supplied.

"Paige Sidney," Mycroft continued, his tone crisp. "There may have been a break-in, possibly worse. I suggest you send a team immediately." He waited for a brief moment as Lestrade, clearly quick on the uptake, searched for the address. "Excellent, thank you," Mycroft said, ending the call. He turned to Alex. "The Scotland Yard is on its way. I'll take you there myself, if you'd like."

Relief washed over Alex. "Thank you," she murmured, barely able to contain her gratitude. She hastily said goodbye to Liz, who remained confined to the bed, and dashed out of the room, not waiting for Mycroft to catch up.

Mycroft, with a sigh of resignation, followed as swiftly as he could, his long strides trying to keep pace with Alex's hurried steps. He couldn't help but feel a gnawing unease, one that came from knowing too much - and still not enough to protect her fully.

Upon arriving at the scene of the crime, Alex hurriedly leaped out of the black limousine. The entire street had been cordoned off with police tape, and numerous officers were scattered along the path.

Officer Tobias Gregson immediately approached her, holding up a hand in a gesture to stop. "You're not allowed here, Missy."

"She's with me," came Mycroft's stern voice, suddenly at her side.

Intimidated, Gregson backed away, lifting the tape to allow them through.

Alex entered the building alongside Mycroft, her heart pounding as they climbed to the third floor, where her colleague Paige's apartment was located. But no sooner had she stepped inside than she froze in place. Mycroft had to catch her as she staggered backward, nearly collapsing.

The living room was drenched in blood. The walls, the ceiling, even the floor - there was not a single untouched spot. The crimson scene was overpowering, like something out of a nightmare. In the center of the room, Paige's body hung grotesquely from the ceiling. Her arms were outstretched and bound by thin ropes and carabiners, making her appear almost crucified, though without a cross, but with a barbaric cruelty that defied words.

Alex couldn't bear to look at the horror any longer. She turned her face into Mycroft's chest, hiding from the ghastly sight. He held her tightly with both arms, bracing her, as if fearing she might faint from the sheer shock.

Inspector Lestrade soon emerged from the bloodstained living room, dressed in a white, sterile suit that covered him from head to toe. The suit was splattered in parts with the same dark red that had stained every inch of the apartment. He stopped before them, a mix of emotions flickering across his face. It was an unusual sight - Mycroft Holmes, usually so detached, was now cradling a woman in his arms, and not just any woman - Alexandra Green, who was notorious for her disdain of him.

Lestrade cleared his throat to make his presence known. Alex, still trembling and unable to face the gruesome scene again, remained close to Mycroft, who gave her a moment of silent support.

Alex turned slowly, trying to focus only on Lestrade. Her eyes brimmed with tears, and a wave of guilt washed over her. She knew she had arrived too late.

Though Mycroft loosened his hold on her, he did not fully let go. He wanted her close. It felt strangely comforting - perhaps the only comfort in this apartment, now awash with death and sorrow.

"We believe there were two assailants," Lestrade began, his voice steady but solemn. "Unfortunately, no one saw or heard anything."

"How long?" Alex's voice trembled. "How long has she been...?" She couldn't bring herself to finish the sentence.

"Seven hours, at least," Lestrade replied quietly.

Alex's face paled. "That was the exact time the bomb went off at my apartment," she whispered, her voice laced with disbelief as she turned to Mycroft, then back to Lestrade. "Find those monsters. Please."

"We're doing everything we can," Lestrade assured her, his tone authoritative but tinged with sympathy. Then, he looked at her with a hint of confusion. "But how did you even know she was in danger? No one reported anything. How could you possibly have known?"

Alex took a deep breath, struggling to keep her voice steady. "Her boyfriend, David Moran, is the son of one of the men who were involved in a car accident with my mother and me all those years ago," she explained. The words were heavy, but Mycroft's presence gave her the strength to speak. She was deeply grateful that he was there, still holding her close in her moment of vulnerability.

Lestrade scratched his head in bewilderment. "I've heard you're good at what you do, but this... this is remarkable. And it certainly gives me a lot of work."

"Remarkable?" Alex echoed, her brow furrowing as she turned her gaze away in anguish. "No. I'm not remarkable. I was too late, and now an innocent person has paid the price for my failure."

After leaving the crime scene behind, Mycroft and Alex sat once more in the backseat of the sleek black limousine.

"Do you know where you'll stay tonight?" he asked, his voice tinged with concern. He didn't want to leave her - especially not in her distressed state - but he also couldn't keep her somewhere against her will.

Alex weakly shook her head, her eyes still distant as she gazed out of the window, though there was little to see as dusk had long since descended. After a long moment, she leaned back, turning her gaze to Mycroft. "I'd prefer a hotel," she admitted quietly, "but I must confess... I'm terrified." Her voice trembled as she shivered. "I'm really scared."

Without hesitation, Mycroft reached out and took her hand, gripping it gently yet firmly, offering both comfort and strength. "Please, come back with me to Southgate," he urged softly. "You'll be safe there."

Her tear-filled eyes looked up at him, searching for reassurance. Mycroft, moved by an emotion that surprised even him, pulled her gently into his arms, holding her close. "I won't let anything happen to you," he whispered, his voice tender yet resolute.

They remained in that embrace for some time, neither moving, both drawing solace from the unexpected closeness between them. It felt oddly natural, as though they had done this countless times before, as if it were the most familiar thing in the world.

"I need a drink," Alex murmured, resting her head against Mycroft's chest.

He chuckled softly, looking down at her with a gentle smile. There was something profoundly different about how he felt in her presence. She made him feel vulnerable, human - yet whole, in a way he hadn't known was possible. It was strange, even unsettling, but it was also beautiful.

"What about Liz?" Alex suddenly asked, her body tensing with worry as she pulled back slightly to look at him.

"She's safe," Mycroft reassured her. "The entire hospital is under lockdown. The Secret Service is overseeing her protection."

He could feel the tension leave her body as she relaxed once more, leaning into him. "Thank you," she whispered, her voice soft, almost inaudible. She nestled back into his embrace, and for the first time in what felt like forever, she allowed herself to enjoy the warmth of his presence - a man she had despised with every fiber of her being only days ago.

For an Ice Man, he's surprisingly warm.

A small smile curled at the corner of Alex's lips. She silently wished that this moment, wrapped in his arms and feeling, perhaps for the first time, truly safe, would never end.

But everything must come to an end.

After a long drive, they finally arrived at Mycroft's estate in Southgate. In the darkness, the grand structure, illuminated from outside, resembled a majestic castle.

Almost like Buckingham Palace.

Mycroft led her into the salon, located just behind the fireplace room on the ground floor. A large bar dominated the space, its glass cabinets filled with an impressive collection of fine spirits. The array of uniquely shaped glasses sat neatly along the bar, almost resembling abstract art. Everything gleamed and sparkled as though the surfaces were covered in diamonds and glistening jewels.

Mycroft positioned himself behind the bar, selecting two glasses and a bottle of expensive Scotch. Alex sat on one of the four barstools, leaning against the smooth, black marble countertop. She watched him intently as he prepared their drinks, handing her one of the glasses when he finished.

"To the past," he said, raising his glass.

"To the past," Alex echoed with a faint smile, clinking her glass against his before taking a strong sip. It was exactly what she needed.

Mycroft moved from behind the bar, sitting on the stool beside her. He watched her as she eagerly downed her drink, not seeming to mind how quickly she consumed it. He knew that if their roles were reversed, he might have done the same. Without hesitation, he refilled her glass.

"Thank you." Alex nodded in appreciation. This time, she drank more slowly, knowing she didn't want to completely lose herself in alcohol - at least, not in front of Mycroft. Yet, at the same time, she didn't care.

Paige is dead.

And it's because of me.

But the worst part is that I couldn't stop it.

Her death is my fault.

She took another sip.

And my apartment... everything inside - destroyed.

Every memory, every keepsake from my mother... all gone.

What else am I supposed to do but drink?

She tried to push those thoughts away and distract herself. "Does Sherlock still have that scar on his arm?" she asked suddenly, trying to change the subject.

Mycroft chuckled at the memory. "Yes, he does. He bled terribly."

"He deserved it." Alex met his eyes. "Siblings should treat each other better."

"But he was right," Mycroft replied, taking a generous gulp of his Scotch. "I was fat."

162

Alex smirked. "Yes, you were. But not anymore. You actually look…" She hesitated, the alcohol loosening her tongue despite her better judgment. "You look really good, Mycroft."

Oh God, did I really just say that?

And did I really just call him Mycroft?

Clearly, I can't handle my alcohol.

But it's true.

He does look damn good.

Mycroft smiled, clearly flustered. It seemed he was searching for the right words, but nothing came. Instead, something else occurred to him. He downed his glass in one swift motion, stood up, and made his way to the record player on a nearby table. Placing the needle on the record, the familiar strains of Johann Strauss II's "The Blue Danube" began to fill the room.

He returned to her, extending his hand. "Dance with me," he said, and though his words sounded more like a command, they were delivered so gently, so charmingly, that Alex couldn't refuse.

She took his hand and allowed herself to be led by him, moving in perfect time to the lilting rhythm of the waltz. Mycroft was, to her surprise, an exceptionally skilled dancer. He rarely had the opportunity to demonstrate this talent, largely because there were few women he would even consider as a partner - and even fewer who would volunteer. But tonight, it seemed as though Alex was his only, perhaps his best, choice.

The two moved gracefully across the floor, their bodies almost seamlessly in sync. Mycroft's arms held her close, eliminating any remaining space between them. As he gazed at her intently, Alex could only bring herself to look up to his lips, unwilling and perhaps too nervous to meet his eyes. His height overpowered her, and the rapid beat of her heart threatened to betray her composure. Her entire body trembled with a nervous energy she couldn't quite control.

And then, just as suddenly as it had begun, the waltz ended, leaving only the soft crackle of the vinyl on the record player. They remained in each other's arms, unmoving. Alex, summoning the courage she didn't know she had, finally looked up into his eyes - and was startled by the intensity of his stare.

"What are you doing to me?" he asked softly, his voice filled with a mixture of confusion and desire, his wide eyes fixed on her as though searching for answers.

"Mycroft..." was all Alex could manage in response. His words and gaze had disarmed her completely.

Without hesitation, he pulled her closer and kissed her. The touch was tentative at first, then deeper, more passionate. His arms tightened around her, pressing his body firmly against hers. The kiss felt like an unraveling - of boundaries, of long-held restraint. And then, in a low, breathless whisper, he murmured a name: "Margaret."

The moment shattered.

Alex recoiled sharply, pulling away from him, her mind spinning.

What...?

Am I really Margaret?

But then, who is Alex?

Who the hell am I?

Her eyes, wide with confusion and hurt, met his, but there were no answers in his gaze. She couldn't stay, couldn't think straight. Without another word, she turned and fled past him, rushing up the stairs to the room she had come to know as her own.

"Alex!" Mycroft called after her, his voice laced with urgency as he followed her up the stairs.

Once inside her room, she slammed the door shut and collapsed against it, struggling to catch her breath. Her heart raced, her thoughts a whirlwind of confusion. On the other side of the door, she could hear Mycroft pounding against it.

164

"Alex, please, open the door! I'm sorry! Please!" His voice, thick with desperation, cut through the silence.

But she couldn't move. She slid to the floor, tears streaming down her face as her emotions overwhelmed her. She could hear the anguish in his voice, but she wasn't ready to face him. Not now. Not after what had just happened.

What's happening to me?
Who am I?
And why did he kiss me?
Why did I want him to kiss me?
I'm supposed to hate him.
This can't be real.
No.
It was the alcohol.
It had to be.
Just the alcohol.
Mycroft Holmes would never kiss anyone.
Especially not me.
He's the Ice Man - he doesn't have feelings.
But I... I have feelings.

She wiped her tears away with trembling hands, trying to regain some semblance of control.

I have feelings for him.

For a long time, she sat huddled against the door, listening to his pleading fade until, at last, she heard him retreat. When the house was finally quiet, she pulled herself up and collapsed onto the bed, emotionally drained. She could no longer fight the questions that swirled in her mind, nor the undeniable truth rising within her heart.

She didn't know what time it was when she finally awoke, a sinking feeling gnawing at her stomach. Reluctantly, Alex left her room, hoping that Mycroft wasn't upset with her.

I don't want to see him.

But I'm starving.

Descending the stairs, she made her way into the living room, where the breakfast table was already set. Yet, there was no sign of Mycroft.

Instead, a man stood by the table with his back to her. He was dressed in a uniform like Mr. Wiggins, but noticeably younger. "Good morning, miss," he said without turning to face her.

Alex glanced around. "Good morning. Where is Myc-," she corrected herself hastily, "Where is Mr. Holmes?" She took a seat at the table, feeling a bit confused.

"Mr. Holmes has relocated to the North Wing," the man responded, his voice tinged with an unsettling undertone, "so you may enjoy your rest as long as you prefer."

He finally turned to face her, and Alex's blood ran cold.

Moran.

She sprang to her feet in sheer panic, attempting to flee the room, but the man was faster. In a swift motion, he grabbed her from behind.

"Mycroft!" she screamed, before his hand clamped tightly over her mouth, silencing her.

Alex struggled with every ounce of strength, but he was far stronger. In her desperate writhing, she managed to kick the edge of the table, sending the delicate tea set crashing to the floor with a deafening noise. The sound echoed through the room like a warning bell.

For a brief moment, his grip loosened, and she wrenched herself free, falling to the floor near the shattered porcelain. Quickly, she grabbed a shard of the broken dish and scratched a small mark into the floorboards. It wasn't much - just half of an "M" - but she knew it would be enough.

Moran laughed coldly. "It'll take more than that to save you, love," he sneered as he roughly seized her again. Fortunately, he hadn't noticed her carving, though to him it would've been meaningless scratches anyway. He dragged her from the room, through the door, and out onto the street. No one came to stop him; there was no one around.

Where is everyone?

Mycroft's staff?

His security?

He would never have left me alone like this.

Where's Mr. Wiggins?

What has Moran done to him?

Waiting by the curb was a dark van, the side door sliding open ominously. Two older men stepped out, their faces etched with cold fury. Their silvery hair gleamed in the dim light, and Alex's heart dropped.

They're alive.

Julius and Sebastian Moran.

She recognized them instantly. Before she could make another move, they grabbed her roughly and shoved her into the van.

No amount of screaming, scratching, or kicking could help her now. She was hopelessly outmatched by the Morans.

By shortly after noon, Mycroft had given Alex ample time, patiently waiting for her to seek him out for the conversation he knew was inevitable. But she didn't, and this absence of action unsettled him more than he cared to admit. He knew Alex far better than he let on, and it was unlike her to avoid confrontation.

Setting the newspaper aside, Mycroft rose from the table and strode out. It took him a while to reach the South Wing of the grand estate, and when he finally entered the empty living room, he froze abruptly.

There was no sign of Alex.

However, the shattered tea set on the floor immediately caught his attention. Mycroft's eyes narrowed as a sense of dread crept over him. He knelt down, carefully examining the shards, and noticed a few scratched lines on the floorboards nearby. He picked up a silver tray that had fallen beside the wreckage and placed it over the markings. The reflection and the jagged lines came together to form a letter.

"M," he muttered under his breath. And then, as if a light had flicked on in his mind, he exclaimed, "Moran!"

In an instant, Mycroft leapt to his feet, pulling out his phone to dial several key contacts within the Secret Service. He began pacing, his usually calculated mind now racing.

For the first time in his life, Mycroft Holmes felt utterly at a loss. How had someone managed to infiltrate his home without detection? This house was supposed to be a fortress, and no one, absolutely no one, should have known that he and Alex were here.

He ran his hands through his hair, pressing them against his temples, as if hoping to squeeze out some solution to this unforeseen crisis. The situation was spiraling out of control, and Mycroft Holmes was not accustomed to losing control.

"Mr. Holmes, Sir!" The breathless voice of Wiggins startled him. Mycroft turned sharply to see his butler standing in the doorway, looking pale and unsteady, wiping blood from a gash on his forehead.

"What is it?" Mycroft snapped, his nerves fraying dangerously thin. His tone was sharper than intended, and Wiggins flinched, stepping back in response.

The shaken man pointed tremblingly toward the hall, his hand still clutching his bloodied cloth. "In the lobby… there are two men…"

Mycroft's face hardened as he moved quickly toward the lobby. His eyes locked onto the figures standing just beyond the entrance.

Inspector Lestrade and his colleague William Doyle stood side by side, an awkward and rather unappealing sight. The tension between them was palpable - neither of them cared for the other, but it seemed fate had forced them into this uncomfortable partnership. It was clear they didn't like it.

"You should come with us," Lestrade said, his expression as stern as ever.

"I have more pressing matters to attend to," Mycroft replied coldly, his patience thin.

Lestrade didn't flinch. "Trust me, Mr. Holmes," he said with an edge of warning in his voice, "you'll want to hear this."

"Where is Alex?" Doyle's eyes flared wide with panic, as if he could read Mycroft's thoughts. "Damn it!" he exclaimed, rushing forward with a fury that broke through all decorum. "What have you done?" His voice was sharp, accusing, as he stormed toward Mycroft. "You bloody idiot-"

"Hey!" Lestrade barked, holding Doyle back with considerable effort. "That's enough!"

"Where is Alex?" Doyle repeated, ignoring his colleague completely and fixing Mycroft with an enraged stare. "Where the hell is she?"

"David Sebastian Moran," came a voice from the doorway. Sherlock Holmes strolled in, his timing, as ever, impeccable. He paused, his sharp gaze resting squarely on his older brother. "Did you really think he wouldn't find her here? The entire world knows this place is *your* residence."

"It's a safe house," Mycroft retorted, his pride visibly wounded. "Very few people know this address."

"Well, apparently one was enough," Sherlock shot back with a piercing look. He didn't flinch under Mycroft's stern expression. "How did she get out of here last time? By bus? Or perhaps she strolled through the countryside for hours? Somehow, she made it back to her flat just in time for a perfectly timed explosion. Convenient, wouldn't you say?"

Mycroft felt a host of scathing retorts rise to his tongue - insults that would easily reduce even Sherlock to silence - but he swallowed them bitterly, as if choking down something as acrid as quinine. Instead, he forced out a single word, weighed down with regret: "Friends." The very word tasted foreign, almost mocking. He recalled something Alex had said to him not so long ago: "What are they good for anyway?"

"To betray us," Sherlock quipped, his voice laced with sardonic amusement, as if the answer had been self-evident all along. Mycroft's eyes darkened, but before he could storm off in pursuit of some ill-defined solution, Sherlock held him back with a firm grip. "Save yourself the trouble, brother," he said, an irrepressible grin tugging at the corners of his lips. "I've already been there."

Lestrade and Doyle exchanged bewildered glances, their confusion evident. The Holmes brothers, as ever, seemed to be performing a baffling act of intellectual sleight-of-hand that neither inspector could quite keep up with.

"Apparently," Sherlock continued, savoring the revelation as if it were a particularly clever punchline, "he passed himself off as your chauffeur - a stand-in, pretending to cover for your usual driver, ensuring, most delightfully, that *you* wouldn't suspect a thing." He met Mycroft's eyes with a penetrating gaze. "So naturally, he asked Miss Markle where you were supposed to be taken and, hopefully, also Alex. Her answer? Southgate." Sherlock's smile broadened. "And that, dear brother, was more than enough."

Mycroft felt his stomach twist. He had always prided himself on being unassailable, untouchable - yet in this moment, he could feel his world, carefully constructed brick by brick, beginning to crumble.

Mycroft's agitation deepened, his uncertainty tightening its grip with alarming intensity. "I have to find her!" he muttered, as if commanding himself to act. He spun in circles like a man unhinged, his brilliant mind clouded by panic. For perhaps the first time in his life, Mycroft Holmes had no idea what to do.

Ordinarily, Sherlock would have reveled in such a spectacle. His all-knowing, ever-composed older brother, unraveling in the face of human emotions he could never quite master - it would have been the kind of moment Sherlock cherished, proof that even the great Mycroft Holmes could be brought down by something as inconvenient as feelings. But this time, things were different. Sherlock understood how much Alex - whom he was certain was, in fact, Margaret - meant to his brother. Though she had irked him as a child with her sharp mind, sharper even than his own at times, there had always been a grudging affection. Watching Mycroft's suffering stirred an unexpected sympathy in him. Still, Sherlock was careful to keep such emotions hidden; exposing them, even now, would be a weakness he wasn't willing to show.

Suddenly, Mycroft seemed to regain control, his expression hardening with resolution. He turned to Lestrade and Doyle, the command in his voice as sharp as a blade. "I want everything you have on David Moran. Every scrap of information on Julius and Sebastian Moran as well. I don't care how trivial it seems - find it. And I want it yesterday." His voice echoed ominously through the grand lobby, the cold authority leaving no room for question.

171

Lestrade and Doyle exchanged quick, uneasy glances before fleeing the room, understanding the gravity of the situation. Despite their mutual dislike for one another, they had no choice but to cooperate. This was beyond personal grudges.

As the door closed behind them, Mycroft turned his back on Sherlock, unwilling to let his brother see the torment etched on his face. "I cannot lose her again," he said, his voice low, quivering with barely contained despair. "I won't survive it a second time."

"We're not children anymore," Sherlock replied, stepping forward in an uncharacteristic attempt to offer comfort. His tone, though still cool, carried a weight of understanding. "This time, we can do something."

Mycroft didn't turn. His pride, as unyielding as the stone walls around him, forbade him from showing Sherlock the depth of his pain. To reveal his vulnerability now would be to admit weakness - and that, more than anything, was a failure he couldn't bear. In this moment, Mycroft Holmes, the formidable force behind the British government - the legendary 'Ice Man' - felt like the weakest man alive. And as he stood there, battling the rising tide of emotion, he found himself hating the man he had become.

Feelings - especially love - had always been his downfall. He had known it ever since the day Margaret had vanished from his life. Since then, he had sworn off such sentiment, fortifying himself with cold logic and detachment. It was how he had earned his reputation, how he had amassed such power. But now, with Margaret – Alexandra - back in his life, all that cold, unassailable strength had crumbled.

And now, there was only one thing that mattered: saving Alexandra Green. He had to make her understand who she truly was - Margaret Trevor, the woman he had loved for as long as he could remember.

X.

THE TRUTH

Her head throbbed terribly as Alex slowly regained consciousness. Through half-closed eyes, she glanced around, disoriented. She found herself in what looked like an old, long-abandoned stable, propped up against a cold concrete wall. The attempt to stand failed immediately; her wrists were bound behind her with thick cable ties, securing her to a large iron ring bolted to the wall. Every slight movement sent searing pain through her wrists, the plastic digging deeper into her skin with each struggle.

"Help!" she screamed, her voice hoarse but desperate. "Help!" Perhaps someone would hear her. Someone who could save her.

And indeed, someone did hear her - though not someone she wanted to see.

David Moran entered, his lips curling into a cruel, demonic smile. He was dressed in a pitch-black suit, pristine white shirt, and a dark navy tie, all impeccably tailored to fit him. The absurdity of such a clean and formal appearance in a filthy, dilapidated setting only highlighted the grotesque nature of the situation.

"What do you want from me?" Alex spat, trying to sound defiant, though her wrists burned under the strain. Fear wasn't something she was about to show, especially since David appeared unarmed - aside from the faint outline of a small knife strapped to his ankle.

"Stop the charade, Margaret." He stepped closer, his voice dripping with mockery. "We're alone. You don't have to pretend anymore. I already know the truth."

"What truth?" Alex snapped, her confusion deepening. He kept calling her Margaret, which was unsettling her even further.

173

Does this have something to do with the car accident?

What truth is he talking about?

Does he think my mother caused the crash?

That's nonsense!

She was innocent.

I saw it myself.

Wait... he was there too.

He must have been...

"You were in the car," Alex whispered, the realization dawning on her like a dark, distant storm cloud.

David crouched down beside her, maintaining eye contact, his knees hovering just above the grimy floor. "Ah, so you do remember," he said smugly, his voice low and menacing. "I knew it."

"What?" Alex's voice wavered, her mind swirling in confusion and fear. "I only remember the accident. That's it."

David moved closer, his face inches from hers, his expression darkening. "Don't lie to me!" he bellowed, fury flashing in his eyes. "You remember more than that! You were there. You *saw* it happen. You can't forget something like that. It's impossible!"

His words, the intensity in his eyes - everything about him - frightened her in ways she couldn't quite understand. What was it that he thought she had seen? What had she forgotten that he was so convinced she remembered?

Tears streamed down her cheeks without her realizing it. "I don't know what you're talking about. What am I supposed to have seen?"

David stared at her in silence, as if he were trying to dissect her, searching for any sign of a lie. Then, after what seemed like an eternity, he stood up. "Remarkable," he muttered, as if he couldn't believe it himself. "She was right after all." He looked down at her with an almost pitying expression. "You really have forgotten everything."

"What have I forgotten? And who are you talking about? Who was right? Paige?" Alex's heart pounded with both fear and confusion.

David let out a cold, cruel laugh. "No," he sneered. "Your mother."

"What?" Alex nearly choked on her words, a mixture of horror and fury swelling inside her. She pulled violently at the cable ties around her wrists, not caring that the rough plastic was cutting into her skin, sending warm blood trickling down her hands. The pain barely registered - what hurt more was the stabbing sensation in her chest, like someone had plunged a stake into her heart. "You killed her!" Alex cried, her voice raw with anguish. She didn't need him to confirm it; his smug, satisfied grin was all the confirmation she needed. "You monster! You murderer! Why? What did she ever do to you? My mother was innocent!" Her voice faltered, breaking into a soft, trembling whisper. "She never hurt anyone..."

"Neither did Paige," David replied, his tone as icy as his smile, twisting the knife in even deeper. "They were simply tools. Means to an end."

"You're insane!" Alex spat, her rage burning through her grief. "You crucified Paige like a deranged lunatic, and you murdered an innocent, defenseless woman. You're a psychopath!"

David's grin widened, a sickening, twisted pleasure lighting up his eyes. He was savoring every moment of her torment. "You're absolutely right, clever girl. I *am* a psychopath. Always have been. It runs in my blood." His voice dripped with dark amusement. He licked his lips, hungry for violence, his bloodlust barely contained. "And now... it's going to be my greatest thrill when I finally get to kill you." He slowly rolled up his sleeves, each motion deliberate and meticulous. "I'm going to take my time with you."

"Not yet!" Another voice rang out sharply. A man stepped forward from the shadows, having watched everything unfold. It was Sebastian Moran, David's father, his presence as sinister as his

175

son's. He moved closer, casting a cold glance at his son. "You don't touch the girl - yet."

Sebastian knelt beside Alex, his eyes gleaming with a predatory gleam. His hand reached out, caressing her cheek with a sickening familiarity, his fingers leaving a trail of cold dread in their wake. "We've got unfinished business, you and I," he whispered, licking his lips with a hunger that made Alex's stomach turn.

She shrank back against the wall, her heart hammering in her chest. Fear coursed through her veins, but behind it was something more - something dark and buried, something connected to the past she had long forgotten but was now dangerously close to remembering.

As he moved closer, his breath and clothes reeking of cheap vodka and stale cigarettes, a memory long buried began to surface in her mind - something she had forced herself to forget for years.

She saw herself, a little girl, barely four years old, running across an open, grassy field. Behind her, Victor, Sherlock, and Mycroft followed, though Mycroft had fallen a little behind. They had been playing a game of tag, their joyful laughter echoing through the air. The little girl, quick and nimble, had easily outrun the boys, disappearing from their view in no time.

"I won!" the young Margaret had called out, her voice filled with triumph. But just as she was about to turn back, strong arms had grabbed her from behind.

It had been Sebastian Moran. There was no doubt in her mind.

The young girl had screamed as if her very soul were being torn apart - screams full of terror and pain - but no one had heard. She had called out desperately for help, shouting for her brother, for Mycroft, even for Sherlock, but no one had come. No one had heard her cries.

A sickening wave of shame and agony followed. Alex's vision blurred as the memory threatened to overwhelm her. But for a single, horrifying second, she was certain she had seen Victor - hidden behind a tree, crouching in terror, watching it all unfold.

He had been there.

He had seen everything.

"Victor," Alex sobbed, the name escaping her lips in a broken whisper as tears streamed down her face. She pushed feebly against the older man, desperate to break free from his filthy grasp.

"See, boy?" Moran sneered, glancing briefly at his son before turning his attention back to Alex. "It doesn't take long to remember when the right memories are... encouraged." He grinned wickedly, grabbing her chin roughly and forcing her to look at him. "Did you miss me?"

Alex, burning with rage and disgust, spat directly in his face, struggling with every ounce of her strength to pull away from his grip.

Sebastian Moran wiped away Alex's spit with an air of complete indifference, brushing it off with his sleeve as if her contempt hadn't touched him in the slightest. In fact, it seemed to please him. He leaned in close, his breath foul and sickeningly near her skin, and with a perverse satisfaction, he licked her from the base of her neck up to her cheek. "Mmm," he groaned, the sound thick with twisted pleasure. "You still taste just as delicious as you did back then."

Alex recoiled as far as her restraints would allow, her stomach churning, head spinning. The terrible memories, long repressed, came flooding back - each fear, every nightmare, all the torment she had spent years trying to bury, surged through her once more. "Victor," she whimpered, barely able to speak. Then, with sudden clarity, something snapped into focus. She raised her eyes, full of fury, and glared at Sebastian Moran with renewed defiance. "You," she hissed. "You killed him. You murdered Victor. Admit it! You killed my brother!" Her voice broke as she shouted, trembling with rage and sorrow.

177

Sebastian chuckled darkly, stepping back just enough to stand beside his son, the mirth never leaving his face. "Clever girl," he sneered. "I didn't think you'd ever remember."

"Why?" Alex cried, tears streaming down her face, unstoppable now. "He was just a child!"

"He saw us - saw you and me," Sebastian said, his voice devoid of any remorse. "I couldn't let him reveal our little secret."

Alex closed her eyes briefly, her mind racing. "Then why am I still alive?" she demanded, unable to understand. "Why didn't you kill me too?"

Sebastian's grin grew more sinister. "We tried," he confessed, his tone as cold as the grave. "It was pure luck that you survived the crash. We were certain you'd never remember."

"But this time, we're making sure," came a deeper voice from the shadows. A third figure stepped into the light - Julius Moran, Sebastian's older brother. His hair was now completely silver, but his smile was just as malevolent as ever. "I do regret what happened to your dear mother," he said, with a mockingly dramatic tone. "Her pleas were so pathetic, they almost made me feel something. Almost. But fortunately, psychopaths like us aren't burdened with emotions."

"You won't get away with this!" Alex shouted, her voice trembling but still clinging to the faintest spark of hope. "Mycroft will find you. And when he does, you'll pay for everything!"

The trio of men erupted into cruel, mocking laughter, the sound echoing ominously around the room.

"I wouldn't be so sure of that," Julius sneered. "Mycroft Holmes, that little fat pig, will - just like back then - arrive too late. If he ever finds us at all."

"And even if he does," Sebastian added with a wicked glint in his eye, "he doesn't know the whole truth. No one does - except for us, and Victor."

"What are you talking about?" the young woman asked, her confusion deepening.

What more is there?

What is this so-called whole truth?

"The world believes someone else murdered Victor," Julius said with a smirk, his eyes gleaming with a sick pleasure. "In fact, the accused is the one most convinced of it. You see, small children are remarkably easy to manipulate - especially when they are exceptionally intelligent." His gaze pierced through Alex, cold and calculating. "Your clever little friends couldn't save you then, and nothing has changed. Today, they'll lose you forever."

"Everything must come to an end, after all," David added with a chuckle, casting an eager glance toward his father and uncle. "Can I kill her now? Please?"

"Not yet," Julius replied, shaking his head with stern finality. "We wouldn't want to be unfair, would we? Let's give her clever friends a little more time. Killing her now would spoil all the fun. We must savor this."

One by one, the three men exited the stall, leaving Alex alone.

The young woman's mind swirled with confusion. Everything felt as though it was spinning out of control. She struggled against her restraints, despite the searing pain in her wrists, but the cable ties only cut deeper into her skin, sending sharp waves of agony through her body. She gasped, her breath catching in her throat, her strength ebbing. Exhausted, Alex slumped against the cold concrete wall, fighting to stay conscious. But it was no use. She could feel her senses slipping away, darkness closing in around her, and at last, she succumbed to unconsciousness.

The bright, joyful laughter of a little girl woke Alex at last. When she opened her eyes, she blinked in astonishment, finding herself in a vast courtyard surrounded by blooming fields. In the distance stood a grand estate - an all-too-familiar building.

Alex knew this place well.

"Get up!" ordered the girl who had suddenly appeared before her.

"Who are you?" Alex asked, frowning as she cautiously rose to her feet. Strangely, the pain that had gripped her so fiercely earlier had vanished completely.

The girl laughed again, a sound like a bell. "I'm you, silly. Margaret." She turned and sprinted across the field. "Come on!" she called, waving for Alex to follow.

Hesitant, Alex trailed after the child.

Am I dead?

What is this?

A memory?

I must be losing my mind.

Alex reached a small hill, and as she stood atop it, she saw, on the other side, three more children. She recognized them instantly - Victor, Sherlock, and Mycroft.

Victor and Sherlock were roughhousing in the tall grass, playing at being superheroes. Mycroft, however, sat against the trunk of a tree, crumbs scattered across his lap, a bag of biscuits resting atop it. As Margaret ran toward him, he wiped his mouth nervously with the back of his hand, swallowed hastily, and brushed the crumbs from his clothes.

"Stop eating so much!" Margaret scolded. "You'll get fat."

Alex moved closer, her steps tentative.

"I already am," Mycroft replied sadly. His eyes were red and slightly swollen, as if he had just been crying. "It doesn't matter anymore."

"Nonsense," Alex blurted suddenly. Back then, she had felt immense pity for him, but now - now it nearly broke her heart. The boy looked up at her with wide, tear-filled eyes, and she knelt beside him. "It *does* matter, do you hear me?" she said gently. She had meant to sound firm, perhaps even stern, but faced with his innocent, vulnerable expression, she simply couldn't bring herself to be harsh. "Don't let the other children drag you down. One day, they'll be envious of you. You'll grow into a powerful, handsome man."

They were the exact same words she had said to him all those years ago.

Wow.

I wasn't just saying that.

I meant it.

I was… telling the truth.

"Who are you?" young Mycroft asked, bewildered, staring at her as if she were some magical being.

"A friend."

"I only have one friend, and that's Margaret."

"I know." Alex smiled and stood up.

Her attention shifted toward Victor and Sherlock, who were playing nearby, too absorbed in their game to notice her approach. She walked through the field and stopped just before the two boys, waiting for them to realize she was there.

"Wow, you've gotten so big," Victor exclaimed, staring up at her in amazement. "Will I be that tall one day?" He removed his oversized superhero helmet, revealing his freckled face.

Alex struggled to hold back her tears. She gazed into her brother's bright eyes, her heart heavy with the knowledge of what was to come. She knelt down in the soft grass, looking at him with a tenderness that nearly broke her. "Yes, of course. Everyone grows tall, even taller than me. I'm actually quite small for my age," she added with a gentle smile.

Victor beamed, delighted by her answer. Without hesitation, he let the helmet fall to the ground and flung his arms around his sister, hugging her tightly as if he'd never let her go. The embrace felt eternal, as though no time had passed since she last held him, though Alex knew it had been over twenty long years since he had died.

She could no longer keep her tears at bay. Holding her brother in her arms again, as if the cruel passage of time had been erased, brought a flood of emotion crashing over her. Every memory of her childhood, every single detail, came rushing back to her - the good, the bad, every hidden corner of her past. She gently pulled Victor closer and whispered, as if speaking the truth aloud for the first time, "I am Margaret. I always have been. I always will be."

Victor pulled back slightly, looking at her with confusion. "What are you talking about? Of course you're Margaret. Who else would you be? Grandma?"

Alex flinched, startled by his innocent remark.

Grandma?

Of course.

Alexandra Green.

That was Grandma.

But why?

"Mom?" she murmured, as though searching for an answer in the sky above. Unconsciously, her eyes followed her thoughts upward. "You just wanted to protect me. Thank you." She smiled, her face wet with tears, but her heart felt lighter, filled with a quiet sense of peace.

"Are you crying?" Sherlock stared at her in disbelief. "Margaret's such a crybaby. Typical girl." He charged at her, brandishing his wooden hammer. "Take that! And that!" He swung at her, but she deftly dodged, jumping to her feet just in time and grabbing a stick from the ground to defend herself.

"Attack!" shouted Victor, rushing forward alongside his best friend, both boys charging at her with gleeful abandon.

It wasn't Alex anymore, fleeing from the playful onslaught of these two boys. It was Margaret Trevor.

I am Margaret.

I always have been.

Suddenly thrust back into reality, Margaret blinked, her mind reeling as she reoriented herself. The old, decaying barn was now submerged in complete darkness. Not a single light flickered in the distance, and the cold, biting autumn wind whistled through the open, glassless windows, carrying with it a chill that gnawed at her bones.

But she had found new hope. That strange dream - or whatever it had been - had reignited something deep within her. It gave her the strength to attempt one more escape. Her fingers began frantically searching the dirt and straw-laden floor, hoping to find something - anything - that could help her cut through the cable ties that bound her wrists. As she clawed through the filth, she suddenly recoiled, hissing in pain. Her fingers had brushed against something sharp, and it had sliced her skin open. Gritting her teeth, Margaret gingerly reached out again, more cautiously this time, and after a few agonizing seconds, her fingers closed around the sharp object.

It was a shard of glass, just large enough to do the job. She worked carefully, her hands trembling as the glass bit into the cable ties. Her wrists screamed in protest, raw and burning from the pressure, but she pressed on. After what felt like an eternity, the ties finally snapped. The instant relief was overwhelming. She drew her hands in front of her, cradling them against her chest as she gingerly ran her fingers over the open cuts, surprised by how warm her own blood felt against her freezing skin.

Margaret was just about to rise and make a run for it when she heard footsteps approaching - slow, deliberate. Panic surged through her, but she forced herself to stay calm. She tucked her hands behind her back, settling into her previous position and slumped against the wall, pretending to be asleep.

The scent hit her before the man did - David. His overbearing aftershave gave him away, announcing his presence even before he stepped into the barn. He crept toward her, kneeling beside her as a sickening smile spread across his face. "Time for a little fun," he whispered, his breath hot against her ear as he began unbuttoning her blouse. His hands, warm and insistent, wandered over her cold skin, making her shiver with disgust.

Margaret remained still, her heart pounding in her chest. She bided her time, waiting for the perfect moment.

As David leaned in closer, his body pressing against hers, Margaret moved in a flash. With no hesitation, she reached down, snatching the knife strapped to his leg, and with every ounce of strength she had, she drove the blade deep into his shoulder.

David recoiled, a scream of agony tearing from his throat as his hand shot to his wounded shoulder. His fingers, slick with blood, wrapped around the hilt of his own knife, now buried deep in his flesh. The shock in his eyes was almost as potent as the pain.

Margaret seized her moment. With a single leap, she was on her feet and bolting from the stall. The darkness swallowed her whole, and though she had no idea where she was or which way to run, it hardly mattered. Panic surged through her, propelling her forward with relentless urgency.

She crashed through the thick undergrowth of a nearby forest, branches clawing at her skin, whipping across her face and arms, but she didn't slow down. Only once did she dare glance back. In

184

the distance, she saw flickering lights - perhaps from torches or flashlights. The sight made her heart race even faster, terror clawing at her chest.

Where am I?

Where can I go?

Her thoughts raced as wildly as her footsteps, her mind clouded with panic and confusion. She zigzagged through the woods, desperately trying to put as much distance between her and her captors as possible.

Then, without warning, her foot caught on an exposed root. She stumbled forward, tumbling headlong down a steep slope. Leaves, dirt, and jagged stones rained down with her as she rolled uncontrollably to the bottom, where she landed, half-submerged, in a shallow, icy stream.

The shock of the freezing water jolted her back to her senses. Gasping, Margaret scrambled to her feet, her entire body trembling from the cold and exertion. Without hesitating, she began running again, this time following the stream's course as far as her weary legs could carry her.

For hours, she pushed herself forward, not daring to stop. Her lungs burned, her legs felt like lead, and hunger gnawed at her stomach with a cruel persistence. Her body was nearing its breaking point.

When was the last time I ate?

The hospital?

No... breakfast at Southgate.

But a single croissant isn't enough to keep me going.

Finally, her strength gave out. Margaret collapsed in the mud, her limbs refusing to obey her commands any longer. She crawled forward on her hands and knees, desperate to escape, but after a few more agonizing feet, she lost all control over her body and fell face-first into the damp earth and leaves beneath her. Darkness, once again, overtook her.

185

The warm rays of the sun finally roused her. Margaret struggled to sit up, every movement filled with pain. It was only now, in the light of day, that she realized just how filthy she was. Her hands were caked in blood up to her elbows, her hair matted with dirt and tangled leaves. Her legs ached terribly, each step a monumental effort. The night's frantic flight had drained her completely, and every few meters she stumbled, catching herself on the trunks of nearby trees before managing to rise again.

How long she had been wandering before she finally emerged onto an open road, she couldn't tell. Morning still, perhaps - she hoped.

A battered silver van approached, crawling slowly down the desolate road. It came to a stop just ahead of her, and a man with short, snow-white hair stepped out cautiously, his eyes filled with concern as he looked at her. "Miss?" he asked gently, his voice thick with worry. "Are you alright?"

From the passenger seat, an elderly woman with a grayish bun emerged, squinting at the scene before her as though her eyesight had long since faded. "Robert?" she called, her voice faint with age. "Robert, what's going on?" Leaning on a cane, she hobbled closer, her eyes widening with shock as she took in the state of the woman before her. "Oh!" she gasped, her face going pale. With great effort, she bent down toward Margaret. "Child, what happened to you?"

Margaret looked up at the strangers, her lips parting as if to respond, but no words came. Her voice was lost, swallowed by exhaustion and trauma. Not a single sound escaped her throat.

"I think we should call the police," Margaret heard the elderly woman say, her voice tinged with panic as she spoke with her husband in the adjoining room. "Who knows what might have happened to her."

A soft, comforting blanket, embroidered with jolly Santas and reindeer, had been draped over her exhausted body. She lay on a wide, white couch, its warmth soothing her chilled frame. Margaret sat up slowly, pressing her hands to her throbbing temples, as her head pounded relentlessly. Everything around her seemed to spin in a dizzying whirl.

Where am I?

What day is it?

How late is it?

Her eyes scanned the quaintly furnished living room, noting the old-fashioned tiled stove and a tall, wooden grandfather clock ticking away in the corner. The time read 3:48 p.m.

I need to get back.

Now.

Margaret tried to stand, but her body, still ravaged by the strain of her ordeal, protested violently. After only two steps, her knees buckled, sending her crashing down onto the plush carpet that covered the polished wooden floor. The sound of her fall was loud enough to draw the attention of the couple from the other room. They hurried over at once.

"Oh, she's awake," the woman said, gently helping Margaret back onto the couch. "How are you feeling?"

"Better. Thank you," Margaret responded, her voice curt as she took in the faces of her rescuers, both kind and worried.

187

"What happened?" the man asked, his brow furrowed with concern.

Margaret hesitated. She didn't want to burden them with the harrowing details of her ordeal. "Where am I?" she asked instead, deflecting the question.

"Northcott, in Bracknell," the man replied.

Bracknell?

That's more than ten hours on foot from London.

Her mind raced, trying to piece together her next move.

What do I do now?

How do I get back?

"We really should take you to a hospital, dear. You look dreadful. What happened to you?" The elderly woman examined Margaret with deep concern.

"No, I'm fine. Really," Margaret replied, shaking her head. "I just need to get back to London quickly." Desperation laced her voice. "I need to speak with Mycroft."

"Mycroft?" The woman looked at her, puzzled. "You mean Mycroft Holmes? You know that young man, child?"

Margaret's eyes brightened with a glimmer of hope. "Yes. Do you, by any chance, have his number?"

"No, not his," the woman replied, walking over to a wooden sideboard where an old rotary phone sat. "But I do have his parents' number. They have a holiday home nearby, and I believe they're staying there at the moment."

Mycroft's parents?

Oh no, this is probably a bad idea.

Before Margaret could object, the woman had already dialed the number. "Hello, it's Moira," she greeted warmly, a smile on her face. "Oh, thank you, dear. We're both well, Robert and I. ... No, I wouldn't dream of canceling Bingo night, not after we've been looking forward to it for months. ... Actually, this is about something else." She turned slightly, her eyes resting on Margaret as she spoke. "We picked up a young girl from the road earlier today. She won't say what happened, but I suspect she's run away from something. And well, she refuses to go to a hospital... Oh, but it does have something to do with you. She mentioned your son. Mycroft." Moira smiled at Margaret. "Really? Oh, that's wonderful! When? Perfect, thank you so much, dear. See you soon." She hung up the phone and turned back toward Margaret and her husband. "Mr. and Mrs. Holmes will be here in a few minutes, dear. They're going to take you to Mycroft."

"That really isn't necessary," Margaret stammered, feeling a deep sense of embarrassment.

"But they're already on their way," the older woman replied. "And you've no idea how excited they are to meet you."

"Why?" Margaret asked, frowning in confusion.

The woman chuckled softly. "They probably think you're Mycroft's girlfriend." She shook her head in mild amusement. It was clear she knew Mycroft well. "That would be quite the occasion. He's never had anything resembling a girlfriend."

"His parents were beginning to worry that he might prefer the other side," her husband chimed in with a grin.

Margaret rolled her eyes.

A little after 4:00 in the afternoon, the doorbell rang. Two elderly figures stepped inside and hurried straight toward Margaret, just as she was finishing the last bite of a slice of raspberry tart.

"Oh!" Mrs. Holmes froze in her tracks, staring at Margaret. "She's not at all how I imagined."

189

"Nor I," added her husband, equally taken aback. "A bit... cleaner, at the very least."

Excuse me?

I can hear you.

That's not exactly polite.

But what did I expect from Mycroft and Sherlock's parents?

That they'd be warm, loving, and utterly normal people?

Nonsense.

Their sons had to get their strange behavior from somewhere, didn't they?

"I did tell you she's been through something," the elderly homeowner chimed in sympathetically.

The Holmeses stepped closer, taking in the sight of Margaret with more care. Suddenly, Mrs. Holmes went pale, gasping as if she'd just seen a ghost.

"Oh my God!" she cried, her voice trembling. "That's Margaret. Margaret Trevor!"

Margaret looked up at them, tears welling in her eyes. The shock of being recognized - after all these years - touched something deep within her, something she hadn't realized was there.

Mrs. Holmes leaned down and pulled her into a tight embrace, not caring about the dirt and grime on Margaret's clothes. "We thought you were dead," she whispered. "Your mother told us you'd died."

Margaret was speechless. She couldn't find the words. Every thought that crossed her mind felt inadequate to explain the confusion and pain swirling inside her.

"You poor thing," Mrs. Holmes said gently, her voice full of compassion. "What happened to you? Does Mycroft know you're alive?"

"Yes," Margaret replied weakly. "He knows. In fact, he knew before I did."

190

Mr. and Mrs. Holmes stared at her in utter confusion. They had no idea what she could possibly mean.

"It's a long story," Margaret dismissed it as if it were a trivial matter. She simply didn't have the strength to explain it all to them.

Better Mycroft explains it to them.

"Alright then, let's get you to Mike," said Mr. Holmes as he helped her to her feet.

Mike?

That sounded odd to her.

Does anyone actually call him that?

It seems so... normal.

And Mycroft Holmes was anything but normal.

With the help of Mycroft's parents, Margaret made her way outside to their car. Before getting in, she turned to thank the kind couple who had taken her in, expressing her gratitude as warmly as she could. Then, they drove off.

It would be an hour-and-a-half drive back, and Mycroft and Sherlock's parents seized the opportunity to pepper Margaret with questions about everything under the sun.

191

XI.

THE MISSING PIECE OF THE PUZZLE

Around six o'clock in the evening, Mr. and Mrs. Holmes finally arrived in London with Margaret. They brought her straight to Mycroft's townhouse in the heart of the city - his usual residence. They had also called ahead, teasingly informing him that they were bringing along a "gift," but they hadn't revealed what it was.

Margaret had warned them that Mycroft would undoubtedly be worried sick about her, especially after all that had transpired. Mrs. Holmes had even heard the tension in his voice during their phone call, but she and her husband, in their mischievous way, had still decided not to give away the surprise.

They're a bit childish.

Strange, but sweet.

If Mycroft were her son, she supposed she'd enjoy teasing him like this as well.

But for her, it wasn't quite as amusing as it was for them.

And for Mycroft, it must be nothing short of torture.

She just hoped he wouldn't be too angry with them.

They climbed out of the car one by one, making their way up the familiar driveway. It was the same brick house that Margaret had broken into only a few days ago. Mr. Holmes pressed the doorbell, and the three of them waited - Mycroft's parents excited, Margaret with a knot of unease twisting in her stomach.

It was Mr. Wiggins who answered the door. The man looked thoroughly startled when he saw Margaret standing there. "Miss Green?" he exclaimed in disbelief. "What a delight to see you! Though, if I may say, you look as though you've just run a marathon through a mud bath. Mr. Holmes has been frantically searching for you. The poor man's beside himself - he hasn't a clue of what to do."

"That's not like him," remarked Mr. Holmes.

"Green?" Mrs. Holmes looked at Margaret curiously. "Child, did you get married?" The very thought seemed to shake her world.

"Wasn't your grandmother's name also Green?" Mr. Holmes asked, peering thoughtfully at Margaret.

"Yes," she nodded. "And no, I didn't get married. It's... well, it's a long and complicated story."

Mrs. Holmes visibly relaxed, relieved beyond measure.

"Are those my parents?" came a familiar voice, sounding slightly tense. Mycroft strode into the lobby, his expression one of restrained impatience. But the moment his eyes landed on Margaret, he froze. "Alex," was all he could manage.

"Margaret," she corrected him with a relieved smile.

Without hesitation, Mycroft pushed past Mr. Wiggins, slipping between his parents, and wrapped Margaret in a tight embrace. The dirt from her clothes smeared across his expensive suit, but he didn't care. She was back, and that was all that mattered to him.

Mrs. Holmes cleared her throat, the sound laced with impatience.

Mycroft had completely forgotten his parents, so overwhelming was his relief at seeing Margaret safe and sound. Not only was she back, but she finally remembered who she truly was. He quickly regained his composure, turning toward them. "Mr. Wiggins, escort my parents to the lounge!" he ordered, slipping momentarily back into his usual, frosty demeanor.

Once Mr. Wiggins had led his parents into the house, Mycroft's attention returned to Margaret. He gently turned her to face him, his gaze filled with palpable relief. "I thought I'd lost you forever," he admitted, his voice softer than she had ever heard it.

193

Margaret smiled warmly, her eyes glinting with affection. "Do you remember my promise?" she asked. "I swore, all those years ago, that I'd never leave you."

"Don't break it," he murmured, his tone full of raw emotion, as he pulled her into another embrace. It was rare for him to show this much vulnerability, but in that moment, nothing else mattered. Then, still holding her close, he led her inside.

"You probably want to know everything that's happened," Margaret said as they paused in the hallway. "And I promise I'll tell you - everything. But first, I'd like to freshen up."

Mycroft chuckled, his eyes softening as he nodded in understanding. "Take your time," he said gently.

Margaret made her way upstairs to wash and change into clean clothes. As she disappeared into the upper floor, Mycroft headed into the lounge where his parents were waiting, attempting to engage them in what he hoped would be a normal conversation - though his thoughts were entirely elsewhere, fixated on the woman he had thought he'd lost for good.

"When did you find out?" his mother asked. She sat on a broad couch beside her husband, a cup of tea in hand, facing their son who crouched on another parallel couch. "Since when did you know that Margaret is still alive?"

"Only a few days ago," Mycroft replied. In the company of his parents, he appeared alarmingly normal.

Margaret stood behind the open door to the lobby, listening to their conversation with keen curiosity.

"And why is she here?" his father pressed. "Why now? After all these years, why has she returned?"

"Margaret was never truly gone," his son declared. "Following the car accident, she suffered from profound amnesia. She forgot everything, absolutely everything."

"So that explains Alexandra Green," Mrs. Holmes deduced thoughtfully.

"Her mother was attempting to protect her."

"From whom?"

Mycroft remained silent, unwilling to divulge the truth to his parents.

"Mycroft Arthur Holmes!" his mother called out sternly. "Respond to me!"

"Moran," he answered curtly.

"But that's impossible!" his father exclaimed in horror. "The Moran brothers perished back then."

"No, they are still alive."

"Oh, how dreadful," Mrs. Holmes murmured, her voice filled with dismay. "The poor child." She looked intently at her son. "Woe to you if anything should happen to her, young man!" She yearned to express her anger, but instead, memories of her son's suffering during Margaret's disappearance nearly broke her heart. "Oh, Mike, I am so sorry," she whispered sympathetically. Then, she smiled reassuringly. "See? I told you everything would work out for the better." Her gaze now fixed on her son with newfound curiosity. "And? What is the situation with you, with Margaret and you?"

"What is there to discuss?" Mycroft retorted, visibly uneasy.

"Oh, my boy," Mrs. Holmes sighed deeply. "Isn't it obvious? She was your first best friend."

"What does that have to do with anything?" Mycroft asked, frowning. "She was just a friend."

Just a friend?
Really?

Margaret could hardly believe the words coming out of his mouth. She had truly thought he harbored feelings for her. But now, it seemed she had been entirely wrong about him.

Why did he kiss me, then?

The alcohol.

So, it really was just the alcohol.

She felt the urge to turn around and leave, to disappear once more. But just as she was about to step away, Mycroft continued. "We were children."

"You suffered terribly when she was gone," Mrs. Holmes interjected. "Why don't you just admit it? It's only human, Mike."

"Please. My name is Mycroft. MYCROFT," he retorted in frustration, pausing briefly to gather his thoughts. "You know me. You both know full well that I'm not capable of something like that."

"Of loving," his mother corrected him sternly. "Not '*something like that*,' Mycroft. Of *loving*." She sighed. "Yes, we know all too well. But she's not just any girl. This is Margaret - your Margaret. My dear boy, it's time you grow up!"

Mycroft said nothing in return. He was at a complete loss for words, uncertain how to respond.

Fortuitously for him, at that very moment, Margaret entered the room, dressed in a long, elegant black gown that he had set aside for her. She made every effort to hide the hurt caused by his words as she gracefully sat down beside him on the couch opposite his parents.

"You look absolutely lovely," Mrs. Holmes remarked, her face lighting up with a warm smile.

"Thank you," Margaret replied with a faint, forced smile of her own.

"And?" Mrs. Holmes pressed. "Will you answer our question now?"

Margaret gave her a puzzled look.

196

"Is there something between the two of you?" the older woman asked, not willing to let the matter drop.

"No," Margaret shot back, her voice sharp and immediate, as though the answer had been waiting on her tongue. She could feel Mycroft's astonished and pained gaze resting on her, but she didn't dare meet his eyes. "We're just friends," she repeated his earlier words, her tone cold and detached.

She had hoped to wound him with those words as deeply as his had hurt her - though it was clear he had spoken them unknowingly. Yet, even as she watched the silent pain flicker in his eyes, it did nothing to ease the ache in her own heart. The hurt remained, raw and unrelenting.

"You two are so strange," Mrs. Holmes said, shaking her head. "Both equally odd." She took a sip of her tea and drew in a deep breath, as though she was preparing to make a grand leap. "Even a blind person could see you're lying. Why can't you just admit it? Surely it's not that difficult."

"Darling," her husband finally interjected, "let them be. They're old enough, I think, to know what's best for them."

Mrs. Holmes sighed, defeated. She knew her husband was right, of course, but she wasn't one to give up easily. She glanced at him and then asked, "But don't you want grandchildren?"

Margaret flushed at the unexpected question. She quickly looked away, hoping Mycroft's parents would change the subject as soon as possible. Mycroft, too, felt a deep discomfort creeping over him.

Margaret stood up abruptly. "Excuse me," she said hastily, and left the room, heading outside. She couldn't bear to stay in the same space with Mycroft and his parents any longer. It was too awkward, too painful.

"Now you've gone too far and frightened the poor girl," Mr. Holmes chided his wife. "Face it, our boys just aren't like everyone else."

197

You've got that right.

Mycroft rose to his feet as well. He followed Margaret outside, where she had sunk down on the lower steps of the staircase, her head resting on her knees. When he sat beside her, she looked up, tears streaming silently down her cheeks.

"I'm sorry," he said softly, his voice weighed down with regret.

"It's fine," she replied, quickly wiping her tears away.

But Mycroft put his arm around her, pulling her gently closer. "No, it's not fine," he said with more urgency. He looked into her eyes, his own filled with sincerity. "I truly am sorry."

"What do you mean?" Margaret asked, confused.

"You're not *just* a friend," Mycroft corrected himself, his earlier words hanging between them. "You're far more than that."

"I know," Margaret whispered, leaning her head against his chest. "I knew it even back then."

Mycroft wrapped his other arm around her, holding her tightly in a protective embrace.

It was in this moment that his parents, standing by the door to the lobby, caught sight of the pair. Unnoticed by either of them, they watched in silence.

"Are you satisfied now?" Mr. Holmes asked his wife, though his voice carried warmth. Mrs. Holmes, utterly overjoyed, smiled brightly as she gazed at her son and Margaret, relief and happiness clear on her face.

After all the formalities at Scotland Yard were settled, the clock in Inspector Lestrade's office read a quarter past two in the morning. Margaret had given her statement, describing to the officers everything she could recall about the old barn's location. Finally, she was allowed to sit in the chair across from Lestrade's desk, and she collapsed into it, utterly drained.

"Well?" Sherlock asked, standing nearby with his brother Mycroft and Dr. Watson. His gaze was sharp, piercing, as if trying to extract the words directly from her mind. "What else is there?"

Margaret looked back at him, confused. "What?"

"The whole truth, Margaret," Sherlock pressed, his eyes demanding an answer, relentless in their scrutiny.

Lestrade adjusted himself in his large black leather chair, exchanging a brief glance with Inspector Doyle, who stood at his side. The look seemed to prompt Doyle to speak.

Doyle cleared his throat, feeling oddly uncomfortable, though he tried to hide it. He stood a little straighter, legs wide apart as if trying to project authority. "Please, tell us everything you remember, Alex-" He coughed quickly, correcting his slip. "-Margaret."

"Everything?" Margaret asked, her gaze questioning as it met his. There was something unusual in Doyle's eyes, a flicker of emotion she hadn't seen from him before.

Is he... worried about me?

The man gave a terse nod.

"Alright," she sighed, exhausted. For the third time now, she would have to recount it all.

"David Moran somehow found his way into the house at Southgate. How he knew I was there, I have no idea." At this, Mycroft and Sherlock exchanged nervous glances, but Margaret didn't notice. Her gaze was distant, focused on some invisible point in the room. "They were three. David, his father Sebastian, and his uncle Julius. I thought they were dead. It was said they died in that car accident." She paused, memories of the crash flashing through her mind. "They wanted to kill me. They knew exactly who I was."

Margaret's voice trembled slightly as she spoke, but she quickly regained composure. Mycroft, standing stiffly beside his brother,

199

clenched his hands behind his back, but he didn't interrupt. His eyes never left her, and the room felt thick with the weight of everything unsaid.

"Why?" asked Lestrade, his voice cutting through the tension.

Margaret looked at him, perplexed.

"Why did they want to kill you? What had you done?"

"I didn't do anything," she replied, her tone rising with a hint of frustration. She could sense in Lestrade's question an implication that she was somehow to blame for her abduction. "The only mistake I made was surviving when they wanted me dead. It wasn't an accident. They planned it all along. I..." Her voice faltered, and the flood of memories from her past crashed into her mind with a sudden and terrifying force, leaving her paralyzed by them. "I... I wasn't... I didn't... they..."

"Margaret," Mycroft's voice broke through softly, as he stepped closer to her. He gently placed a hand on her shoulder, waiting for her to meet his eyes. His gaze was tender, filled with a warmth she hadn't expected. "Please, continue. You need to tell us."

His closeness was comforting, for the first time. It no longer felt strange or out of place. It felt right, like a familiar anchor in the storm of her thoughts.

"I was only four," Margaret's voice wavered, laden with anguish. "We were playing tag." Her eyes moved from Sherlock to Mycroft, searching their faces. "Do you remember? I was too fast, and I ran into the woods."

"We searched for you for two hours," Sherlock recalled instantly, his face growing pale as realization dawned. "What happened then?"

Margaret took a breath, steadying herself, her body trembling as the memories flooded back. "I ran deep into the trees, trying to hide, but I didn't know... I didn't know he was there, waiting."

Both Mycroft and Sherlock went rigid, their eyes locked onto hers, the weight of what she was about to say settling heavily in the room.

"Sebastian Moran," she whispered, her voice raw. "He found me. And then... he..."

The room fell into an oppressive silence, each word of hers landing like a blow. Sherlock's jaw clenched, Mycroft's hand tightened on her shoulder, the only tether keeping her from collapsing under the weight of her memories.

"I screamed for you. Over and over, I screamed." Her voice cracked, the pain unbearable. "But you never heard me," she whispered, her voice cracking under the weight of her words. "He followed me, and he... he raped me." Margaret felt Mycroft's fingers tighten around her shoulder, his grip growing firmer as if to hold her steady. "And Victor..." She choked on her tears, unable to keep them at bay any longer. "Victor saw it. He saw everything." She looked up at Mycroft, her eyes filled with unbearable sorrow. "He killed Victor to keep him quiet. My brother..." Her voice broke, and she turned her gaze away from Mycroft, her heart heavy with guilt. "He died because of me." She trembled with despair. "I wasn't strong enough," she sobbed, collapsing into her grief.

Mycroft knelt beside her, drawing her into his arms with a tenderness that belied the stoic man he usually was. He gently stroked her back, his voice soft but firm. "No, it wasn't your fault."

Margaret clung to him for a moment, seeking the solace he offered, before she wiped her tears and turned toward Lestrade and Doyle, her eyes pleading. "Please. You have to find them," she begged, her voice desperate.

Lestrade, visibly moved, nodded solemnly. "We will do everything in our power. You have my word." His sympathy was genuine, but as he glanced at the scene before him - Margaret in the arms of Mycroft Holmes - he couldn't shake the strange dissonance of it. The image of Mycroft, usually so cold and distant, now holding this woman with such care unsettled him deeply. He couldn't quite place why, but something felt... incomplete.

Something wasn't right. Something was missing.

Margaret shifted her gaze between Mycroft and Sherlock. She could see it in their eyes too - they all felt it, as if a critical piece of the puzzle still eluded them.

It was Dr. Watson who finally spoke, his voice cutting through the lingering tension. "What about Montaigne?"

Inspector Doyle responded, "MP Shepard is safe. We've confirmed his security."

"It was never about Shepard," Sherlock interjected, his voice sharp with certainty. "He was just a pawn, a distraction."

All eyes turned toward him, hanging on his every word.

"The real target," Sherlock continued, his tone darkening as he pieced it all together, "was Margaret. Everything was designed to draw her into a trap."

"The Moran brothers are not his employers," Margaret said thoughtfully, her mind piecing the puzzle together. "He said 'his employer,' singular, which rules them out entirely. And it wasn't David either. Without his father and uncle, he wouldn't have done anything. He simply doesn't have the nerve."

She could still hear David's voice from the night before, echoing loudly in her mind: *'Can I kill her now? Please?'*

The memory of his voice sent a shudder through her.

"So, there's someone else involved?" Dr. Watson asked, his confusion evident. He was trying to follow the swift exchange of ideas but was having trouble keeping up. "Someone else who wants you dead?" He looked at Margaret with concern.

She nodded silently.

"Who could that be?" Lestrade mused aloud, furrowing his brow.

"The list isn't exactly short," Doyle chimed in. He was slightly taken aback when the others turned to him as if he'd said something inappropriate. "Margaret's put a lot of criminals behind bars over the past five years - bank robbers, pickpockets, drug lords, serial killers - just to name a few. None of them are big fans of hers."

"They're all locked away," Margaret responded, shaking her head. She was certain it wasn't one of them. "This goes beyond just me." She turned to Sherlock, her eyes searching his. "Do you remember what I said to you in Newgate?"

Sherlock's face paled, the memory clearly unwelcome. "I do," he said, his voice tight. "What links you and Mycroft?"

"You?" Mycroft looked at his brother, puzzled. He thought for a moment, but quickly came to the same conclusion. "Indeed."

"Okay, wait just a minute," Dr. Watson interjected, raising his hands in protest. "How in the world did you arrive at that conclusion? Surely there are other connections between the two of you? This sounds utterly insane."

"It's not," Margaret said calmly, rising to her feet. She stood in the center of the room, ensuring everyone could see her clearly. "Victor is dead. He was the first and only link between Mycroft and me. But he's gone now. Sherlock was Victor's best friend. Through Sherlock, I met Mycroft." She glanced at Mycroft and gave him a soft smile. "Even though we didn't get along at first." She sighed deeply. "Sherlock and Victor - they're our connection. The only one."

"How does that help us?" Doyle asked, clearly still baffled. He wasn't the only one, though. His irritation at the revelation that Margaret and Mycroft had been childhood friends was barely concealed. The underlying jealousy Doyle harbored toward the elder Holmes was painfully obvious to anyone paying attention.

Of course, Mycroft had noticed immediately. He was far too perceptive to miss the way Doyle looked at Margaret, trying - but failing - to keep his feelings under control.

"I have no idea," Margaret replied, her voice tinged with frustration. She truly didn't know.

"So, what does this mean?" Doyle pressed, his impatience flaring up. His temper was getting the best of him, and it showed as he arched an eyebrow. "Are all three of you in danger now? Well, that's just brilliant."

"That's your contribution?" Mycroft snapped, his voice laced with unexpected fury.

Everyone turned to him, startled by the sudden outburst. He had gone from composed to enraged in the blink of an eye.

"Three of the brightest minds in all of London - no, probably the entire world - are standing in this room," Doyle continued with a sneer, glaring at Mycroft. "And none of you have the faintest idea what's really going on? That's ridiculous. I don't need an IQ of 200 to know something doesn't add up. You must know *something*. This can't all be a blank slate."

"Intelligence and knowledge are not the same thing," Sherlock retorted coldly, clearly insulted by Doyle's condescending tone, which was aimed at him just as much as at Mycroft. "And no human being has an IQ of 200. That's a myth. Psychologically impossible."

"So, someone's trying to kill Mycroft Holmes and Margaret Trevor because of some connection they share?" Doyle shot Sherlock a pointed look.

Trevor?

"No," Margaret interrupted, her voice thoughtful but soft enough to draw everyone's attention. "He didn't call me Trevor." She was piecing it together. "He called me Miss Green. Montaigne. He doesn't know who I really am. Which means his employer doesn't know either."

"That doesn't narrow down the suspects much," Doyle said, his tone still icy.

Damn.

204

He's right.

"Alright," Lestrade said with a weary sigh, standing up from his chair, his joints creaking in protest. He glanced at his watch - nearly half past two in the morning. He yawned and stretched, clearly exhausted. "Until we capture the Moran brothers, we won't get much further on this. Speculation and conspiracy theories aren't going to help us." He shot a stern look at Doyle. "And insults definitely aren't."

Doyle met his gaze with a defiant glare but said nothing.

"It's late," Lestrade continued, his voice heavy with fatigue. "Go home. We can pick this up tomorrow. Without the Moran brothers, staying up all night won't do us any good." He rubbed the back of his neck, his face unmistakably showing that all he wanted was to collapse into bed. "Good night, everyone," he said, in a tone that brooked no argument.

As Mycroft, Sherlock, John, and Margaret stepped out of the police station, a sleek black limousine with tinted windows awaited them by the curb. The four of them paused in a loose circle just outside the entrance.

"So, what now?" asked Dr. Watson, eyeing the car warily. "Are we really just going home? There's still a hired killer out there gunning for you both."

"You should stay with us, Dr. Watson," Mycroft suggested. "It would be best if we all remain together for the next few days. I have certain connections within MI6 that should ensure we get at least one peaceful night."

205

"With *you* in the same house?" Sherlock scoffed, his face twisting into a mocking grimace. "I'd rather sleep under a bridge, to be honest."

"Enough of this nonsense," Mycroft snapped, his patience wearing thin. He was exhausted and in no mood for bickering with his younger brother at this late hour. "You're coming with us, and that's final. No arguments."

"You know," Margaret interjected, her tone serious as she looked directly at Sherlock, "if Montaigne gets to you first, you'll never figure out who's really behind all of this. So, just this once, could you possibly listen to your brother?" Her voice softened, a touch of almost maternal concern in her gaze. Without waiting for a response, she turned and walked toward the black limousine.

The three men exchanged raised eyebrows, each caught off guard by her sudden authority. Mycroft, in particular, found himself both surprised and - truth be told - utterly captivated by her demeanor. Yes, he admired her more than he cared to admit. Without further protest, he followed her silently. John and Sherlock, after a moment's hesitation, trailed behind and climbed into the car as well.

During the long drive, none of them spoke much. They were all exhausted, though none would admit it, and the thought of a warm, comfortable bed was the only thing on their minds. Margaret sat by the door, her head resting against Mycroft's chest. She had already fallen asleep by the time he gently draped his arm around her. But her dreams were anything but peaceful - they were filled with tension and terror.

In her dream, she was a little girl again, sprinting through a dark forest. "You'll never catch me! You'll never catch me! You're too slow!" she shouted, laughing as she darted between the trees.

When she glanced back to see her pursuers lagging far behind, her foot caught on a jagged stone that jutted from the ground. She tumbled down a steep embankment and, when she came to a stop, two men loomed over her. Their towering forms cast long, menacing shadows across the forest floor.

"Let's play a game," one of them said. It was Sebastian Moran.

Margaret flinched involuntarily in her sleep.

Mycroft, noticing her sudden movement, glanced down at her with concern. He knew there was nothing he could do to help her. Waking her might be worse; she needed rest, just as much as he did.

"Come on, Maggie," the man in her dream continued, kneeling down to bring his ravenous eyes level with hers.

The terrified child scrambled to her feet and fled in the opposite direction, away from the two men.

"You can't escape us!" they called out in unison, their voices echoing ominously as they pursued her. "There's no way out for you."

Margaret ran without stopping, her heart pounding in her chest. She suddenly found herself on an old, decrepit cemetery. Rows upon rows of gravestones stood, tangled with cobwebs, shrouded in a thick, creeping fog that veiled the far end of the yard.

The girl tiptoed nervously past the gravestones, each step more hesitant than the last. She stopped at one particular grave.

Margaret Trevor, born yesterday, died today, was engraved in golden letters.

As the child leaned in to examine the inscription more closely, the ground beneath her crumbled. She plummeted into the abyss.

Margaret jolted awake, drenched in sweat. The sensation of falling had finally wrenched her from the nightmare.

"Are you alright?" Mycroft asked, his arm still securely wrapped around her. He gazed down at her with concern.

She nodded. "Just a bad dream," she murmured, settling herself more comfortably against his chest. Her hand slipped around his waist, and she nestled into the warmth of his body. It didn't bother her that Sherlock and Dr. Watson were staring, as if she were doing something scandalous. She didn't care at all.

"Do you realize what my parents think of us?" Mycroft whispered in her ear, his breath soft against her skin.

"Yes," Margaret smiled and looked up at him, her eyes twinkling. "They think we're normal."

Sherlock cleared his throat loudly, casting them a disdainful glance. "While you two are busy pretending to be ordinary people, there are maniacs out there plotting our murder. I would very much appreciate it if you'd stop playing house and help me figure out the last missing piece of this puzzle."

John rolled his eyes, exhausted and clearly annoyed. "It's almost three in the morning, Sherlock."

"Thank you, John. I can read the time," Sherlock snapped, his frustration barely concealed. The thought of someone out there plotting to kill them gnawed at him, kept him on edge. "So? What do you propose we do?" He shot a sharp look between Mycroft and Margaret.

Mycroft arched an eyebrow. "For now? Absolutely nothing. It's late. We'll discuss this in the morning."

"What if there *is* no morning?" Sherlock retorted, his voice laced with unease. "What if by tomorrow it's already too late?"

"What exactly do you want us to do?" his older brother asked, keeping his voice steady.

"I don't know," Sherlock admitted, clearly agitated. "Something. Anything. Just not… *this*," he said, his eyes narrowing in disdain at the sight of Mycroft and Margaret sitting arm in arm, as if this whole situation weren't life-threatening.

"Very well," said Margaret, sitting up straighter and slipping out of Mycroft's protective embrace. "There's nothing more we can do tonight, Sherlock, no matter how much you brood over it. But I do have an idea for tomorrow." She paused, waiting until she had the full attention of all three men before continuing. "The Moran brothers have undoubtedly fled the old farm by now. David is likely seeking medical attention - after all, he does have a hole in his shoulder. Finding him won't be too difficult. It's the other two I'm more concerned about. Last night, they didn't strike me as the type to leave their plans half-finished. In fact," she hesitated, her tone growing more somber, "I'm afraid they wanted me to escape. They didn't let David kill me - not yet. That means they still have something in store."

"So, you believe the Moran brothers are connected to Montaigne after all?" Dr. Watson asked, leaning forward with interest.

"Not directly, but there's some link between them. I'm sure of it," Margaret replied.

Sherlock, pacing in thought, spoke next. "So, if we catch them, we may very well get Montaigne too. The question is, how do we go about that?"

"Well, that's where things get tricky," Margaret said thoughtfully.

Mycroft's gaze lingered on her, his brow furrowed in concern. He didn't like where this was going - he didn't need her to spell out her plan to understand what she intended. The thought of it made him uneasy, a gnawing anxiety that tightened in his chest.

"You're thinking of using yourself as bait," Mycroft said quietly, his voice tinged with apprehension, and the room grew still as the weight of his words settled on them all.

209

XII.

THE WITCH

The Céleste, a Michelin-starred restaurant nestled within The Lanesborough Hotel at Hyde Park Corner in Belgravia, catered exclusively to London's political elite and the wealthiest of government officials. It was the kind of establishment where the clink of fine crystal and the murmur of quiet, dignified conversation filled the air. Mycroft Holmes was a regular patron here, well known among the other high-ranking guests. But tonight was different. For the first time in his life, Mycroft was not dining alone.

Though he had certainly shared a meal with women before - business associates, diplomats, even politicians - this particular woman was different. There was something special about her, something the staff noticed immediately. She wasn't just another business partner.

As they entered, Mycroft, ever the gentleman, held the door for her, guiding her gracefully by the arm through the opulent dining room. Every table was occupied, and many of the guests recognized Mycroft at once. His presence was commanding as always, yet tonight, with this woman by his side, he seemed somehow more complete, though neither of them paid the curious glances from around the room any mind.

The maître d' approached them with a beaming smile. "Mr. Holmes," he said, practically glowing with the privilege of greeting him. Indeed, Mycroft Holmes was a distinguished guest at the Céleste. "A very good evening to you," he continued before turning to acknowledge the woman beside him, dressed elegantly in a long, midnight-blue gown. "What a charming companion," he added with a courteous nod. "Please, follow me. I'll take you to your table."

Without a word, Mycroft and his guest followed him to a secluded corner of the room, where a table for two awaited them, set with the finest silverware and adorned with soft candlelight - a setting intimate, romantic even.

As they settled into their seats, a young waiter appeared with two menus. "May I offer you something to drink?" he asked, visibly nervous. The waiter, new to the Céleste, seemed almost intimidated by Mycroft's presence, his hands trembling slightly as he stood by.

"A large bottle of sparkling water," Mycroft commanded with his usual authoritative tone. "And a bottle of Château Barrique, as per my usual selection."

The young waiter nodded frantically, his nervous energy palpable, and hurried off, eager to fulfill the order without delay.

"I hope you're aware we have plenty of witnesses," Mycroft began, his tone serious as he glanced at his companion across the table. "We're sitting here on display for the whole world to see."

"That was precisely the plan," Margaret replied with a playful smile. She seemed to be relishing the game. "Trust me, Mycroft. Everything will unfold exactly as we've planned."

"I sincerely hope you're right," Mycroft spoke with a hint of reluctance, his discomfort palpable. "I feel like I've got a giant target painted on my forehead."

"Relax," Margaret reassured him, still smiling. "The three most brilliant minds in all of Britain - or possibly the entire world - crafted this plan. What could possibly go wrong?"

"We could all end up dead."

"Not all of us," Margaret mused, her smile fading slightly as she considered his words. "Just me."

Mycroft reached across the table, taking her hand in his with a gentle but firm grip. "I trust you," he said softly, his voice filled with uncharacteristic warmth. "And I won't let anyone get close enough to harm you."

"Has it occurred to either of you," Dr. Watson's voice interrupted from a nearby table, his back turned to them, "that Montaigne and the Moran brothers might already know this is a trap?" He was cleverly disguised with a moustache, barely recognizable except for his familiar voice.

"Yes, John," Sherlock muttered under his breath as he approached the table, also in disguise as a waiter. "While you were napping this afternoon, we ran through sixteen possible scenarios and calculated each in painstaking detail." He placed the water and wine on the table with the precision of an experienced sommelier. His voice was low, meant not to attract attention as he played his role perfectly. "Everything has been planned down to the smallest detail."

"I still don't feel good about it," John protested, his brow furrowed beneath the false moustache.

"Neither do I," Margaret admitted, her usual bravado faltering. Only then did the others notice that she was trembling slightly. The confidence she had exuded earlier was merely a facade. Beneath it, she was genuinely frightened. "But it's too late to turn back now."

Sherlock finished pouring the wine and straightened up, his sharp eyes meeting Margaret's. "Fear is useful," he said quietly. "It keeps us sharp. But it doesn't change the plan."

Margaret gave a small nod, though the unease in her eyes remained. The stakes were higher than ever, and they all knew it. She took a generous sip from her glass.

Mycroft gave her a horrified look. "I don't recall the part of the plan where you get drunk," he said sharply.

Margaret quickly followed her wine with a gulp of water. "Sorry, Mycroft. I never said it was a *good* plan."

"Wonderful," Dr. Watson chimed in sarcastically. "Now you're losing your nerve. This will end in disaster."

"Oh, do be quiet," Mycroft snapped, irritation flickering across his face. "We've only been here for five minutes. There's plenty of time."

"I wouldn't be so sure," Sherlock interjected, scanning the room intently. "See that waiter? The young one? He's far too nervous for someone just serving wine." Without waiting for a response, Sherlock began making his way toward the waiter.

"Sherlock!" Mycroft hissed, barely containing his frustration. "That wasn't part of the plan!"

"Let him be," Margaret murmured, taking another sip of her wine. "What trouble could he possibly cause?"

John chuckled behind them, as if she had said something amusing. "You clearly don't know Sherlock Holmes very well," he remarked dryly.

"Enough!" Mycroft snapped, his icy demeanor returning in full force. "Can we focus on what's important?"

"What's important," Margaret countered, setting her glass down with a delicate clink, "is that we both enjoy this dinner. Is that within your capabilities, *Mike*?"

"Don't call me that!" Mycroft growled, his tone darkening.

"Why not? Because 'Mike' sounds too *normal* for your ears?" Margaret smirked. "I don't think it's a bad name, but it definitely doesn't suit you. You've never been normal - not even back when you ate two entire bags of marshmallows at that picnic in our garden."

Mycroft, visibly agitated, snatched the wine glass from her hand. "Enough! Stop behaving like this!"

"And how am I behaving?" Margaret retorted, her irritation rising to match his. A few nearby guests turned to glance at them, intrigued by the sudden outburst. John, on the other hand, buried his face in his hands, embarrassed by the scene unfolding. Undeterred, Margaret grabbed Mycroft's glass in return. "You're such a boring stiff," she declared, downing the entire contents in one swift

213

motion. Margaret's voice cut through the murmurs of the restaurant, her tone both defiant and slightly slurred.

Mycroft stared at her, utterly appalled. "What do you think you're doing?" he hissed, his face turning pale. "You're embarrassing me in front of everyone here. Have you no shame?"

Margaret, undeterred, refilled her wine glass with a smug, almost playful grin. "Not a bit," she replied casually, sipping from the glass as if it were nothing more than water. She rose unsteadily from her chair and swayed around the table until she was seated right beside him. With one hand still holding the glass, she gently placed the other on his knee, her fingers tracing a slow, deliberate pattern. "Don't you like this?" she asked teasingly.

Mycroft flinched at the contact, his cheeks flushing a deep shade of red. He was mortified, his usual composed demeanor slipping away in the face of her brazen behavior. And yet, despite his discomfort, there was no denying the flicker of desire that accompanied his shame. He quickly grabbed her wrist, pulling her hand away from his leg, freeing himself from her delicate touch.

Startled by his abrupt reaction, Margaret jerked back, spilling a splash of wine across her dress. She sprang to her feet, outrage written all over her face. "Look what you've done!" she shouted, her voice loud enough to turn heads. And before he could utter a word in his defense, her hand cracked across his face in a stinging slap. Without hesitation, she stormed off, her steps erratic and unsteady as she made her way out of the room.

"Brilliant plan," Dr. Watson remarked, his lips twitching into an amused smile as he watched Mycroft rub his reddening cheek. The slap had clearly stung more than just his pride.

Margaret, meanwhile, stumbled into the ladies' restroom, her mind still reeling from the scene she had just caused. She wobbled toward the sink, staring at her reflection in the mirror. Her hair was disheveled, and the dark red stain on her dress seemed to mock her. She tried, in vain, to rub it away, muttering to herself all the while.

She glanced around the room and realized she was alone.

Good.

Very good.

Margaret turned back to the sink, her back now facing the stall doors behind her. But in the mirror, she caught a glimpse of one of the doors slowly opening. Silently, a figure dressed entirely in black crept toward her. Before she could react, a pair of strong hands wrapped around her throat, squeezing with terrifying force. She didn't need to see his face to know who it was.

Sebastian Moran.

"Looks like someone's had a bit too much to drink," he sneered, his breath hot against her ear, his grip tightening.

Perfect.

He bought it.

In a flash, Margaret twisted out of his grasp, using his surprise to her advantage. With a series of swift, calculated strikes, she brought Moran crashing to the floor. She wasted no time, straddling his chest, her movements precise and practiced. From a hidden holster strapped to her ankle, she pulled out a small pistol, pressing the barrel firmly against his forehead.

"Did you miss me?" she asked, her voice dripping with triumph, a cold smile spreading across her lips.

The man stared at her in utter bewilderment. Margaret had truly caught him off guard. He had assumed she was drunk, an easy target for him to overpower. But he had gravely miscalculated.

"Did you enjoy our little performance?" Margaret asked as she rose from her crouch, her voice laced with quiet menace. "Now, where's your brother?"

"Right here," came a cold voice from behind her. Julius Moran stood there, his gun aimed directly at her, ready to fire.

Before Margaret could react, one of the stall doors swung open with force, slamming into Julius. The man crumpled to the ground, unconscious, his weapon clattering to the floor.

215

Sherlock Holmes emerged from the stall, a wicked grin playing on his lips as he bent down to retrieve the fallen gun. "In theory," he said, twirling the weapon expertly in his hand, "this seemed far more complicated. But I must say, your improvisation was nothing short of Hollywood-worthy." His eyes sparkled with mischief as he glanced at Margaret.

Margaret allowed herself a small, satisfied smile. "I'm afraid the slap I gave Mycroft might not have gone over quite as well," she replied, amused. "Though, by now, he should be used to it, don't you think?"

"You did *what*?" Lestrade bellowed in utter disbelief as Sebastian and Julius Moran were being escorted away in handcuffs beside him. "Are you all completely out of your minds? That could have ended very differently!"

"The plan was perfectly calculated," Sherlock defended, speaking on behalf of the group.

"That was sheer luck," Doyle retorted, standing beside Lestrade with a scowl etched on his face. He was far from pleased. "What were you thinking?"

"We were just trying to lighten your workload," Margaret replied, a hint of sarcasm in her voice.

"You could've all been killed!" Doyle snapped, clearly on edge.

"Not all of us," Dr. Watson interjected calmly, glancing at Margaret. "Just Margaret."

"Are you all stark raving mad?" Doyle's frustration boiled over. "The lot of you?"

"We had everything under control from start to finish," Mycroft said, his tone calm yet authoritative, the kind that brooked no argument.

"You've got a death wish," Lestrade shook his head, bewildered.

"And you're just too slow," Margaret fired back at both Lestrade and Doyle, her words sharp and unapologetic. "If we'd waited around for Scotland Yard to apprehend the Moran brothers, we'd likely be corpses by now. So instead of hurling insults, you should be *thanking* us."

"*Thanking* you?" Doyle repeated, his voice tinged with outrage, as if the very idea was absurd. He took a few steps toward Margaret, stopping just inches from her. His eyes blazed with fury. "You're not an agent, not a detective, not even a bloody officer," he spat, disdain dripping from his words. "You're a simple secretary - nothing more."

Margaret leaned in even closer, meeting his fiery gaze with a childlike grin that bordered on mockery. "Then isn't it all the more embarrassing for you that I got to them first?"

Doyle visibly struggled to keep his temper in check. With a sharp turn, he stormed off, taking several officers with him.

"It goes without saying, we'll be having a word with them," Mycroft said coldly, his gaze locking onto Lestrade, towering over him both literally and metaphorically.

Lestrade opened his mouth, prepared to argue, but closed it just as quickly. There was no point. He knew well enough that going up against Mycroft Holmes was a battle he could never win. Holmes stood far above him - above anyone, really - and there was no arguing with that kind of power.

That same evening, Julius and Sebastian Moran were interrogated in separate rooms. Sebastian had the dubious honor of facing Mycroft and Margaret, while Doyle stood sulking in the corner, clearly displeased at being sidelined. Sherlock and Dr. Watson handled Julius, with Inspector Lestrade watching intently from behind, his arms crossed in quiet observation.

"Victor Trevor," Sherlock began, his voice cold and demanding. "What did you do to him?"

"Me?" Julius feigned confusion, his eyes narrowing slightly. "I did nothing to him. Haven't you already found his killer? You should know who it is."

"Who killed him?" Sherlock pressed, the sharpness in his tone cutting through the air.

"It wasn't me, I can tell you that much," Julius replied with an air of casual indifference. "And it certainly wasn't my brother either."

"Perhaps your nephew, then?" John prodded, his eyes keen for any sign of a lie.

Julius let out a condescending laugh. "Oh, please. Little Dave was only eight years old at the time. How could he have possibly killed a boy nearly his own age? I don't understand why you're dredging this up. It's been over twenty years. No one cares who killed Victor anymore. No one even remembers the boy."

"I remember him," Sherlock's voice grew taut with barely restrained fury. "He was my best friend."

"Oh," Julius mocked sympathy with a thin smile. "I didn't know that. But really, it can't be that bad. You've got a new best friend now, don't you?" He shot a smirk at John. "No harm done."

Sherlock's fist came crashing down on the table, his restraint finally snapping. "Who killed Victor?" he shouted, leaning in toward Julius, his eyes wild with rage. "Who?"

Julius leaned back in his chair, utterly unfazed by Sherlock's outburst. "She did," he said, his voice calm, almost bored.

"She? Who do you mean?" Sherlock's frustration was palpable, his voice edged with desperation.

Julius chuckled darkly, his smile twisting into something more sinister. "Oh, you know exactly who I mean, Sherlock. You know her all too well."

"Who is he talking about?" John asked, clearly confused as he turned to Sherlock.

"Margaret," Sherlock replied, his voice noticeably calmer now, as if a crucial piece of the puzzle had just fallen into place. It was as though Julius had unwittingly revealed more than he intended. Sherlock stepped back to stand beside Dr. Watson, his eyes narrowing in contemplation as they studied their captive. "He'll never admit it. He'll go to his grave insisting that she was the one."

"Then what do we do with him?" John asked, casting a wary glance between Sherlock and Julius, his voice edged with frustration.

Sherlock remained silent for a moment, his mind clearly racing. He watched Julius, whose smirk hadn't faded, a man all too comfortable in his web of lies and deceit. Finally, Sherlock spoke, his voice low and calculating.

"We wait," he said simply. Then he turned toward Lestrade, who had been observing in tense silence. "We have enough to hold him, don't we?"

Lestrade nodded, though his brow furrowed in concern. "Yes, but it won't last forever. We need something more concrete."

Sherlock's lips curved into a cold, determined smile. "Don't worry. We'll get it. He knows something he's dying to keep buried, and soon enough, we'll dig it out."

Julius met Sherlock's gaze, unblinking and unperturbed, his eyes gleaming with dark amusement. "You think you're so clever, Holmes. But this isn't one of your little mysteries. Some secrets are meant to stay buried."

Sherlock raised an eyebrow, unfazed by Julius' bravado. "Oh, I'm counting on it," he replied, his voice laced with menace. "Because when they're uncovered, they're always far more damning than anyone could imagine."

In the adjoining room, Mycroft and Margaret sat side by side at the table that dominated the center of the room. Opposite them, Sebastian Moran sat shackled in handcuffs, his demeanor as smug as ever. Inspector Doyle stood brooding in the corner, arms crossed, his face a storm of dissatisfaction.

"So, are you two going to play good cop, bad cop with me now?" Sebastian sneered, his gaze flicking between them. "How cute. You almost look like a couple."

Mycroft stiffened at the suggestion, unwilling to engage in the petty taunt. "Where is Thomas Montaigne?" His voice was sharp, cutting through Sebastian's jabs with practiced indifference. He knew Moran's words were nothing more than a distraction.

"How should I know?" Moran replied, his tone thick with false disinterest.

"Where is he?" Mycroft repeated, colder this time.

Sebastian, clearly enjoying the back-and-forth, leaned forward towards Margaret, licking his lips with predatory satisfaction as he fixed his gaze on her. "And what about you, darling? No words from you tonight? Shame, really. I was looking forward to this little rendezvous. Has something taken your voice?"

Mycroft's expression darkened, but before he could respond, Margaret spoke, her voice cutting through the air like ice: "Victor Trevor."

Sebastian reclined in his chair, as though the name brought back fond memories. "Ah, yes. Sweet little Victor. I liked him. Such a pity he had to leave us so soon." He turned his unsettling gaze back to Margaret. "It must be excruciating, losing your own brother. And then to forget all of it, only to be forced to relive that pain later. Amazing, isn't it? What the mind can do? Simply... fascinating."

Margaret remained unnervingly still, her eyes boring into the man before her, unmoved by his provocations.

"Why did you kill him?" Mycroft persisted, his voice taut with restrained fury.

Sebastian rolled his eyes with exaggerated boredom. "Honestly? I'm sitting here with two of the brightest minds I know. You, Mycroft Holmes, are surprisingly one of them. Who would've thought that the chubby oddball would grow into something formidable? You fascinate me, really. What's your secret? Starvation? Self-control? How did you do it?"

"Answer the question!" Mycroft snapped, his patience wearing dangerously thin.

"Oh, struck a nerve, have I?" Sebastian grinned, his eyes glittering with malice. "My sincerest apologies. But no, I didn't kill Victor. Why would I? Whoever's been feeding you that nonsense must be quite deluded."

The laughter that followed was as hollow and chilling as the man himself.

Margaret clenched both fists tightly, her entire body tensing with barely contained fury. She said nothing, but the storm inside her was palpable.

"Don't bother denying it," Mycroft warned, his voice cold as ice. "We have enough evidence to implicate you."

"Evidence?" Sebastian scoffed, laughing harshly. "What evidence? The word of *her*? A silly, foolish girl who doesn't even know her place? No judge, no jury would ever believe her." He

221

leaned forward, his eyes flashing with malice as they bore into Margaret. "You ridiculous child. Do you really think you can outsmart me? You failed once, and you'll fail again. I defeated you a long time ago - we both know that. No one will believe your story, so don't even try. It's pointless, just a waste of time. Look at you – weak. You're not nearly as clever as people say. If you were, I'd already be behind bars. But you? You're nothing but a cheap imitation of Sherlock Holmes, a naive little girl who thinks she can play detective with her childish fantasies. What do you know? Do you think anyone takes you seriously? You're just a girl. This world belongs to men. Men lead, men fight wars, men die for their country. And women? You lot stand on the sidelines, crying your pretty little tears."

Margaret's eyes narrowed, her voice steady but sharp as a blade. "A woman."

"What?" Sebastian's sneer faltered, confusion flashing across his face.

Margaret turned to Mycroft. "Montaigne's employer - it's a woman."

"No," Sebastian shouted, his voice rising in panic. His face drained of all color. "That's not true."

A sly smile crept across Margaret's lips. "Oh, but it is. You've just given yourself away," she said, her gaze unwavering. "You despise her. You hate her even more than you hate me, because she's smarter than you. She's more capable." Margaret's brow furrowed as she studied him intently. "No, it's more than hate. You're afraid of her. Who is she?"

"As if I'd ever tell you," Sebastian spat, his tone dripping with disdain. "You think you can impress me with your little tricks? How amusing. You see so much in the tiniest details, but you're blind to what's right in front of you."

What?

222

The words echoed in her mind, a cold shiver running down her spine. Montaigne had said something similar.

He's playing with me.

Margaret shot a glance at Mycroft. "He won't tell us anything," she said flatly, rising from her seat. "It's pointless." Without another word, she strode towards the door.

"Goodbye, little miss," Sebastian called mockingly after her.

Mycroft's gaze hardened as he stood. Without a second glance at Moran, he hurried after Margaret into the hallway.

Around the same time, Sherlock and Dr. Watson emerged from their respective interrogation room, both wearing the same look of frustration that mirrored Mycroft's and Margaret's.

"He's not talking, is he?" Margaret asked, directing her gaze toward Sherlock.

"Oh, he's talking," Sherlock replied dryly. "He's just saying all the wrong things. He claims you killed Victor."

"Of course," Mycroft interjected, "he won't betray his own brother."

"Is that so?" Sherlock snapped, irritation flaring. "Do brothers normally do that, Mycroft? Perhaps you could take a page from their book."

Margaret took a few steps away from the group, lost in thought, her shoes echoing softly as she paced down the corridor.

"Sherlock," John said, raising his voice slightly in a warning tone.

"What?" Sherlock shot back, his patience clearly thinning.

"Now's not the time for this," John urged.

"I'll decide when it's the time," Sherlock retorted.

"For once, he's right," Mycroft agreed with John, his voice calm but firm.

"And now you're siding with him?" Sherlock exclaimed, his frustration boiling over.

223

"Enough!" Margaret's voice rang out, sharp and full of anguish as she spun around to face them. Her eyes burned with a mix of fury and pain, the intensity of her emotion silencing the three men immediately. They stood frozen, staring at her in stunned silence. Just as Inspector Lestrade and his colleague Doyle emerged from the rooms, Margaret turned to them, her voice trembling with urgency. "What about David Moran?" she asked, her voice tight with desperation. "Have you found him yet?"

Lestrade shook his head solemnly. "No, we haven't."

"Check every hospital!" she pleaded, her composure slipping.

"He won't go to a regular hospital," Mycroft said, thinking aloud. "Not if he wants to remain hidden."

"To avoid being tracked, he'll seek out places that operate more anonymously," Sherlock added, picking up on his brother's line of thought. "Volunteer clinics, homeless shelters with medical staff - those are where you should start looking."

Lestrade nodded in agreement and headed off to relay the instructions, leaving Doyle lingering behind. He approached Margaret, his expression softening as he saw the turmoil in her eyes.

"Listen," Doyle began gently, "I'm sorry for what's happened, but this is bigger than you. You need to step back from this."

"I can't," Margaret's voice broke as she looked at him, tears welling up in her eyes. "This is all my fault. They're after me. I did something wrong."

The vulnerability in her words cut through the tension, leaving the room heavy with the weight of her guilt.

"You haven't done anything wrong," Doyle insisted softly, trying to soothe her.

"In the eyes of that woman, I have," Margaret retorted sharply. "And right now, her opinion is the only one that matters."

"Please," Doyle pleaded, his concern evident. "Step away from this. Go somewhere far from here, let us handle it."

"You just don't get it, do you?" Margaret's voice grew taut with frustration. "This woman will find me, no matter where I hide. She's always one step ahead of me. I'm not going to give her the satisfaction of running away."

"Alex..." Doyle began, but the instant he realized his mistake, it was too late.

"My name is Margaret!" she snapped, her voice a whip of raw anger. "I am Margaret. Alexandra Green has been dead for years." She fixed him with a piercing glare. Though Doyle had only been trying to help, his words grated on her nerves. Once, perhaps, she had felt something for him - more than she had wanted to admit - but those feelings had evaporated. Now, she could only feel contempt. Her dark gaze made it clear how little she thought of him now. "You don't know anything, Doyle. Nothing. So shut up and do your damn job!"

With that, she stormed past him, her heels clicking angrily against the pavement as she made her way outside the police station.

Her hands trembled as she fished out a battered pack of cigarettes from the inside pocket of her coat. She slid one between her lips, searching her other pockets for a lighter but finding none. "Damn it," she muttered under her breath.

Just as she was about to give up and put the cigarette back, Mycroft appeared, holding out a lit lighter for her. She gratefully lit her cigarette from the flame, taking a deep drag that immediately seemed to calm her frayed nerves. "Thanks," she said, exhaling a cloud of smoke.

Mycroft lit his own cigarette and offered a small, knowing smile. "For someone who quit, it's curious how you always manage to have a pack on you."

"Not always," she defended herself. "Only for the past few days." She watched as her smoke mingled with his in the chilly air, a strange comfort in the quiet. His presence alone steadied her. "It feels like everything's shifting, like everything I thought was solid is turning into something else, as if I'm living someone else's life."

"That's perfectly understandable," Mycroft said gently, his tone unusually tender. "You spent nearly your entire life living as someone else."

"And yet, deep down, I always knew." Margaret turned to face him, her eyes locking onto his. "Somewhere inside, I always knew who I really was. I just didn't want to admit it."

"Why not?" Mycroft asked, his curiosity evident, though his voice remained as soft as a whisper.

"Do you remember when you asked me what you had ever done to me?"

"It wasn't all that long ago," Mycroft replied, his tone carrying the faintest trace of his usual haughty inflection. "And you never answered my question." He paused for a moment, his inquisitive eyes narrowing slightly. "Why not?"

"Because I didn't know the answer at the time - at least, not consciously," Margaret admitted, her gaze never wavering from his. "You never did anything to me, neither you nor Sherlock. But somewhere deep inside, I blamed you both for Victor's death. That was the reason."

"And here I thought it was because Sherlock and I are smarter than you," Mycroft teased with a sly smirk.

Margaret gave him a playful shove on the shoulder, laughing. "Don't be ridiculous. Everyone knows I'm the clever one out of the three of us."

"Is that so?" Mycroft raised an eyebrow, feigning suspicion but unable to suppress his grin. "Perhaps it's only because you're a woman, and women tend to get preferential treatment."

"Intelligence has nothing to do with gender," Margaret shot back, glancing out onto the dimly lit street. "And besides, you don't actually believe that."

226

For a while, they fell into a comfortable silence, finishing their cigarettes, each lost in their own thoughts.

Margaret's mind lingered on the events of the last few hours. Sebastian Moran had revealed more than he intended, unaware that she had already crossed paths with Thomas Montaigne. It confirmed what she had begun to suspect - the Moran brothers were nothing more than pawns, manipulated by Montaigne's employer, who had likely kept them in the dark about the full scope of her plan, using their long-harbored hatred for Margaret to her advantage.

"They're just puppets in this game," Margaret mused aloud, her voice distant. "Julius and Sebastian Moran - mere pawns on the chessboard. The real move is yet to come."

Mycroft glanced at her, intrigued. Though he had suspected something similar, he hadn't pieced it together quite as clearly.

"He used nearly the exact same words as Montaigne," Margaret continued, her mind working through the puzzle. "*You see so much in the smallest detail, but you're missing what's right in front of you.* That's what Montaigne said to me - the night before he broke into your house." She turned to Mycroft, her expression darkening. "That can't be a coincidence. But Moran said it for a different reason. If he knew Montaigne had spoken to me, he would've chosen different words. Which means those words come from their employer. The question is - what is she trying to tell us?"

Mycroft's eyes narrowed, the weight of her deduction sinking in. "Indeed," he murmured. "The true meaning remains elusive, but one thing is certain - this game isn't over. And our opponent is far from finished. It must be tied to what happened back then, with Victor. What transpired at Abbey House." Mycroft's voice was low with contemplation. Unlike Margaret, he remembered everything about that time with painful clarity - at least, everything concerning him. And that was what troubled him most. He couldn't pinpoint anything that justified the elaborate nightmare they now found themselves in.

Margaret felt the same frustration. The fragmented memories slowly resurfacing in her mind were like pieces of a puzzle that refused to fit. Surely, Victor's murder was at the heart of it all - she already knew the identity of the real killer and the reasons behind it. Why then, this twisted game? The more she strained to recall the past, the deeper her uncertainty grew, and with it, a rising sense of dread.

Dread?

Why am I afraid?

What else happened back then?

"Did you have a dog back then?" she asked suddenly, as if hoping this simple detail might explain her growing fear. But Mycroft shook his head, gazing at her with a puzzled expression that crushed her faint hope. "Why did I avoid your house then? We were best friends, weren't we? So why was I rarely there? I mean, even before Victor and Sebastian Moran. What was it that scared me?"

Mycroft's face darkened as the memory resurfaced, something buried so deeply that even he had almost forgotten. "It was a long time ago - so long, in fact, that I've nearly forgotten it myself. Annabelle Sacker... the daughter of our first housekeeper. We used to call her 'the Witch.' She had... a talent for something terrible. She could manipulate people, bend their will with nothing but her words."

"What did she do? I don't remember her at all," Margaret asked, her voice trembling.

Mycroft hesitated, his gaze softening with the weight of the truth he was about to deliver. He hadn't wanted to tell her - it was too painful. But he knew that eventually, the full truth would come out, and it was better she heard it from him now. "Your father," he began, his voice breaking slightly. "When you and your parents first visited us... she got into your father's head. She convinced him... that he should kill your mother first, and then you."

228

Margaret froze, her eyes wide with horror.

"He fought it for as long as he could," Mycroft continued, his voice a strained whisper, "until one night-"

"-until he shot himself," Margaret finished for him, her voice barely audible as the familiar, terrible piece of the past clicked into place. That part, she had never forgotten. "She... that girl, she's the reason he's dead?" she asked, her voice cracking as tears began to stream down her face. "How is that possible?"

Mycroft couldn't bring himself to answer immediately, his own pain reflected in her stricken gaze. The past had been cruel, but now it seemed that its claws had come for them again, dragging forgotten horrors back to the surface.

"There are only a handful of people in the world capable of such mind control," Mycroft began gravely. "And Annabelle was exceptional at it - dangerously so."

"What else happened?" Margaret's voice trembled as she fought to keep her composure. "What did she do?"

Mycroft paled visibly, as though dredging up a memory too painful to bear. "She tried to make Sherlock jump off a cliff," he said, his voice hollow, each word weighted with the burden of a long-buried torment.

"She didn't succeed, did she?" Margaret's question hung in the air, but one look at Mycroft's haunted expression told her the answer. She gasped, horrified. "Oh my God."

"He stood there," Mycroft continued distantly, as though reliving the nightmare in his mind, "right at the edge, at the highest point. Below him, jagged rocks jutted out, and the icy waves crashed mercilessly against them. He just stood there, frozen, for seventeen hours. Motionless. Silent." He let out a deep, shuddering breath. "Thankfully, he doesn't remember it. He was only two years old then. And I'm grateful for that, because... it was the worst day of my life."

Margaret was stunned into silence. She had never seen Mycroft reveal such raw emotion, had never seen how deeply he cared for Sherlock. It struck her powerfully, this unexpected glimpse into the genuine, fraternal love he harbored for his brother.

Sherlock should see this now.

He should know just how much he truly means to his older brother.

The thought of sibling love stirred something painful in her heart. The ache of Victor's absence had never felt more profound than it did in this moment.

In the end, family is all that matters.

But what if you have no family left?

The bitter realization hit her like a blow, and the weight of it was almost unbearable. Her brother had been murdered as a child. Her father had taken his own life in a desperate attempt to save her and her mother. And her mother - her dear mother - had passed away five years ago, though Margaret had long since stopped believing it was a natural death, despite what the doctors had claimed.

She was truly alone now, and the cold truth of it gnawed at her soul.

"What happened then?" Margaret forced herself to focus, desperately trying to steer her thoughts away from the abyss threatening to swallow her.

"I climbed up to him," Mycroft began, his voice distant, as though he were watching the scene play out before him. "And I talked to him. Seventeen hours we spoke, Margaret. Seventeen long hours. Our parents were beside themselves when they found us, but they knew, they both knew there was nothing they could do. And then..." He paused, taking a deep breath, as if bracing himself for what came next. "Then he jumped. 'Love you, Mikey,' he said, just before he let go. If I hadn't been close enough, if I hadn't caught him by the arm and pulled him back-"

Mycroft's words trailed off into silence, the weight of the memory too much to bear. "For days, weeks, even months afterward, all he did was cry. Our parents were ready to send him to a doctor, to have him treated. But then, one day, he met Victor... and he started to laugh again."

Margaret turned away from him, her eyes stinging as she fought to hold back her tears. "I didn't know," she said, her voice barely a whisper, shaky with emotion. "The loss of a brother-" She choked on the words, trying to keep her composure. "It's a pain like no other, an emptiness that can never be filled. It tears a hole in your heart, a deep, black void, and it eats you alive from the inside, until you're nothing but an empty shell. You're lucky to still have Sherlock." She let out a tortured sigh. "I would give anything to see Victor again, even just once." She swallowed the grief, wiped her tears quickly, and turned back to face Mycroft. "Could it really have something to do with this Annabelle?" Margaret's confusion gnawed at her. "She must know who I am. Why did Montaigne call me Miss Green, then?"

"To deceive you," Mycroft replied, his voice full of quiet certainty. "If it is indeed her, then she's trying to mislead you at every turn. She knows you far too well, and-" He hesitated, locking eyes with Margaret, his expression grave. "She hated you."

"But why? What did I ever do to her?" Margaret's voice cracked with desperation.

"You were too clever for her. You always have been. You're like Sherlock and me - you stood between her and us." Mycroft's words cut through the haze of confusion like a knife.

"But I don't even remember her," Margaret protested, the frustration and helplessness mounting inside her.

"It doesn't matter," Mycroft said softly. "She hates you for the simple reason that you exist. For being who you are."

231

"She's blaming me?" Margaret asked, her confusion evident as she stared at Mycroft. "What happened to her after my father killed himself because of her?"

"She was committed to a psychiatric institution," Mycroft replied, his voice measured. "My family even covered the costs at the time."

"And what became of her? Is she still there? Don't tell me you forgot about her, Mycroft. That's not like you. I know you. You could never forget someone who almost murdered your brother."

"She was transferred to a different facility in Switzerland about fifteen years ago. Beyond my jurisdiction now. As an outsider, I have no rights regarding her anymore."

"And her mother?" Margaret pressed.

"She passed away last year. Lung cancer."

Margaret paused, thinking. "Then at least we know what triggered all this. Her mother's death." Mycroft frowned at her, trying to follow her reasoning. "She's clearly unwell, mentally. The loss of her mother must have caused severe psychological damage. I'd wager she's twisted all past events in her mind, convincing herself that we're somehow responsible for her mother's death."

"A distorted perception of reality," Mycroft mused, nodding. "If that's true, she's even more dangerous than I feared."

Just then, Dr. Watson and Sherlock emerged from the building, both looking slightly disheveled.

"What took you so long in there?" Margaret asked, eyeing Sherlock suspiciously, sensing from his furtive glance that he'd likely done something... underhanded.

"Gregson owes me a favor," Sherlock muttered nonchalantly, offering no further explanation as he began striding down the pavement away from the police station.

The others hesitated but quickly followed him, unsure of what exactly their enigmatic companion had just done - save for John, who seemed to know but kept quiet.

232

Margaret couldn't help but exchange a look with Mycroft as they walked. "Whatever he's done," she muttered, "I hope it works."

Mycroft simply sighed. "With Sherlock, one can only hope."

XIII.

THE BRUCE PARTINGTON CASE

"Must I truly do everything myself?" his employer's voice shrieked down the phone line. She was so loud that anyone passing by might think Montaigne had the speaker on.

"I've done exactly what you asked of me," the man replied, attempting to defend himself.

"Not quite. Mycroft Holmes is still alive."

"That was the plan, wasn't it? You specifically instructed me *not* to eliminate him yet."

"Ah, yes," the woman snapped, briefly pausing as if to recall her own instructions. "Change of plans. You're going to kill Alexandra Green. Tonight. I'll send you her exact location shortly. I want it done on-site, and I have no doubt she'll be in the same building as Mycroft Holmes. Do it there. And make sure there's plenty of blood. Is that clear?"

"What do you have against her?" the man asked, his voice laced with a rare note of curiosity.

"That's none of your concern!" she spat back, her tone sharp with impatience. "I was under the impression you were a professional. I was assured you don't ask stupid questions."

"Typically, I don't," he retorted, now feeling the sting of his own error. "But my usual targets are criminals or killers. I don't typically have innocent people on my list."

"What makes you so certain Alexandra Green is innocent? You don't know her. I, on the other hand, know her all too well. She's a vile person - she murdered her own brother," she lied with chilling conviction, her words dripping with venom. Montaigne believed her without a second thought. "Do what I've told you, and maybe,

234

just maybe, I'll show you some leniency." She hung up abruptly, leaving him in the flickering silence of the London street.

Montaigne strolled down a dimly lit sidewalk in central London, his hand still gripping the phone as if trying to absorb the intensity of her command. He slipped it back into his coat pocket, but it buzzed almost immediately. A message from his employer flashed on the screen, containing nothing more than an address: a street name and a house number.

"It's just five minutes from here," he muttered to himself, quickening his pace. As he walked, he began to envision the task ahead. He always carried a knife and a pistol, both reliable companions in his line of work. Tonight, he would use the knife. It would create more blood - precisely what she wanted. But it would also increase the risk. That was the part he relished. The danger, the adrenaline. He craved it, almost as much as the act itself.

Montaigne stood before the address, taking in the sight of the grand, silent building. No lights were on. "Who's still awake at two in the morning?" he muttered. "Well, aside from someone like me." With the agility of a seasoned climber, he scaled the drainpipe, his movements fluid and calculated. He made his way to a small ledge just beneath a window. He had already noticed from below that one window on the third floor was left slightly ajar.

"You're making this far too easy," he thought, slipping through the narrow gap and landing quietly in a wide hallway.

As soon as his feet touched the floor, a motion sensor flicked the lights on, casting an eerie glow over the hallway. The walls were adorned with unsettling oil paintings of gloomy landscapes, and far too many antique vases were lined up along the sides, their delicate shapes barely noticeable in the shadows.

Montaigne didn't know exactly which room his target was in, so he moved stealthily, creeping past each door with a practiced silence, pausing now and then to listen for any sign of life. "A murderer, they say," he mused to himself. "Didn't expect that. Odd, though - her eyes told me something different. There was guilt there, a lot of it. Perhaps it was for that? Could she really have killed her own brother? How twisted must someone be to do that?" He shook his head, his resolve hardening. "That makes it easier. She deserves what's coming. She's going to bleed for this."

Sherlock and Dr. Watson had long since retired for the night, likely deep in sleep by now. Mycroft and Margaret, however, had settled into the cozy confines of the library after returning from Scotland Yard. They sat across from one another, engrossed in ancient tomes and dusty manuscripts, the firelight flickering lazily in the dim room.

By two in the morning, exhaustion finally caught up with Margaret. She stifled a yawn, stretched, and rose from her chair. "Good night," she murmured, not particularly caring whether Mycroft even noticed. He was so absorbed in his reading that he barely acknowledged her departure.

Margaret didn't mind his lack of response. She was far too tired to be bothered by such things. Her body ached for sleep, and as she trudged up the stairs, her mind was already half-drifting into dreams. She wandered down the long, dimly lit corridor, her gaze lazily drifting over the dark, oil-painted portraits hanging on the walls - art that, in her drowsy state, seemed more sinister than beautiful, like eerie, twisted imitations of Van Gogh's world.

Halfway down the hallway, the lights suddenly blinked out, plunging her into total darkness.

"Stupid motion sensor," she muttered to herself, frowning. "I *am* moving. Do I need to dance to get your attention?"

She was too weary to be genuinely annoyed, but the inconvenience only added to her foggy frustration. She trailed her fingers along the wallpaper and wooden paneling as she blindly continued forward, her steps slow and hesitant. Then, without warning, her foot slammed into something hard. A sharp pain shot through her toes, and before she could even curse, she heard the unmistakable sound of a vase crashing to the floor, shattering into a thousand pieces.

"Dammit!" she hissed, wincing at the thought of how expensive that vase had likely been.

Mycroft will kill me for this.

She stood frozen for a moment, hoping that he hadn't heard the commotion coming from upstairs. Sighing, she knelt cautiously, groping around in the dark to gather the shards. But she hadn't even managed to collect two pieces before one of them sliced deep into her palm.

"Dammit!" she cursed again, this time more sharply as the pain flared.

She was about to stand when she suddenly froze, every nerve alert. There, at the far end of the corridor, she heard it - the faintest sound of breathing. Quiet, deliberate.

Her exhaustion vanished in an instant, replaced by an acute awareness of the danger lurking in the shadows. Margaret's heart pounded in her chest as she strained her ears, certain that she wasn't alone anymore.

"Who's there?" Margaret demanded, abandoning the shattered vase as she swiftly rose to her feet. "If that's you, Sherlock, this isn't funny." She peered into the oppressive darkness but could see nothing.

That's not Sherlock.

An icy dread crawled up her spine, and panic surged within her. In a split second, her mind raced through her options, calculating her next move.

237

My room is too far from here - and too close to whoever that is.
Whoever they are, they'll reach the door before I can.
Sherlock and Watson are directly upstairs - so too far away.
But Mycroft... he's awake.
He's my only hope.

She pivoted abruptly and sprinted down the hallway, but before she could cover any real distance, a hand grabbed her from behind, yanking her to the ground. The overpowering stench of whiskey and cheap cigars filled her nostrils.

Montaigne.

Margaret landed hard amidst the shards of the broken vase, her already injured hand slicing open again as it hit the sharp pieces. Without hesitation, she grasped the nearest shard, oblivious to the fresh cut it made in her palm. Her survival instincts kicked in, drowning out the pain. She crouched, then lashed out with the shard, plunging it into the unseen assailant behind her.

A man screamed in agony and recoiled, his grip instantly loosening.

Margaret couldn't see where she had struck him in the pitch-black hallway, but she didn't care. The attack had worked - she was free. She scrambled to her feet and bolted towards the staircase. As she neared the light, she braced herself against the banister, her bloodied hand leaving smudges on the wood. She cast a single glance back into the shadows behind her. But the darkness revealed nothing.

With her heart racing and her hand throbbing painfully, Margaret descended the stairs as fast as her legs would carry her, bursting into the library and slamming the door shut behind her.

The noise startled Mycroft, who jerked upright, his eyes widening in confusion as he saw her.

Margaret, pale as a ghost and trembling uncontrollably, stood by the door, blood dripping from her right hand onto the polished floor. Her breath came in ragged gasps, and she clutched her in-

238

jured hand to her chest as if to keep herself from unraveling entirely.

"What happened?" Mycroft asked, his voice laced with shock.

"He's here," she managed to say between gasps. "Montaigne."

Mycroft's face twisted in horror. Without wasting a second, he pulled Margaret away from the door, sat her down in the chair he had been reading in just moments before, then swiftly returned to the door, locking it from the inside. His movements were quick and deliberate as he rushed to one of the overstuffed bookshelves and pulled out a thick, black leather-bound book.

Margaret watched in confusion.

Why a book?

Shouldn't he be reaching for a weapon?

But then, the mystery was solved. Hidden inside the hollowed-out pages was a revolver, along with a box of ammunition. Mycroft calmly loaded the weapon, his hands moving with the precision of someone well-versed in such actions. He moved back toward the door, glancing at Margaret with an intensity that was as protective as it was commanding.

"Lock the door behind me! Let no one in!" he ordered firmly, opening the door just a crack.

"Mycroft!" Margaret cried, fear gripping her as she sprang to her feet, rushing toward him.

He turned sharply, catching her by the shoulder with his free hand. "You stay here!" he said, his eyes locking onto hers with an unyielding seriousness.

"But-"

"No!" he cut her off, his tone steely and unrelenting. "Do as I say!" With that, he vanished into the dark corridor, leaving her no choice but to seal the library door behind him.

Shaking with panic, Margaret pressed her hands to her temples, pacing nervously in the now eerily quiet room. The adrenaline coursing through her veins momentarily dulled the pain in her right hand, but as she glanced down, she saw the blood still flowing freely from the gashes she had received. The sharp, throbbing ache returned with full force.

Desperate for anything to distract her from Montaigne's lurking presence, she scoured the room - searching for another weapon, a first-aid kit, something, anything. But the library held nothing but rows upon rows of dusty old books.

Her gaze drifted to a small side table next to the armchair. Mycroft's phone lay there, silent and undisturbed. She had paid it no mind until it vibrated suddenly, displaying "DI Lestrade" on the screen before fading back to black. Without hesitation, she grabbed the phone, but quickly found herself frustrated - it was locked, and only Mycroft's fingerprint could unlock it.

Cursing under her breath, she put the phone back in its place, pulling out her own and dialing Lestrade's number.

"Miss Trevor," Lestrade answered, his voice tinged with surprise. "You're still awake? Has Mycroft told you what's happened? He was supposed to keep it to himself. I'm... I'm sorry things have escalated this far. But rest assured, we're handling it. My team is already on the search for her."

Liz.

Damn it!

"If anything happens to her," Margaret hissed, her voice trembling with fury, "you'll be a dead man. And Doyle too. How could you let this happen? The Secret Service was supposed to be protecting her!" She took a shaky breath, her heart pounding with a mix of rage and helplessness. "Do you at least have any news about David Moran?"

"Not yet," Lestrade admitted, sounding equally tense. "But Gregson's working on a promising lead. We're closing in."

"Is that it?" Margaret asked, her voice trembling with barely suppressed anxiety.

Lestrade, sounding more than a little irritated, responded, "And what exactly do you expect? That we walk out there, and Moran will simply be waiting for us with open arms? If you were on the run, would you make it that easy?"

Before Margaret could answer, a deafening shot rang out in the background.

Mycroft!

She flinched violently, her heart racing in terror.

Montaigne.

The gravity of the situation crashed over her. She had momentarily forgotten the peril they were in.

"What was that?" Lestrade's voice crackled through the phone, now sharp with alarm. He had heard the shot as clearly as she had. "Did someone just fire a gun? What in God's name is happening over there?"

"Montaigne's here!" Margaret's voice trembled, her body shaking uncontrollably as the reality of the danger hit her with full force.

"What?!" Lestrade shouted in disbelief. "And you're just telling me now? I'm on my way!" The call ended abruptly.

Another shot echoed through the corridors, followed by the unmistakable sound of shattering glass. The crash reverberated in Margaret's chest, as if the walls themselves were trembling in fear.

Her mind raced. Mycroft. The thought of him facing Montaigne alone was unbearable. Even though Mycroft had a gun and the skillset of a former top-tier intelligence agent, Thomas Montaigne was no ordinary adversary - he was a trained assassin, cold, calculating, and ruthless. Margaret's heart pounded as she wrestled with her fear. Mycroft could be hurt - or worse. She couldn't just stand by and wait for someone else to act. The very idea of losing him, knowing she could have done something, was impossible to bear.

Her hands trembled as she opened the library door and stepped into the dimly lit corridor, the soft light of the house casting ominous shadows. The stairwell loomed at the end of the hall, a gateway to whatever chaos awaited above. She had no weapon, nothing to defend herself with. Her eyes darted around until they landed on an old black umbrella propped in a nearby stand. It wasn't much, but it was something. Grabbing it with a firm grip, she hurried toward the stairs.

Another shot rang out, louder this time, the unmistakable crack of a bullet tearing into the wooden paneling nearby. The air felt thick with tension, and every instinct told her to run in the opposite direction. But she couldn't. Mycroft was up there, and she wasn't going to leave him alone.

As Margaret raced up the stairs, her mind filled with fragments of half-formed plans and desperate thoughts. She reached the landing, her breaths shallow and rapid. A few steps ahead, the hallway stretched out before her, filled with silence once more, but she knew Montaigne was close. She could feel his presence, lurking just beyond the veil of darkness.

Her heart hammered in her chest. Would she find Mycroft alive - or would she be too late?

Before Margaret could react, someone grabbed her and pushed her into a corner, pinning her against the wall. A hand swiftly clamped over her mouth, silencing any cry she might have made. The darkness enveloped them both, but the proximity of the stranger allowed her to feel the fine texture of an expensive tailored suit brushing against her discount sweater. Relief surged through her - it was Mycroft. There was no mistaking him.

Silence fell between them. Neither moved. The tension in the air thickened as they stood frozen in place. Then, with a soft hum, the motion-sensor lights flickered on, illuminating the hallway.

Margaret blinked, her eyes adjusting to the sudden brightness. She looked up to find Mycroft standing directly in front of her, his hands still gripping her shoulders tightly. His gaze bore into hers, the unmistakable blend of fear and concern etched into every line of his face. He was clearly shaken by what had just occurred.

"What the hell is all this about?" Sherlock's voice echoed down from the third floor. He descended the stairs quickly, his sharp eyes taking in the scene. When he saw his brother and Margaret pressed so close together, he stopped midway. His lips curled into what was almost a sneer, but then his gaze fell on Margaret's bloodied right hand, gripping a black umbrella like a lifeline. The caustic remark he'd been about to make died on his tongue. He paused, unusually speechless for once.

Mycroft stepped back, releasing Margaret as his attention shifted down the corridor. The destruction was evident - broken vases scattered across the floor, some paintings lying shattered and trampled beside their frames, and at the far end, a windowpane had been smashed, shards of glass glinting in the dim light. But of Thomas Montaigne, there was no sign.

"Is this chaotic gunfire something that runs in the family?" John Watson's groggy voice drifted toward them as he stumbled down the stairs, half asleep. "It's nearly three in the morning. Can't you people just sleep like normal humans? Or are you all completely mad?"

"Montaigne was here," Margaret explained, her voice tense as she exchanged a glance with Mycroft.

At the mention of that name, both Sherlock and John blanched, their faces drained of color.

"Enough!" Mycroft snapped, his frustration boiling over. "This ends now, once and for all." Without another word, he turned on his heel and stormed downstairs, heading straight for the library to retrieve his phone. "I'm increasing the security level immediately."

As he vanished from sight, John noticed the severity of the wound on Margaret's hand, the blood steadily dripping onto the floor. "That needs bandaging," he said, more awake now, and gently took her by the arm, guiding her down the stairs.

Sherlock, seemingly unmoved by the chaos, yawned as he turned to head back upstairs. "Well then, good night," he muttered nonchalantly, waving them off as he resumed his trek to the upper floor, leaving the others to deal with the aftermath.

Mycroft grasped his phone, quickly reading through the message from Inspector Lestrade before dialing him immediately.

"Are you alright?" Lestrade's voice came through, breathless and urgent, as though he were running down a street.

"Elizabeth Markle has disappeared - Margaret's closest friend," Mycroft replied, his voice strained. "Why are you asking if *I* am alright?"

"What about Montaigne? Did you catch him?" Lestrade pressed, his concern palpable.

Mycroft's confusion deepened. "How do you know about Montaigne…?" A sudden thought struck him. Glancing at his phone, he noticed the smear of blood on its surface. "Margaret," he deduced grimly.

"We'll be there in a moment," Lestrade called out, his voice strained with effort. And indeed, just then, the doorbell rang.

Mycroft pocketed his phone and walked to the door. Standing there was Lestrade, flanked by a squad of about fifteen armed officers. Mycroft's eyes narrowed in mild irritation. "You're too late," he muttered, exasperated, rolling his eyes. "He's already gone." Without another word, Mycroft turned and led the group inside.

He headed straight for the kitchen, where Margaret was perched on the edge of a table, her wounded hand being carefully bandaged by John Watson.

Lestrade followed Mycroft in, his expression unreadable. Mycroft's gaze locked on Margaret, and there was no mistaking the displeasure in his tone. "You were on my phone," he said, his voice edged with stern reproach.

"All I saw was Inspector Lestrade's number," Margaret replied defensively.

"Then you don't know…" Relief washed over Mycroft's face, but it was short-lived.

Margaret stood abruptly, fury blazing in her eyes. "Oh, I know!" She stormed toward him, her voice shaking with anger and hurt. "You told me she was safe!" she shouted, her voice rising. "You gave me your word, and I *trusted* you!" The rage swelled within her, almost uncontrollable. "If anything happens to Liz, Mycroft, you'll have a serious problem with me!"

She brushed past him, her anger tangible as it radiated off her.

"Margaret, please, wait," Mycroft pleaded, reaching out and catching her by the wrist.

"Let me go!" she snapped, her tone fierce. She wanted nothing more than to slap him, but her injured hand throbbed in protest, and her other hand was still firmly held by him. "I don't want to hear *anything* right now. No 'I'm sorry,' no excuses. You can keep your empty words to yourself. Liz is more than just a friend – she's the only family I have left. She's always been there for me, even when she was at her lowest. Without her, I have *no one*."

Mycroft's grip faltered, and he released her.

"If she dies," Margaret continued, her voice low and dangerous, "that blood is on *your* hands. And when I'm done with you, you'll wish you had never been born." With that, she stormed upstairs, her fury trailing behind her like a dark cloud.

The room remained still for a moment, the weight of her words hanging in the air. Mycroft stood frozen, uncharacteristically shaken, as Lestrade watched him with a mixture of sympathy and helplessness. Watson, silent in the corner, could only shake his head, knowing there was little anyone could do to console her now.

"Women," muttered Lestrade after a long pause, shaking his head. "They're truly peculiar creatures."

John shot him a disdainful glance. "She may be peculiar, but by God, she's right." He threw Mycroft a disappointed look and then turned to head upstairs.

As he passed Margaret's room, he paused. From behind the door, he could hear the muffled sound of her crying. John hesitated for a moment, torn between the instinct to give her space and the urge to offer her comfort. He knew it might seem intrusive but leaving her alone in this state felt even worse.

He knocked softly. The sobbing quieted but did not cease. After a brief hesitation, he opened the door and stepped inside.

Margaret sat huddled in the corner, curled up on the floor, a broken figure consumed by sorrow. Her tears flowed freely, her body shaking with the weight of grief.

Dr. Watson said nothing. He understood that words, no matter how well-intentioned, would offer her little solace right now. Instead, he crossed the room quietly, sat down beside her on the cold floor, and gently wrapped an arm around her, pulling her into a comforting embrace.

"She can't die," Margaret whispered through her sobs. "Liz is all I have left."

"She won't," John assured her softly, his voice steady and filled with compassion. He gently stroked her shoulder, offering what little comfort he could. "We won't let anything happen to her."

For a moment, neither spoke. The room was filled only with the quiet sound of Margaret's weeping and the soft, steady breathing of John beside her, his presence a silent anchor in the storm of her anguish.

"What?" Montaigne answered the call, irritation lacing his voice as he darted through a dimly lit alley. "What now? First, you demand I kill her, then you change your mind. What am I supposed to do now? Turn back again? Listen, Lady! I don't care how much you're paying me if you're going to change your orders every five minutes. It's been over two weeks since I last took someone out. If you don't give me a proper assignment soon, you'll have to find someone else for this circus."

His caller laughed, the sound light but dripping with menace. "You can't simply walk away, Thomas. Have you forgotten what I'm capable of? You've witnessed firsthand the destruction I can cause with nothing more than my words. I promise you, I'll make it my mission to torment you until your dying breath, something I would personally find quite enjoyable. So, I suggest you choose your words carefully. Any one of them might be your last. It would be such a waste to spend a bullet on you, don't you think? Besides," she added with a sinister grin that was nearly audible, "I am a woman. It is my prerogative to change my mind. Now, if you've calmed yourself, I have a target for you. One that you may dispatch immediately, and I swear on everything I hold dear, I won't be changing my mind this time."

Montaigne's grip tightened on the phone, still agitated but listening closely.

"This individual is someone who, unfortunately for me, knows Alexandra Green a bit too well. They pose a threat, and it's imperative that this problem is... removed. You may handle it however you see fit, but it must be done tonight. Do we understand each other?"

Her voice held the finality of a judge passing a sentence, leaving no room for debate.

The next morning, Sherlock sat cross-legged on the cobblestone driveway outside his brother's estate. His eyes were closed, as though he were meditating, utterly indifferent to the bemused stares of passersby who looked at him as if he'd escaped from an asylum. He appeared oblivious, his mind completely elsewhere, lost in the labyrinth of his own thoughts. His mental journey through his mind palace gave the impression of a man wandering aimlessly through a maze, searching for an elusive truth. The notion that someone other than Moriarty or the Moran brothers wanted him dead both puzzled and unsettled him. Despite the enemies he'd accumulated over the years, none of them seemed to fit this new threat.

"What do Mycroft, Margaret, and I have in common? Aside from Victor? What else was there? I know something else happened, but it must have been before the incident with Victor," he mused, his mind racing. "She was hardly ever at our house. Why? Was she afraid? Afraid of what? Or better yet, of whom? Who else was there back then?"

Before he could follow this train of thought any further, the front door swung open, and Margaret stepped outside, cigarette in hand, ready to light it. She paused, her brow furrowing in confusion when she saw him seated on the ground.

"Sherlock?" she called out, uncertain. "What are you doing?"

To her surprise, Sherlock sprang to his feet, his usual brooding demeanor replaced by sudden energy. He darted over to her, plucked the cigarette from her hand, and lit it for himself without hesitation, taking a deep drag before asking abruptly, "What were you afraid of?"

Margaret frowned, caught off guard. "What?" She retrieved another cigarette from the pack, her last one, and lit it with a flick of her lighter. With a casual flick, she tossed the now-empty carton into a nearby bin.

"Back then," Sherlock clarified. "Abbey House. Why did you visit us so rarely? Victor was there almost every day."

"Of course, he was," Margaret replied, watching as her own cloud of smoke dissipated into the crisp morning air. "He was your best friend."

"And you were Mycroft's best friend. So why didn't you come around more often? Who were you afraid of? It couldn't have been me - I doubt you'd bite someone you're frightened of."

Margaret smiled, a glimmer of nostalgia in her eyes. "You cried like a little girl."

"I was six!" Sherlock retorted, offended.

"And I was only four," Margaret shot back, clearly amused as she recalled the memory.

Sherlock rolled up his sleeve, revealing the deep bite marks, the scars still starkly visible. "You bit down like an animal."

"You called Mycroft an animal, so it was only fair. Honestly, you should have been kinder to your brother."

Sherlock sighed dramatically, rolling his eyes. "You sound just like my parents. 'Don't be so cruel to Mycroft. He's your elder brother,'" he mimicked his mother's voice with a surprisingly accurate imitation.

Margaret chuckled, amused by his impression, but her tone shifted to seriousness. "Older brothers are the best thing anyone can have."

"Not when they're named Mycroft Holmes," Sherlock replied with theatrical disdain.

"Especially when they're named Mycroft Holmes," Margaret said, her voice firm.

For a moment, Sherlock stared at her, puzzled by the intensity with which she defended his brother. It didn't quite make sense to him, but he suspected it might be because Margaret had a certain fondness for Mycroft. After a brief pause, he realized something. "You still haven't answered my question."

Margaret shook her head, irritated.

You two are more alike than you realize.

"What were you afraid of back then?" Sherlock pressed, his voice sharper now.

"Ask your brother," she replied, exasperation lacing her words. "I can't remember her."

"Her?" Sherlock's curiosity sharpened instantly.

"Annabelle Sacker," Margaret said, watching his reaction. "Does that name mean anything to you?"

"The witch," Sherlock whispered, a chill running down his spine as he recalled the name. He couldn't help the involuntary shudder that overtook him.

"You remember her?" Margaret asked, surprised and somewhat alarmed. Did Sherlock know what she had done to him all those years ago?

"She killed your father," Sherlock replied, his voice tinged with an uncharacteristic fragility. His usually pale face turned even whiter as he spoke the words. He didn't recall much more about her, but the mere memory of Annabelle filled him with a sense of dread he couldn't shake. "Terrifying what a child is capable of."

Margaret swallowed hard, struggling to push down the painful memories. After a deep breath, she said, "I believe she's behind everything that's happening now."

250

Sherlock froze. The thought had never crossed his mind until that moment, though now it seemed the only explanation that made sense. Perhaps he had avoided it because, deep down, the idea of her involvement terrified him more than anything else. "If you're right," he said, his voice strained, "then we're in far deeper trouble than we thought." The cigarette he held did little to calm his nerves. "Annabelle is capable of horrors. It'll be nearly impossible to stop her. Our intellect won't save us here. She's above us - far above us. She'll outwit us and destroy us."

"But you stopped her once before," Margaret reminded him, trying to instill a shred of hope in his increasingly anxious mind.

"Back then, she was still a child," Sherlock muttered grimly. "Now, she's a grown woman. That makes her unstoppable."

"So, there's nothing we can do?" Margaret's voice trembled with frustration, the edge of hopelessness creeping in. "Are we supposed to just sit here and wait for her to kill us? Damn it!" Her eyes locked onto Sherlock's with a fierce intensity. "You're *Sherlock Holmes*," she said firmly, as though the very name itself was a weapon. "If anyone is her equal, it's you." Margaret was desperate to rekindle the fire in him, to pull him out of this unsettling defeat. "I've followed all your cases, Sherlock. No matter what she's capable of, she can't outmatch you."

Sherlock stared at her, stunned into silence. He ground the cigarette butt under his shoe, staring down at the crushed filter, and in some way, he seemed to resemble it - flattened, used up. "You don't know her," he murmured, his gaze still fixed on the ground. "No one is her equal. Least of all me."

"Why are you so terrified of her?" Margaret asked, perplexed. She'd never seen him like this - so bent, so strained. It was as though he had become someone entirely different. "She killed my father, not yours." Although Margaret knew what Annabelle had done to Sherlock all those years ago, she couldn't help but push. She needed to know why the mere memory of that woman haunted him so deeply. "What did she do to *you*?"

Sherlock shifted nervously, unable to meet her gaze. His feet shuffled against the cobblestones, as though he could somehow escape the onslaught of images flooding his mind - long-buried memories he had fought so hard to forget. The scenes sharpened, sending a tremor through his frame. His voice wavered as he whispered, "Victor." It was soft, barely audible, the name of his long-dead friend breaking from his lips like the whimper of a child who had just glimpsed a ghost.

"Sherlock." Margaret's tone softened as she placed a hand gently on his shoulder. "What happened?" Her heart ached to see him like this. She had never witnessed such vulnerability in him before.

"He stayed with us once - just once," Sherlock managed, his words short, clipped with tension. "And she was there. She talked to him. For a long time. It was... horrific." He shivered, as though the cold fingers of that memory still clutched at his heart. "He was different after that." His voice broke entirely, and the rest of his sentence dissolved into silence. The memory was too raw, too unbearable to voice.

"What happened next?" Margaret's voice was a whisper now, hoping against hope that Sherlock might continue.

But it was Mycroft's voice that answered from the doorway behind them, grave and solemn. "She convinced Victor to kill Sherlock."

Margaret's breath caught in her throat.

Mycroft stepped further into the light, his presence casting a long shadow over the both of them. "When I found them," he continued, his words heavy with memory, "Victor was on top of Sherlock, his hands wrapped around his throat, squeezing with all his might, while the witch stood beside him, ordering him to press harder."

Margaret stumbled back, her mind reeling. The revelation struck her like a blow. Her own brother - Victor - had once tried to murder Sherlock, his best friend. The weight of that truth settled

252

over her like a suffocating blanket, crushing her under the enormity of it. Her heart twisted painfully.

She felt as though the ground had opened beneath her, and everything she thought she knew had shifted. Victor - her beloved Victor - had been twisted into something monstrous by the dark manipulations of Annabelle Sacker. The pain of that knowledge cut her deeper than any physical wound. She felt utterly shattered.

"I didn't know," she whispered, her voice thick with grief. The image of her brother, trying to kill Sherlock, broke something inside her. Tears brimmed in her eyes as the full weight of her loss settled over her heart. And the looming shadow of Annabelle Sacker felt more terrifying than ever.

"It wasn't his fault," Mycroft said, stepping forward from the shadows. He had quickly recognized the weight Margaret was carrying from this revelation. "Victor had no control over his actions. She manipulated him. There was nothing he could have done. None of us could have."

"How is that possible?" Margaret's voice trembled with disbelief. "She was just a child. How could she do something like that?"

"Annabelle Sacker was never *just* a child," Sherlock interjected, turning toward them. His eyes were dark, seething with the deep hatred he had carried for years. "She was born a witch."

Margaret took a few steps away from the brothers, her mind racing as she tried to piece together what it all meant. Annabelle had tried to kill Sherlock twice now. But why? What was it about him that provoked such obsession?

Was she merely bored?

Or did Sherlock's intelligence threaten her in some way?

And why hadn't Annabelle targeted Mycroft or herself in the same way?

No, it had to be about him.

Suddenly, she spun on her heel and looked directly at Mycroft, a question burning in her eyes. "What else did she do?" she asked, her voice thick with suspicion.

Mycroft's face grew tense, his usual air of composure cracking ever so slightly, but he didn't answer.

"Mycroft!" she demanded, her tone sharper. "What did she do to you? It can't all have been about Sherlock. If it were, my father's death wouldn't make any sense..."

Her words stopped abruptly as a chilling realization took root. For the first time, she understood the real reason behind it all.

"It's because of *you*," she whispered, staring at him intently. "She wanted to make *you* suffer. Victor's attempt on Sherlock's life, my father's death - meant to take my mother and me with him. All of it traces back to one common thread - *you*, Mycroft. She wanted you to watch us all suffer. She wanted you to feel that pain." Margaret paused, studying him with an intensity that made the air feel heavier, more suffocating. "So, tell me," she continued in a quieter voice, almost a plea. "Why? What is the reason for all of this?"

Mycroft stiffened and instinctively took a step back, as if retreating into the distant recesses of his memory. The image of something long buried rose sharply to the surface, a scene from a time when Sherlock had just been born and Annabelle, barely two months into her stay at Abbey House with her mother, had been nothing more than a curious, unpredictable child.

He could see it now, as clearly as if an old film reel were playing before his eyes.

Mycroft, only seven at the time and all gangly limbs, had spent the entire afternoon chasing a vibrant butterfly through the knee-high grass of the estate. He had pursued it with all the intensity and precision of a young boy lost in his world of curiosity.

Annabelle, just five years old then, had appeared suddenly, emerging from the house with her wide, inquisitive eyes.

"Do you want to play?" she had asked, her voice innocent yet piercing, as though the mere sound of it disrupted the delicate balance of the world around them.

Her presence alone, however, had startled the beautiful yellow butterfly he had been tracking for hours. It fluttered away in an instant. Mycroft, utterly dismayed, had stomped the ground in frustration.

"No!" he had shouted at her, his eyes still following the butter-fly with a longing gaze as it vanished beyond his reach. "You scared it away!" His young voice trembled with anger as he turned on her. "All those hours... wasted!"

"I'm sorry, Mikey," Annabelle had whimpered, her eyes wide with regret, though there was a lurking sharpness behind them even then. "I didn't mean to."

"That doesn't help," Mycroft had snapped, turning his back on her with cold indifference. He stalked away, furious, muttering under his breath, "Stupid girl." His words had not been loud, but they had been just loud enough for her to hear.

"I'm not stupid!" she had screamed, her small voice now raw with hurt. In a sudden, fierce burst of emotion, Annabelle had charged at him, her tiny hands shoving Mycroft to the ground with more force than any child her age should have possessed.

Before he could even comprehend what had happened, she was on top of him, her fists raining down in a violent flurry. "I'm not stupid!" she had screamed again and again, her voice filled with a disturbing mixture of anger and desperation.

Mycroft, overwhelmed and terrified, had cried out for help, flailing wildly under her assault. But in that moment, he had been powerless against her. Powerless against the rage that had exploded from her in a way that made no sense for a child so young.

His mother and Mrs. Sacker had rushed out of the house, drawn by Mycroft's desperate cries for help. Mrs. Sacker had

255

struggled to pull her daughter away from him, while Mrs. Holmes, deeply concerned, gathered her injured son into her arms.

"I hate you!" Annabelle had screeched, her small face contorted with fury. "I'm not stupid! You're the stupid one! You'll pay for this! I hate you!" Her screams were abruptly silenced when her mother, blushing with embarrassment, clamped a trembling hand over her daughter's mouth.

"I'm terribly sorry, Mrs. Holmes," Mrs. Sacker had stammered, her voice trembling with anxiety. "My little Annie isn't usually like this. I don't know what came over her. Please, forgive her." She pleaded, lowering her head in shame.

For a moment, Mycroft's mother had stood frozen, staring at the scene with wide-eyed shock. Then her gaze turned sharply toward her son, her expression hardening with disapproval.

"What did you do to the poor girl?" she demanded, her voice sharp with accusation. "Shame on you, boy! I didn't raise you to behave like this."

"I didn't do anything!" Mycroft had protested, his voice thin and shaking. "I didn't do anything to her."

"Liar!" Annabelle had shrieked again, her voice filled with venom. "You're a nasty liar! He didn't want to play with me! He said I was stupid!" she sobbed, looking up at her mother with tear-filled eyes.

Mrs. Holmes, without another word, grabbed Mycroft by the ear and pulled him to his feet. "Mycroft Arthur Holmes!" she scolded, her tone filled with authority. "How dare you say such a thing? Go to your room immediately! I expect you to reflect on what you've done. And at dinner, you will apologize to Annabelle properly and sincerely."

Just as it had happened all those years ago, Mycroft recounted the story to his brother and Margaret. In his youth, he hadn't understood that he had done anything wrong, but now, he saw things in a different light. "It's my fault," he admitted in a state of shock.

"No, it's not," Margaret swiftly interjected. Her anger toward him had entirely dissipated. In that moment, she had completely forgotten about her friend Liz. "Annabelle is a psychopath, Mycroft. It wouldn't have made a difference if you'd been kinder to her back then. She simply needed a target, and unfortunately, that was you." She couldn't continue, for her phone suddenly rang. She pulled it from her jacket pocket and glanced at the display. A wave of relief, mixed with anxiety, washed over her as she answered. "Liz? Where are you?"

"Please help me," Liz whispered in fear. "It's so dark here."

Margaret quickly put the call on speaker so Sherlock and Mycroft could hear as well. "Can you see anything? Is there a window where you are? Or can you hear anything nearby?"

"I can hear water, like a large river flowing. There's a wide bridge with lots of people on it, but none of them see or hear me."

"A bridge with lots of people," Sherlock repeated quietly to himself, sifting through his mental map of London. In record time, he identified several possible locations. "What about inside?" he asked. "I assume you're in a building, or the people would at least hear you. What does the room look like?"

"It's dark. There's only a narrow window, and no other light. Everything feels damp and smells moldy. The walls seem really old."

Sherlock processed the information with lightning speed, fitting each clue into place. "That's the old printing house by the Thames," he declared with unwavering certainty. "From there, you can see directly across to the Millennium Bridge. The building has been abandoned for years, slated for demolition, but its foundations are protected as a historic site."

"Stay calm!" Margaret commanded, her voice firm yet comforting. "We're coming for you, and we'll get you out of there."

"Please hurry," Liz pleaded, her voice breaking into sobs. "She'll be back any moment and..." Static crackled, abruptly cutting off the connection.

"Liz? Liz!" Margaret shouted into the phone, but there was no response. "Damn it."

Sherlock and Mycroft, who had only been half-dressed in their haste, dashed back into the house to properly attire themselves. Margaret followed swiftly, her unease intensifying with every step. By the time the brothers reappeared, fully dressed and ready, her sense of dread had blossomed into something much darker. Before they could rush headlong into danger, she stopped them at the door, her voice firm with suspicion.

"How did you know it was the printing house, Sherlock? There are plenty of bridges crossing the Thames, and numerous buildings within sight of them."

"I solved a case there a few years ago," Sherlock replied.

"The Bruce-Partington case," Mycroft recalled. "It was all over the news back then."

"This can't be a coincidence," Margaret said, her mind racing. "Why would Annabelle choose that exact location? It's almost certainly a trap."

Mycroft narrowed his eyes, sharing a quick glance with his brother. "She's right."

"Possibly." Sherlock pulled out his phone and dialed quickly. Holding it to his ear, he waited for the line to connect. "Inspector Lestrade? Meet us at the old printing house near Millennium Bridge. Elizabeth Markle is being held there." He listened intently as Lestrade spoke, his expression darkening. His eyes widened in shock, then briefly closed as if absorbing bad news. "When?... Who?... Damn it! We'll meet you there." He hung up and turned to Margaret, his face grim. "David Moran is dead."

"What? How?" Margaret's voice trembled, disbelief filling her eyes.

"There were no fingerprints, no physical traces, but there was blood. A lot of it. They suspect Thomas Montaigne, but there's no concrete evidence," Sherlock explained as he moved past her and strode out into the street. The others followed swiftly, their pace quickened by the urgency of the situation. Sherlock's mind was racing. "It's odd, though," he mused aloud. "Why would Montaigne kill Moran? They were on the same side, weren't they?"

"Perhaps he knew too much," Mycroft speculated, his voice steady.

"Too much about what?" Margaret asked, her confusion evident.

Sherlock, with a swift, deliberate motion, hailed a passing taxi as they reached the curb. "About you," he answered, holding the door open for her with the practiced ease of a gentleman.

"That doesn't make any sense," Margaret muttered as she slid into the back seat, followed closely by the Holmes brothers.

"Where to?" the driver asked, his voice carrying a subtle Asian accent.

"3 Bankside, Southwark Street," Sherlock replied sharply, causing the driver to pull away immediately. Then, turning his attention back to Margaret and Mycroft, Sherlock continued as if no interruption had occurred. "It doesn't *need* to make sense," he remarked, the intensity in his voice undeniable. "Annabelle Sacker is a deranged psychopath. Nothing she does or says will ever make sense to a rational mind. But that's precisely the point. Her behavior tells us everything we need to know. She's completely unhinged, acting on impulse, without a shred of consideration for the consequences. If her actions *did* follow some sort of logic, then we'd have to assume someone else was pulling the strings. But as it stands, it's just her. Alone."

"She seems dangerous enough on her own," Margaret said, her voice edged with discomfort.

"But we're three," Mycroft replied, his tone firm with determination. "And the brightest minds in all of Britain."

Margaret glanced around the small confines of the taxi, suddenly realizing something was missing from their team. "Where's Dr. Watson?" she asked, her brow furrowing in concern.

"Working," Sherlock said dismissively, as if that were explanation enough. "Probably somewhere in a clinic or tending to some animal. He's a doctor, doing what doctors do."

"Alone?" Margaret's skepticism deepened. A knot of worry tightened in her stomach - she feared Watson might be in danger as well.

"Inspector Doyle is with him," Sherlock added, waving off her concern. "Not that John needs any help. He's quite capable of handling himself."

Since entering the cab, a peculiar smell had begun to permeate the air, faint at first but now growing stronger. It was a sharp, exotic blend of spices - aniseed, cloves, something almost intoxicating. The scent thickened with each breath they took.

"What is that? Do you smell it?" Margaret asked, her voice muffled as she raised a hand to cover her mouth and nose. Her question lingered in the air as an unsettling white mist began pouring from the taxi's air vents, slowly but steadily enveloping the back seat in an eerie fog.

The mist coiled around them, thickening by the second. Margaret felt the sudden, irresistible pull of fatigue. Her eyelids grew heavy. Mycroft's head lolled to the side, and Sherlock, always sharp, tried to shake it off, but even he couldn't resist the swift onset of unconsciousness. One by one, they succumbed to the fumes, slipping helplessly into the dark.

XIV.

ANNABELLE

The pungent smell of chemicals and toxins filled her nostrils as Margaret slowly regained consciousness. Groggy and disoriented, she pushed herself up, her head spinning as she tried to make sense of her surroundings. She was in a small, starkly lit room, two of its walls made of thick, transparent glass. The other two walls were of cold, unyielding concrete, and behind her was a door, heavy and unwelcoming.

Fear gripped her as she looked straight ahead. Through the glass, she saw Sherlock and Mycroft sitting opposite her, bound to their chairs, their hands tightly fastened to the armrests. Thick strips of tape were cruelly slapped across their mouths. Both brothers were staring at her, their eyes filled with desperation.

Panicked, Margaret scrambled to her feet, rushing towards the glass. She pressed her hands against it, but the barrier refused to yield, solid and indifferent to her struggle.

"It's pointless, my dear," said a voice. The sound was like smoke curling in the air - low, distorted, and deliberately ominous. A figure emerged from the shadows, stepping into the room with the Holmes brothers. The woman's face was obscured, and her movements, though graceful, carried a cold, calculated menace. "That's bulletproof glass," she continued with a smirk in her voice. "Even a pistol couldn't scratch it."

"Who are you? What do you want?" Margaret shouted, her voice edged with panic. Though she couldn't yet see the woman's face, she could tell by her slight frame, her voice and the sharp click of high heels that it was a woman.

The figure let out a soft, mocking laugh. "You really don't remember me, do you?" she said, her voice filled with malice. "After all the suffering I've caused you?"

Margaret's breath caught in her throat. Recognition hit her like a shock of cold water. "Annabelle," she whispered, her eyes widening in disbelief. "Why are we here?"

Annabelle Sacker, still concealed by the shadow, tilted her head slightly, as if amused by the question. "Do you really not know?" she asked, almost disappointed. "Can you not even *imagine* why I would bring the three of you here? Of all people?"

Margaret's mind spiraled into chaos, her thoughts careening wildly.

Why?

What had they done to her? Why *them*? Why were *they* the ones in this nightmarish prison?

'Mycroft must die,' Margaret recalled the chilling message she had seen in her mind's eye, the words haunting her like a dark prophecy.

Mycroft?

Why him?

Why not Sherlock?

Why not me?

Her eyes darted between the two brothers, tied up and helpless. She was free - unbound. Why?

What is she planning?

Margaret's pulse raced as her thoughts spun into confusion. Was she meant to witness Mycroft's death, to be tormented by it? But then why that cryptic message? Was it because Mycroft had saved Sherlock all those years ago?

None of it made sense. The harder she tried to piece together the puzzle, the more disjointed her thoughts became, like the pieces were being deliberately scrambled.

262

Annabelle, sensing Margaret's disarray, stepped further into the light but kept her face in shadow, reveling in her captive's inner turmoil. "You're overthinking it, Margaret," she taunted, her voice like poison. "It's simpler than you realize. This isn't about logic. It's about pain - *your* pain."

Margaret's heart pounded in her chest, her mind drowning in a torrent of questions and fear.

"I thought you were supposed to be clever," Annabelle sneered, her voice dripping with malice. "I was told you were smarter than Sherlock - smarter even than his brother, Mycroft." She laughed, a sound full of contempt. "But it seems they lied to me. You're nothing but a fool. Ordinary, dull, and dim-witted."

Margaret heard her, but the words hardly registered. Instead, her eyes swept across the room, taking in her surroundings with sharper focus. They were all trapped within a maze of interconnected glass containers. Each square chamber was separated by thick, transparent walls, and at various points along these partitions, Margaret noticed hinges - door mechanisms disguised within the glass structure. Her eyes flicked back to the glass in front of her. It wasn't just a wall; it was a door that separated her chamber from the one where Sherlock and Mycroft sat bound and gagged. Meanwhile, Annabelle stood in her own separate compartment, insulated from the others, with only one exit behind her.

"No," Margaret finally spoke, her voice steady. "I'm not like Sherlock, and I'm certainly not like Mycroft. Whoever said I was clever doesn't know the first thing about intelligence. I'm just a simple secretary."

Annabelle cackled, the sound dark and malevolent, as if the very devil had risen from the depths. Margaret had played right into her hands. "Ah, humility - the first step toward self-realization. In the end, you're just like all the other ordinary people, aren't you? How disappointing." She paused, relishing the moment. "I had hoped for so much more. Everyone needs an adversary, don't they? A true nemesis. Sherlock has Moriarty. Mycroft has Sherlock. And you, Margaret, you have me. And you have had me for the past five years."

With that, Annabelle stepped out of the shadows, her voice returning to its normal pitch. Margaret's heart stopped. The figure before her wasn't Annabelle Sacker after all - it was Elizabeth Markle, her best friend.

Liz tilted her head slightly, allowing Margaret a clearer look at her face. "For over five years, I've been right in front of you, and you never noticed. You're so infinitely clever, and yet you failed to see what was right before your eyes."

"Liz!" Margaret gasped, rushing to the glass and pressing her hands against it. "What is this? I don't understand. Why?"

"Of course you don't understand," Liz spat back, her voice twisted with bitterness. "You're far too stupid to grasp it. But that's not your fault, is it? Stupidity runs in your family." She took a few slow steps toward Margaret, her eyes gleaming with cruel intent. "Just like your father. Instead of saving his own life by killing you and your mother, he took the coward's way out and killed himself. If he were alive today, if he knew what he'd really done to the two of you, I'm sure he would've made a different choice. He could've spared you both so much suffering. What an incredibly selfish man he was."

"Stop!" Margaret cried, her voice breaking as old wounds were ripped open, her father's memory crashing back into her like a tidal wave of grief. But the most insidious part was that she could feel herself starting to believe Liz's words.

Would it have been better?

Would we have been spared all this pain?

The thought clung to her, dark and oppressive.

"What do you want?" she asked, struggling to shake off the growing shadow of doubt.

264

Liz, or Annabelle - or whoever this woman had become - smiled coldly. "I want you to understand," she said. "To understand what it feels like to be nothing. To be broken."

She took a few steps to the side, stopping before a panel of switches and buttons on the wall. Without hesitation, she flipped a small lever.

Behind Margaret, a compartment at eye level slid open, revealing a small, dark object. Unsure, she turned her head to glance at it, her instincts screaming caution. Slowly, she approached.

"Take it!" Liz commanded, her voice sharp and unforgiving.

Margaret reached into the compartment and pulled out a pistol. The cold weight of the weapon in her hand sent a chill through her, making her acutely aware of the gravity of what was to come. As she turned back toward Sherlock and Mycroft, the glass partition that separated them groaned open with a soft, eerie creak.

"You have exactly one bullet," Liz said, her voice dripping with twisted glee. "Only one of them will die today. And you, Margaret, get to decide who. Sherlock or Mycroft."

Margaret's heart pounded as she stepped closer to the brothers, her mind waging a war within itself. She kept the gun lowered, unable to raise it against either of them. She halted before them, their faces etched with desperation, their eyes silently pleading for her to make a choice. But Margaret's own eyes, filled with helplessness, begged for an answer - anything to tell her what to do. "I can't," she whispered, her voice fragile. "I'm not a murderer."

Liz laughed, a cold, cruel sound that echoed through the room like a predator toying with its prey. "Look at it another way, my dear," she purred. "You only need to kill one of them. By doing so, you'll save the other. Isn't that something? A small mercy. So, who will it be? Sherlock - the stubborn, drug-addled genius with his delightful sociopathic tendencies? Or Mycroft - the most powerful man in London?" Her grin widened, devilish. "It's hardly a difficult choice. I see it in your eyes." Liz's gaze pierced Margaret, as if she were an exhibit in some twisted carnival. "Love outweighs reason, doesn't it?"

She knows.

The realization hit Margaret like a bolt of lightning. Liz's words unraveled everything in an instant.

That's why the message.

That's why Mycroft.

She had known all along. Known how much Mycroft meant to Margaret, even when she had buried those feelings deep, tried to forget.

Liz had always known.

Margaret had been nothing more than a pawn in Liz's twisted game, a puppet dangling on strings that had been pulled years before.

"You want me to kill Sherlock," Margaret said, never breaking eye contact with him. Her voice was steady, though her hands trembled. "You know me. You know Mycroft. You knew I'd choose him." Slowly, she raised the pistol, pointing it directly at Sherlock. Her hand quivered slightly as the tension in her body turned her limbs to stone. "You've driven me mad so many times," she said softly to Sherlock. "Everyone compares me to you - or worse, calls me some cheap female imitation. It's always been you. And I never stopped blaming you. For Victor." Her voice faltered. "I thought… I always thought he died because of you. But I was wrong." Her hand lowered, the pistol falling limply at her side, and her gaze dropped to the floor. "I can't do it. I won't."

"Why not?" Liz's voice was sharp, incredulous. She hadn't anticipated this.

Margaret looked up, her expression filled with a sorrow that ran deeper than any hatred. "Because," she said, her voice gaining strength, "I'm not like you. I don't kill to win. And I won't play your game." She looked at Sherlock and Mycroft, both still bound, their fates teetering in the balance. "They don't deserve this. Neither of them."

Liz's amusement drained from her face, replaced by a cold, calculating fury. "Then you've just sealed your own fate," she hissed, stepping toward Margaret with lethal intent. "This is your last chance! Choose one of them, or all three of you will die today."

"If I kill Sherlock, then Mycroft dies too," Margaret said, her gaze fixed on the floor. Slowly, she raised her eyes to Sherlock, who was staring at his brother with a look of confusion. He had no idea how much he truly meant to Mycroft, no real understanding of the bond they shared. But family always came first, always. "And if I kill Mycroft," Margaret continued, her voice quivering with anguish, "then I die." Her eyes brimmed with tears as she locked them on Mycroft. "No matter what I choose, two lives are lost. Which leaves only one option."

Mycroft shifted nervously in his chair, the realization of what she was about to do hitting him like a cold wave. He thrashed against his bonds, screaming through the tape that muffled his voice. He could see it in her eyes, and it terrified him. He couldn't allow this - he had promised her.

Margaret lifted the pistol and pressed it to her temple, her gaze never leaving Mycroft's. In her pained eyes, he saw her silent farewell, and it tore through him like a blade. It felt as though her heart was being ripped from her chest. "This is my choice," she whispered.

Liz's eyes widened with a mixture of surprise and twisted amusement. "Oh!" she exclaimed, her voice gleeful, as if savoring an unexpected twist in her cruel game. "How thrilling."

"I'm sorry, Mycroft," Margaret choked out, her voice heavy with sorrow. Her hand trembled as she kept the gun to her head. "Please, forgive me," she whispered.

Mycroft's muffled roars grew frantic, his body thrashing wildly as he tried, in vain, to break free from the chair. He knew, beyond any doubt, what she was about to do. He shouted through the gag, his words coming out in desperate, garbled fragments: "No! Don't! Please, no!"

"It has to be this way," Margaret said, her face etched with torment. "One day, it won't hurt as much. You've lost me once before, and you survived. You'll survive this, but not Sherlock's death. I know you. And without you, I won't survive either."

Mycroft continued to struggle, his eyes wide with horror, his hands and feet thrashing violently against the restraints. His muffled cries - begging, pleading - were heartbreaking, a desperate man trying to halt the inevitable.

But I have to do this.

And you know it too.

"I'm sorry," Margaret said softly, placing her finger on the trigger. Her eyes never left his, even as memories flashed before her in a whirlwind - fragments of her past with him, jumbled and bittersweet.

I love you, Mycroft.

Those words were caught painfully in her throat, weighing her down as though they might crush her. She couldn't speak them; she knew they would only deepen his agony. Instead, she thought of how she might make it easier for him to say goodbye, how she could lessen his suffering. She didn't want him to live with the pain of her loss. "Actually... I'm not sorry."

Mycroft's eyes widened in disbelief. For a moment, he hoped he had misheard her, but the resolute look in her eyes shattered that hope. She meant it. The pain of that realization rippled through him, and he froze, staring at her in shock.

Margaret held his gaze, her heart breaking, but her resolve solidified. This was her final act, and she needed him to understand - to live with it, without guilt, without torment. "You and I... how did you ever imagine it would work?" Her voice trembled, but it was firm, each word measured as she stared into Mycroft's eyes. "We're not like the others. We're not normal, and we never will be. Love is like cancer. It clings to you, never lets go, and in the end, it kills you. We will never be capable of loving each other, Mycroft. You know that as well as I do. You're terrified of it - just like me. Emotions cloud judgment. Emotions make us weak. They destroy us. They destroy *me*." She took a deep breath, her chest tight with the weight of her next words. "Even though we are so much alike, we could never live together. Yes, I like you, but nothing more." Her voice cracked, the lie almost too painful to speak. "I do not love you."

Mycroft shook his head violently, refusing to accept what she was saying. He could see through her words - or at least he believed he could. He had to. He couldn't bear to believe she was telling the truth.

"Forgive me," she whispered. Her finger remained on the trigger, poised for the final, irreversible step. Margaret closed her eyes. Her lips trembled. She pulled the trigger.

Mycroft's scream tore through the air, but then... silence. No gunshot. No searing pain. Nothing.

There was no explosion of sound, no bullet leaving the barrel. The room remained still, as if time itself had frozen.

Liz's laughter cut through the quiet like a blade. Sharp. Mocking.

Margaret's eyes fluttered open, confused and alive. Her heart pounded in her chest, but she was unharmed. "What?" She looked at the gun in her hand, utterly bewildered. Fumbling, she pulled the magazine out. It was empty.

"Did you really think I'd hand you a loaded gun?" Liz asked, her voice dripping with malicious amusement as she strolled forward, her glee barely contained. "I knew exactly what you'd do. I know you too well. You're so *predictable*. So utterly... *boring*."

Rage surged through Margaret like a wildfire. She hurled herself toward the glass wall, fists pounding against it in fury. "You!"

she screamed. "How could you? Why are you doing this?" She struck the glass so hard that all the interconnected chambers rattled from the impact. The glass trembled under her blows.

Why is it moving?

Panic turned to realization.

Bulletproof glass doesn't move like that.

This isn't real.

It's a trick.

Her eyes blazed with newfound determination as she gripped the pistol tighter and began smashing it against the glass, each strike more furious than the last.

"NO!" Liz's voice cracked with panic, her previous confidence unraveling. Her eyes darted frantically around the room, realizing her ruse had been exposed. "Damn it!" she cursed, her plan falling apart before her eyes. Without another word, she bolted across the room, fleeing through a wide door at the far end, disappearing into the shadows above.

Margaret watched her go, breathless, but she wasn't done yet. She *couldn't* be. This was far from over.

Sherlock and Mycroft thrashed against their restraints, stamping and shouting as loud as their bonds would allow. But Margaret was consumed by a rage so intense that their cries barely reached her. All she saw, all she could focus on, was the glass wall between her and her quarry. With the butt of the pistol, she hammered the glass with relentless fury. A loud groan echoed through the chamber, the glass buckling under her assault before finally shattering into a thousand glittering shards that scattered across the floor like broken dreams.

The moment the opening was large enough, Margaret leapt through, heedless of the jagged edges still clinging to the frame. Without so much as a glance back at the Holmes brothers - now abandoned to their fate - she darted up the staircase in pursuit of

Liz, or rather, Annabelle Sacker, the woman who had been hiding behind a mask all these years.

As her feet pounded up the steps, thoughts swirled in her mind, chaotic and relentless. The distant wail of police sirens barely registered in her consciousness, muffled as though they were a world away, even though they were rapidly approaching.

What have I done to her?

The question gnawed at her, fierce and unyielding.

What is the reason for all of this?

She tried to make sense of it as she ascended, two steps at a time, her breath ragged with both effort and fury.

Does this all come back to Victor?

She's furious with Mycroft for saving Sherlock all those years ago... but what does she want from me?

The betrayal cut deep. Liz, the woman she'd thought was her best friend, had been nothing more than a puppet master - Annabelle Sacker, hiding in plain sight. Margaret's heart twisted painfully at the realization.

Has she used me all this time just to get to Sherlock?

The thought was suffocating. Margaret had always believed in her friendship with Liz, had trusted her, confided in her. Now, all of it seemed tainted, a web of lies spun with one goal in mind - destruction.

But why?

Margaret's eyes narrowed as she reached the landing, her mind snapping back to the present. The answer still eluded her, but one thing had become brutally clear: Annabelle wasn't just trying to destroy Sherlock and Mycroft. She was coming after Margaret too, targeting her in ways Margaret hadn't even fully grasped yet.

And whatever the reason, whatever long-buried hatred fueled Annabelle's twisted game, Margaret was determined to put an end to it, once and for all.

Margaret stepped onto the rooftop, her breath clouding in the frigid air. A biting wind whipped through her hair, its chill cutting deep. Above, the night sky was clear, dotted with stars, while the restless city of London buzzed far below, unaware of the dangerous game unfolding.

Liz stood motionless at the edge of the rooftop, her back to Margaret. She stared silently down at the dizzying drop, her figure cast in shadow.

"It's over," Margaret called out, her voice hoarse and breathless from the chase. She cautiously stepped closer. "Scotland Yard is on the way. The building's surrounded."

Liz turned slowly, her eyes burning with hatred and anguish. Her lips curled into a wicked grin, a cruel mockery of any human emotion. "Over?" she spat, her voice dripping with venom. "It's not over for me. Not yet."

"Why are you doing this?" Margaret's voice trembled, not from fear but from the deep hurt of betrayal. "What have I ever done to you?"

"You let him die," Liz's voice was low, simmering with fury. "You stood by and did *nothing*. You, with all your cleverness, couldn't even save your own brother."

"I was four years old!" Margaret cried, her voice breaking. "What could I have done?"

"You could have protected him!" Liz's voice rose, shaking with rage. "That's what siblings do - they protect each other. But no, you thought only of yourself, just like you're doing now. Instead of freeing your so-called friends, you chase after me. You've always been selfish. You lived your entire life as someone else and didn't even realize it. How could you forget your own brother?"

Margaret flinched, the accusation cutting deeper than any blade. "I didn't forget him on purpose," she said, her voice quieter, filled with raw pain. "It was the car accident... That's why I couldn't remember. I lost everything that day."

Liz faltered, her certainty cracking. "What car accident?" she demanded, her voice wavering.

Margaret took a slow, steadying breath. "It was after Victor died. I looked for him the whole day, running through the rain, desperate. My mother came to get me, late that night, and the Moran brothers - they tried to kill us. You know this."

"No!" Liz screamed, her voice wild with disbelief. "You're lying! That never happened!" Her grip on reality seemed to slip, her hands shaking violently. "You just *forgot* him. You let him die, and now you want to rewrite history to ease your guilt. This is your fault - *all* of it!"

Margaret took a cautious step forward, hands raised in a placating gesture, but Liz's reaction was instant. She whipped out a pistol from her coat pocket, the cold metal gleaming under the city lights. Her hand was steady as she aimed it directly at Margaret's head.

"Stay where you are!" Liz barked, her voice sharp with panic and rage. "One more step and I'll put a hole right through that clever little brain of yours."

Margaret froze, her heart pounding in her chest. "Please, Liz," she said softly, her voice full of quiet desperation. "You have to believe me. I'm telling you the truth."

But Liz's eyes were wild, her mind spinning out of control. The weapon trembled in her hand as the weight of everything - years of manipulation, lies, and twisted vengeance - bore down on her. "No," she hissed, her breath coming in ragged gasps. "You're lying. You've always been lying."

Margaret's heart pounded in her chest as she faced her, the gun still pointed at her. Liz's words felt like daggers, twisting deep into her already broken soul.

273

"Do you really think I could ever forget Victor?" Margaret's voice cracked, raw with the pain she could no longer contain. "Since the moment my memories of him returned, not a single second has passed where I haven't thought of him. I miss him more than words can say. And every time I have to remind myself that he's truly gone, that I'll never see him again - it feels like I'm losing him all over again. How dare you say I've forgotten him?"

Liz's eyes narrowed, watching Margaret intently. The weapon trembled slightly in her grip, but she didn't lower it completely. It was clear that she was weighing her next move, plotting one last twist to escape the tangled web she had spun. Slowly, her expression softened, as if a new, sinister idea had formed in her mind. "What would you give to see him again - just once? What would you sacrifice for that chance?"

Margaret's brow furrowed in confusion, her grief clouding her mind. "Everything," she whispered, the ache in her voice palpable. "Anything - and more."

"Even your life?" Liz's voice was calm, almost soothing. Margaret hesitated, her mind reeling, as if struggling to process the question. Seeing her uncertainty, Liz's lips curled into a wicked grin, sensing that she had finally ensnared her old friend in her trap. "They're all gone, Margaret - your father, your mother, your brother. You're alone. Completely and utterly alone. Wouldn't it be better to join them?"

The gun in Liz's hand dipped ever so slightly, her words like venom sinking into Margaret's thoughts. "They've been waiting for you, you know. For so long. They miss you far more than you could ever miss them."

Margaret's eyes glazed over, her breath shallow as Liz's manipulative words took root. She turned mechanically, moving toward the edge of the rooftop. The wind whipped at her hair and clothes, but she barely felt it. Grief had blinded her, and Liz's voice was all she could hear now, leading her like a siren's call.

"Yes," Liz crooned, her voice lowering to a soft, sinister whisper. "Step closer. They're waiting for you, longing to see you again." She watched with sadistic pleasure as Margaret mounted the low parapet, standing at the very edge, staring down at the abyss below.

The flashing blue lights of police cars blinked far below, their beams flickering in the night, barely registering in Margaret's dazed mind. A gathering of officers milled around the vehicles, but Margaret paid them no heed.

Liz took a step forward, savoring the moment. "Remember Victor's voice? His sweet, innocent smile? They're all waiting for you, Margaret. They've missed you so much. Don't make them wait any longer. Jump! Be with them again."

Margaret teetered at the edge, her arms hanging limply at her sides. She looked down at the ground far below, her mind swirling with memories of Victor - his laughter, his kind face, his tragic death. She could almost hear him now, his voice calling her, beckoning her to follow him into the void.

Liz's voice turned darker, more insidious. "Can't you hear him, Margaret? He's calling out to you. Your father is, too. They're all waiting, just for you. Follow their voices! Jump!"

"Margaret!" Mycroft's voice cut through the chilling night, filled with a desperation that shook even the wind. He raced up the stairs, breathless, his eyes wide with panic as he reached the rooftop.

But it was too late - Margaret was already at the edge, her toes hanging over the abyss, the world below ready to claim her.

"Don't do it!" he begged, standing as close as he dared to the two women, his gaze fixed on Margaret.

"I have to," Margaret murmured, her voice distant, her eyes locked on the dark void beneath her. Tears streamed silently down her cheeks, but she was too far gone to notice. "They're calling me. I need to go to them."

275

"No, they're not! Those voices - they aren't real. That's Anna-belle. No one is calling you!" Mycroft's voice trembled, but his tone was urgent, desperate to reach her through the fog of delusion.

"But I must!" Margaret sobbed, her entire body trembling with despair. "I have no one left. They're all dead, and they've been waiting for me for so long."

"They can wait longer!" Mycroft pleaded, his voice a fragile thread of hope. "Listen to me! Listen to the sound of my voice!"

"I can hear Victor," she whispered, her words filled with long-ing. "He wants me to come. I'm so sorry."

"No!" Mycroft shouted, stepping closer, his heart hammering in his chest as he fought to keep his voice steady.

"There's only one place left for me," Margaret continued, her voice hollow. "With them, I won't be alone anymore."

"You're not alone here either," Mycroft said gently, his eyes locked on her with an intensity that nearly broke him. "You have me."

Liz, who had been silently observing with a growing unease, couldn't allow this. Mycroft's words threatened to unravel every-thing. Her voice rose sharply, trembling with barely concealed frustration. "He's lying!" she spat. "Don't listen to him. He's al-ways used you, Margaret. In Mycroft Holmes's eyes, you've never meant anything. He doesn't want to free you - he wants to trap you here, in this miserable world, so you can keep suffering. That's all he's ever wanted. Can't you see?"

Margaret, who had been swaying dangerously at the edge, took Liz's venomous words as truth. She stepped closer to the precipice, her toes now fully over the ledge. The wind gusted violently around her, making it hard to balance. But still, she stood, barely holding her ground as the abyss beckoned.

"Let her go, Mycroft!" Liz commanded, her voice a serpent's hiss. "Let her find peace with her family. Let her go where she belongs. You can't save her. Save her by letting her go! It's the only way. Besides," Liz's voice turned cruel, dripping with malice, "she doesn't love you. She's told you herself - she never has, and she never will. No one will. You're a cold, heartless man, unworthy of love."

Her words slithered around Margaret like chains, pulling her deeper into her despair, further from the ledge of sanity. All the while, none of them noticed Sherlock, moving stealthily across the rooftop. His sharp, calculating eyes took in the scene as he crept closer, his footsteps as silent as the wind.

When he was finally near enough, and Liz's vile words had reached a crescendo, Sherlock had to do something. "That's quite enough!" he barked, and with one swift, decisive motion, he delivered a blow that sent Liz crashing to the ground, her twisted smile wiped from her face as she fell unconscious.

Freed from the spell Liz had cast over her, Margaret blinked, the fog of her mind lifting. But the sudden clarity came at a terrible cost. Realizing where she stood, she panicked, her body tipping dangerously forward as she lost her balance. Her arms flailed wildly, but it was no use. The rooftop vanished from under her feet as she plunged into the yawning abyss below.

"Mycroft!" she screamed, her voice lost to the wind as her body plummeted towards the dark streets below.

Mycroft lunged forward, his heart hammering in his chest as he leaned over the edge of the building. At the very last second, he grabbed Margaret's wrist with an iron grip, as if his entire existence depended on it.

Margaret dangled precariously, her body pressed against the cold, unforgiving side of the building. A wave of pure, paralyzing terror surged through her, rooting her to the spot. She glanced down into the abyss below, and the vertigo of the drop sent a fresh surge of panic crashing over her.

"Margaret!" Mycroft shouted, his voice sharp with urgency. "Look at me!"

With great effort, her eyes slowly rose to meet his. "Please," she whispered, her voice trembling with fear. "Don't let me fall."

"I won't," Mycroft said, his tone unwavering, filled with a fierce determination. "I promised you I wouldn't lose you again, and I intend to keep that promise."

Desperately, Margaret tried to find something - anything - to grab onto with her free hand, but the smooth surface offered no hold. Her grip in his hand began to slip, inch by inch, and panic flared anew in her chest. She could feel herself sliding away from him. Her voice was soft but filled with regret. "I'm sorry," she gasped, her breath hitching in fear. "I lied to you before."

"I know," Mycroft replied, his lips curling into the faintest of smiles. "I know, because I love you too."

Margaret's eyes widened in shock. Those were the last words she had expected to hear from him, especially in this moment. But hearing them, coming from him, gave her a spark of hope, a lifeline she hadn't realized she needed.

"I don't care what anyone else thinks or says," Mycroft continued, his voice softening. "Not even what I once thought myself. Love isn't a weakness - not when you love the right person. And you're the right person for me, Margaret. You always have been, and you always will be." He exhaled deeply, as though a heavy weight had been lifted from his chest. Then his eyes sharpened, and he extended his other hand to her. "Take my hand," he commanded, his voice steady and clear.

"I can't," she whispered, her voice tight with despair. She knew she didn't have the strength. The distance was too great, her muscles too weak. If she tried, she would slip from his grasp, and that would be the end. She would fall, and she would die. But despite the fear gripping her, she didn't want that end.

"You can," Mycroft insisted, his tone leaving no room for doubt. "You *will*. Just try."

278

"That'll make your grip slip," she protested, her logical mind already calculating the outcome, her voice trembling. "It won't work."

"Forget what you know. Forget the statistics, the calculations, and all your logic," Mycroft said, his voice thick with emotion. "Just do what your heart tells you. Do what you want."

For a moment, the world seemed to freeze. The sounds of the city below faded into nothing. Margaret stared up at him, her mind racing, torn between the safety of inaction and the terrifying unknown of trusting him, of trusting herself.

And then, with every ounce of strength left in her, she made her choice.

Margaret gazed into Mycroft's pain-ridden eyes, knowing he couldn't hold onto her much longer. She had mere seconds before her strength failed her, before gravity would pull her away from him forever. But in that fleeting moment, she shut out the inevitable, focusing only on the one overwhelming truth.

I don't want to die.

That thought alone consumed her, becoming the single driving force that pushed everything else from her mind. Margaret drew in a deep breath, held it, and with every ounce of will left, swung her free arm upward, desperately trying to grasp Mycroft's outstretched hand. Her fingers grazed his, but she missed. She slipped further, the icy grip of death creeping closer.

It won't be enough.

I'm going to die.

Tears streamed down her face as she locked eyes with Mycroft once more. And even as despair tightened its hold around her, she forced a trembling smile. "I'm sorry," she whispered, her voice breaking.

"No!" Mycroft shouted, instantly knowing the fatal resignation that had settled over her. He lunged forward, straining to hold onto her, but his foot slipped, nearly sending him over the edge with her.

His heart pounded in his chest as he fought to steady himself, his grip faltering.

"I love you," Margaret's voice floated up, soft yet final, as her fingers slipped from his. In that terrible instant, she fell.

Mycroft's scream tore through the night. His soul shuddered violently, every part of him wanting to leap after her, to join her in the descent. But Sherlock, swift and unrelenting, grabbed him by the shoulders and dragged him back from the edge of the roof, pulling him away from the abyss.

Mycroft stood there, dazed and disoriented, staring at the empty space where Margaret had once been. The silence around him pressed in, suffocating, deafening. He had just lost everything - his entire world had shattered in that cruel, fleeting moment. The woman he loved, the one he had already lost once before in the most heart-wrenching way, was now gone forever. And in that crushing, unbearable instant, Mycroft knew with cold, brutal clarity that no force in this world, no power known to man, could ever bring her back.

She was gone. Forever.

In the days that followed, Mycroft Holmes seemed to vanish from the world. He had retreated to his vast estate in Southgate, far beyond the reach of the city, where no one - especially his brother - could find or reach him.

Sherlock, although just as shattered by Margaret's loss, had managed to hold himself together. Unlike Mycroft, he found solace in the distractions of daily news reports, which, though fleeting, had at least dulled his pain enough to keep him functional.

For days, Sherlock had made attempts to contact his brother. He had left voicemails, sent emails, and even resorted to writing an old-fashioned letter in his finest hand. But not a single word came back. Mycroft's silence was absolute.

By the time Sherlock had half-seriously considered buying a carrier pigeon and training it to deliver messages to his brother, Dr. Watson intervened, appealing to reason. He urged Sherlock to stop playing games and visit Mycroft in person, before it was too late.

And so, Sherlock now stood before the immense front door of Mycroft's secluded manor, the latest issue of the *Daily Mirror* folded tightly in his hand, as if clinging to it would give him the resolve to continue. He pressed the doorbell, the faint chime echoing through the frosty air.

"I'll regret this," Sherlock muttered to himself. "But if I don't do it, I'll regret it even more. I've got no choice - into the lion's cage it is." He sighed deeply. "Let's just hope I'm not too late."

A chill ran down his spine as memories of Margaret's sudden disappearance after the car accident surfaced in his mind.

"I've never seen him so broken, so completely destroyed," he thought bitterly. "Losing her... it changed him. It made him into the man he is today." Then, a new thought struck him like a lightning bolt. "Perhaps it's better if he doesn't know... Just like before. Yes, I should leave. I should turn back now."

Sherlock had already begun to turn away, his steps quiet on the gravel path, when the great door creaked open behind him. From a narrow crack, a shadowed figure peered out.

It was Mr. Wiggins, draped in black from head to toe, who stood at the door like a shadow of despair. His posture slouched until he recognized who the unexpected guest truly was. In an instant, he straightened himself and cleared his throat. "Mr. Holmes," he called out, almost relieved at Sherlock's appearance. "What brings the rare honor of your visit?"

"Gossip and scandals," Sherlock replied with a mischievous grin as he walked back toward the butler. *Brace yourself,* he thought grimly. With a flourish, he raised the newspaper in his hand so that the headlines - bold and unmistakable - were visible to Wiggins.

"Oh!" Mr. Wiggins' eyes widened in shock. He clutched his face with trembling hands, clearly appalled by what he had just seen. "That… that cannot be," he stammered, still grappling with the headline's implications. "Please, come in," he added quickly, stepping aside and closing the door behind Sherlock as he ushered him into the manor.